Praise for MR COMMITMENT

'Something near to mid-period Woody Allen ... a delicate blend of realism and whimsy ... funny and clever ... it's refreshing to find a male writer working in this genre'
Guardian

'Funny, sharply observed and right in tune with ageing adolescents clinging desperately to the wreckage of their youth. This is a winner'
Yorkshire Evening Post

'Told in an easy, chatty style ... the lighter moments in *Mr Commitment* say more about what's wrong with the modern twentysomething male than any amount of earnest introspection ever could'
Express

'Unputdownable ... coloured with cool, rueful wit'
She

'Would you swap your fridge full of beer and an eclectic record collection for trips to Ikea and a series of dull dinner parties? Would you hell!
Pick of the Week, *Marie Claire*

'Gayle's book has the ability to touch the parts other books fail to reach ... the funny bits will make you laugh out loud while the beautiful moments will make you remember all those you've loved before ... Unmissable'
B-Magazine

Praise for MY LEGENDARY GIRLFRIEND

'Full of belly-laughs and painfully acute observations'
Independent on Sunday

'If you like *Gregory's Girl* . . . then this novel has your name on it'
Sunday Times

'Hilarious debut'
Cosmopolitan

'Comic . . . fizzy. Here comes the male Bridget Jones'
Mirror

'Wonderfully contagious, humorous and astute'
The Bookseller

Praise for MY LEGENDARY GIRLFRIEND

'Can't help but win you over'
Company

'Gayle handles the tale impressively and in the almost-Biblically desolate Will, he has created a character who would cheer Holden Caulfield up'
GQ

'Bridget Jones for the boys'
Observer

'Fresh and funny'
Ben Richards

'A fresh, funny debut for anyone with their roots in realism, but their souls desperately holding out for a movie life'
Birmingham Evening Post

Also by Mike Gayle

My Legendary Girlfriend

About the author

Previously an Agony Uncle, Mike Gayle is a freelance journalist who has contributed to a variety of magazines including *FHM*, *The Sunday Times Style* and *Cosmopolitan*. He is the author of one previous novel, the bestselling *My Legendary Girlfriend*.

Mr Commitment

Mike Gayle

FLAME
Hodder & Stoughton

The lines from *The Cassell Dictionary of Contemporary Quotations*,
1996, ed Robert Andrews, are reproduced by permission of
Cassell PLC
The line from *The Collins Dictionary of Quotations*, ed. A. Norman
Jeffries and Martin Gray © 1995, is reproduced by permission of
HarperCollins *Publishers* Ltd

First published in Great Britain in 1999
by Hodder and Stoughton
First published in paperback in 2000
by Hodder and Stoughton
A division of Hodder Headline

A Flame Paperback

15 17 19 20 18 16 14

A CIP catalogue record for this title is available
from the British Library.

ISBN 0 340 73516 3

Printed and bound in Great Britain by
Mackays of Chatham PLC, Chatham, Kent

Hodder and Stoughton
A division of Hodder Headline
338 Euston Road
London NW1 3BH

For Mum and Dad

Acknowledgements

Very, very special thanks for everything as always to Claire. Very special thanks for all their hard work to Phil Pride and all @ Hodder (brilliant job on the cover!), Agent on a Motorcycle, her assistant Euan Thorneycroft and all @ Curtis Brown, and my mate, Jackie Behan. Special thanks for help, advice and general nonsense to Helen Lamont, Fergus and Catherine 'Hello B' McDonnell. Special thanks for nice things said and done to Sid Cannon, Lisa Keogh, Emma Unsworth, Neil O'Sullivan, Sheila Goulding, the girl I spoke to on the Manchester to Birmingham train reading *MLG*, Pip, Lorna, Danuta Kean and Leah Hardy. Last but not least, second verse same as the first thanks to everyone I thanked last time round.

The music sounds better with all of you.

Do you know the difference between involvement and commitment? Think of eggs and bacon. The chicken was involved. The pig was committed.

—Martina Navratilova

A long-forgotten conversation

Her: (Pause.) Do you love me?

Me: Of course I do.

Her: How much?

Me: I don't know . . . loads. To infinity and then some.

Her: (Contentedly.) Good.

Me: That's that sorted, then.

Her: (Playfully.) So what would you do if I ever split up with you?

Me: Are you going to do that?

Her: No.

Me: Then why are we talking about it?

Her: It's called conversation. People do it all the time.

Me: So let me get this straight, the question is what would I do if you hypothetically dumped me?

Her: Yes.

Me: Hypothetically nothing.

Her: Nothing?

Me: Well, as we're mad about each other it'd take me doing something pretty stupid for you to want to get rid of me. (Pause.) Like if I started biting my own toenails or something. I'd dump me if I started doing that.

Her: Do you always have to be so logical?

Me: (Laughs.) I'd be devastated. Destroyed. Dismantled. And other words beginning with 'D'.

Her: But what would you *do*?

Me: Do? [Pause.] I would do everything in my power to get you back.

Her: Like what?

Me: Climbing the highest mountain, crossing scorching deserts, fighting man-eating tigers – that sort of thing. Granted there aren't that many tigers, mountains or deserts in Muswell Hill. But you get my drift.

Her: What if the odds were impossible?

Me: Then I'd die trying.

Her: What if I told you I didn't love you any more?

Me: I wouldn't believe you.

Her: But you wouldn't ever give up trying?

Me: Nah. Some things you can't give up on, can you?

Her: Mr Duffy, you've answered every single question correctly.

Me: Great, so what do I win?

Her: Me.

Let's talk about us

'Have I missed something here?'

It was an ordinary Thursday evening in January – at least I thought so. I was round at my girlfriend Mel's flat and it was to her that I'd aimed my question, as for some unknown reason she'd just turned off the TV even though I'd quite clearly been watching it. What really wound me up, however, was the fact that she'd used the remote control to do it, adding insult to injury. It was an unofficial rule of ours that I looked after all TV channel-changing duties – in the same way that Mel got first grazing rights on the top layer of any box of chocolates that came into our possession. We'd arrived at these and various other rules through a process of trial and error over the course of our four-year relationship. These rules made me happy. I always knew where I stood. But when you abandon rules there's bound to be chaos, and right now what I had on my hands was a serious case of anarchy.

My obviously deranged beloved pursed her perfect full lips together and blew into the end of the remote haughtily as if she'd just battled the TV for my attention and won. *There's no need for you to be quite so pleased with yourself*, I thought. After all, it was only a repeat of *Star Trek* – the episode where Kirk and co. go back in time to earth in early 1920s America and Spock has to wear a woolly hat to cover his pointy ears. A young Joan Collins is in it, and Kirk, surprise, surprise, snogs her. I wasn't a Trekkie but I'd seen this episode a million times before and the more I thought about it the more irritated I became that Mel had curtailed my intergalactic viewing pleasure.

Mel, who had disappeared into her bedroom when I'd arrived at her Clapham flat, only to reappear an hour later and turn off the TV, was now looking at me intently as if studying some unknown creature under a micro-scope. Her face bore the look not of someone annoyed, or angry but intrigued. Even so, I signalled an internal green alert and continued to feel on edge. She stood up – still holding the remote control – and walked across the room to the table in the corner where a bottle of Chardonnay sat. She poured out two glasses of wine, put them on the coffee table, seated herself on my lap and kissed me.

Watching her carefully I began to wonder if she was trying to seduce me. Being seduced was a nice idea, but she really had no need to go to all this effort. When it came to Mel – who was beautiful in a wonderfully understated kind of way – Easy was indeed my first, last and middle name. *No, this isn't about seduction*, I decided. *This is about me doing something wrong.* There was something about this whole situation that had a suggestion of forgot-ten anniversary about it, only it wasn't our anniversary. Was it?

'It's not our anniversary,' I said unsteadily, attempting to add a dash of confidence to my voice. 'That's not until June eleventh.'

'The eighteenth actually.'

'Oh.'

She smiled and kissed me again.

'It's not your birthday, either . . . that's not until April sixth.'

'Nearly,' she smiled. 'The fifth.'

'Oh.'

She smiled and kissed me once more.

'It's not my birthday, is it?' I said, grasping at nothing. 'I can't be so crap that I've actually forgotten my own birthday, surely?'

'What are you like?' said Mel, laughing. 'Your birthday isn't until October the seventh.'

All out of commemorative occasions, I continued to rack my brains. Mel loved any excuse for a celebration. It was bound to be something strange like the anniversary of the first time we had a Chinese takeaway, or four years to the day since we first cooked for each other or . . .

'I've got it,' I said victoriously. 'It's the anniversary of the day I first told you I loved you.'

'It is?' said Mel quizzically. 'Are you sure?'

'I dunno,' I sighed and shrugged my shoulders. All I could remember about the day in question was that it had been the Friday Channel Four repeated the very first episode of *Cheers*. I'd been looking forward to the moment all week and then five minutes before it was about to begin, I'd felt a sudden urge to tell Mel about the intense emotional turmoil she was causing within my normally placid frame. Such was the sense of exhilaration caused by my outburst, that we ended up missing *Cheers* altogether. It was worth it though. Well worth it.

After some moments of quiet contemplation attempting to work out why Mel had turned off the TV, was sitting on my lap and acting so strangely, I resorted to basic questioning in order to try and find out what was wrong, carefully avoiding the question I really wanted to ask: 'Why have you turned off *Star Trek?*'

Like a panther of passion stalking her prey, she leaned forward and kissed me again, slowly, carefully and seductively. Maybe she was trying to seduce me after all.

'Can't a woman be nice to her boyfriend once in a while?' she purred.

'No . . . I mean . . . yes.' I looked at the TV forlornly. 'I mean if that's all it is.'

'I do have an agenda,' she replied whilst gaily fondling my ear lobes.

I knew it . . .

'So what is it?' I asked carefully.

'It's us.'

'Us?'

'Us,' she said calmly. 'Let's talk about us.'

I felt my whole frame sink heavily into the sofa. I'd suspected she was up to something and I was right. Mel had invited me round to her flat on a Thursday night under false pretences. I thought we were going to watch TV and order a Chinese takeaway (me: Chicken Kung Po; her: King Prawn Egg Foo Yung) and moan about our days at work because that's what we always did on Thursdays. But it wasn't to be. Now we were in this horrendous situation where she wanted to talk about 'Us' while all I wanted was to watch *Star Trek*.

Us.

There was never a good reason to talk about 'Us'. Talking about 'Us' always ended up as talking about 'me'. Mel would, metaphorically speaking, get out her list entitled 'Things that are wrong with Duffy: Part 1', and go through it item by item. I would of course nod and murmur in the right places and promise to reform, because generally speaking they were usually reasonable requests along the lines of 'Will you pick your clothes up off the floor?, 'How about washing out the bath sometimes?' and 'Why don't you look at me the way you used to when we first met?'

Us.

'Duffy?' Mel asked. 'How long have we been going out . . . together, that is?'

I knew the answer to her question but racked my brains for additional information in case this was a trick. 'Four wonderful years,' I ventured tentatively.

'Exactly,' she replied. Against my will my mind began to drift – right about now Spock would be heading to the hardware store to buy some chicken wire to aid his efforts to construct a primitive communicator out of a radio set. 'Four years is a long time, you know—'

I interrupted, even though it was very bad to interrupt. I didn't like where this was going at all. 'It's not that long. If you were a four-year-old child you wouldn't even have started going to school yet. You wouldn't be able to read or write but you could probably just about tie your shoelaces . . .'

'Duffy, don't drivel on, will you?' She glared at me, exasperated, then removed herself from my lap and rested her bottom on the arm of the sofa instead, with her stockinged feet on the cushion next to me. 'You know what I'm getting at.'

I shrugged silently, turning my whole body into a question mark.

'Do I have to spell it out?'

'No . . . yes . . . maybe.'

'Duffy, do you love me?'

'Is that all this is about?' I asked incredulously. 'You've got no worries there.' I was pleased that was all. Mel quite frequently asked me if I loved her. Sometimes I think she got a bit insecure about 'us' and needed a little reassurance from me which I was always pleased to give. I reached out and held her hand and whispered closely into her ear, 'I love you. I love you. I love you.'

She smiled, leaned forward to kiss me and whispered back, 'Then let's get married.'

My first impulse as the words rocketed around my skull, causing all manner of brain damage, was to run.

My second impulse (a little more subtle) was to hide.

My third impulse (admittedly far less subtle) was to run and hide.

Maybe my crap impulses were due to my being a Libran. I hoped so. A dismal astrological sign was a greater source of comfort than simple cowardice.

In the end I didn't run or hide, because that would've really annoyed her, so I went with the only other option available to me – to curl up into a ball and hope she didn't want to do too much damage.

'You want to get married?'

'I do,' she said, laughing.

'To me?'

'The one and only Ben Duffy.' She stood up from the sofa, and pulled the hem of her skirt up slightly before getting down on one knee on the carpet. 'I'm a modern woman, Duffy. Modern women don't have to wait to be asked any more.' She cleared her throat, knocked back a huge gulp of wine and held my hand. 'Will you Benjamin Dominic Duffy do me the honour of becoming my lawful wedded bloke, to have and to hold till death do us part?'

Till death do us part.

How did that ever get into the wedding ceremony? Prior to this moment it had been my fullest intention to live for as long as possible – where was the incentive now?

Till death do us part.

Why couldn't they have put in something less restrictive, like 'renewable on a four-year basis', or 'until either party gets bored' or, at worst, 'for the foreseeable future'?

Till death do us part.

That is what you call a long time.

'I thought you didn't believe in marriage,' I said, regaining my wits. 'Didn't you once call it "an outmoded concept created by a patriarchal society to keep women in their place"?' I was paraphrasing the contents of one of those late-night debates we'd had somewhere in year one. I always knew remembering that conversation would come in handy one day.

'Well, I changed my mind,' snapped Mel as if she considered this reason enough. 'Duffy, we're both twenty-eight. We aren't kids any more. I want to settle down . . . I don't mean that . . . I want to settle up . . . I want a proper life.'

Those perfect lips of hers were now pressed together once again, this time in confusion. This obviously wasn't the reaction she'd been expecting. I didn't understand where this had come from. I didn't understand at all. I studied her face to see if I could locate the answer there.

'Don't look at me like that,' said Mel sternly.

'Like what?' I protested.

'Like this.' She pulled a face which was both amusing and incredibly accurate. 'Like I'm a tinned food without a label. Like I've just dropped in from another planet. Like I'm acting like a "bloody woman".'

I adjusted my look accordingly.

'I know what I've said in the past about marriage. You don't need to remind me what I've said before. I know it doesn't make sense. But it's what I want, Duffy. You want me to be ashamed of wanting to be with you for the rest of my life, like it's some sort of weakness. I know I can live life on my own,

Duffy. I don't need to prove anything to anyone. But I don't want to live on my own. I want to live with you.'

Whilst carefully maintaining my nonjudgemental facial expression, I studied her face again, hoping for some sign that she was winding me up – that at some point she was practically going to wet herself laughing and say, 'Had you going there, didn't I?' I waited for this moment, but of course it didn't arrive because Mel was as serious as the *Nine o'Clock News*.

'Are you sure?' I asked timidly.

She nodded. 'Yes. Aren't you?'

'Yes,' I said instinctively. And then, 'No.' And then, 'What I mean is . . .'

She took another long sip from her wine and swallowed hard. 'What you mean is you're not sure.'

I hesitated cautiously, hoping to make certain 'not sure' was an acceptable response and not one that could and would be taken down and used as evidence against me. Once again I examined Mel's features for clues. There were none. The inner workings of Mel's mind were a total enigma to me. I'd often tried to get in there, in the attempt better to understand, but I could never bring all the strands together into a consistent book of law, because as far as I could work out she was making this stuff up as she went along.

Eventually I went with the 'not sure' option. 'It's just that . . . well . . . I just know that if we change things somewhere down the line you'll discover just how annoying I really am. This way we keep an air of mystery about ourselves.'

She set her wine glass down on the table in front of me with force and sat on the armchair opposite, with her arms crossed. 'Believe me, Duffy, there is no air of mystery. I've wiped sick off your chin, watched you cut your toenails and seen with my own eyes the animalistic way you devour bacon and egg sandwiches. And I still love you. But that's not the point. The point is, do you love me enough to commit to me for the rest of your life? I want you to be truthful. I really don't want to put any pressure on you, but I have to tell you I can't wait for ever for you to make up your mind.'

Leaning forward on the sofa, with my head resting on my hands and my elbows resting on my knees, I tried desperately to find the words I wanted to use to express how I felt, but there were none. At least none that were anywhere near satisfactory. 'You're all that I want,' I said.

'And . . .'

'And that's it. Why do we have to get married? Can't we just . . .'

'Move in together?' She'd thought this one out. I was running to every escape route I could think of, only to discover she'd got there first. 'We've been together four years and we're not even living under the same roof, Duff. You know I've tried to talk to you about this more times than I care to remember but you've always avoided the issue. I even changed tactics. I stopped mentioning it, hoping that you'd suggest we move in together in your own time. But you never did. Now it's too late for temporary measures. It's too late to dip your toe in and check the water temperature. It's all or nothing. Now or never. So what do you want to do?'

I didn't answer and remained steeped in silence, half worrying about where this was going to end up, and bizarrely half worrying about what was going on with the crew of the *Enterprise.*

Mel stood up and began pacing the room nervously, sniffing back tears. 'You just don't want things to change, do you, Duffy?' she said, trying to remain controlled. 'You want everything to stay the same. Well, it can't.'

I still didn't respond. Instead I wondered whether if I'd

insisted on watching *Star Trek* any of this would be happening now. We would've had a row but nowhere near as destructive as what was going on here. Eventually, that is once the silence had become too uncomfortable even for me and the crew of the *Enterprise*, I said the only thing I could think of which was, 'I love you.' These words had always helped me out in the past, and now more than ever I needed them to work their magic. I needed them to stop this situation from getting out of hand.

'You can say that you love me, but do you mean it? I dare you. I dare you to show me that you love me.' Then she started crying. Or more accurately she started to try not to cry and failed abysmally. Each and every tear was a tear of resentment. She didn't want them shed for me. She didn't want them wasted.

Instinctively I wanted to put my arms around her and tell her everything was going to be all right, but I couldn't, because quite frighteningly, for the first time since we started going out, I wasn't sure everything was. Without looking at me, Mel picked up the remote, switched the TV back on and disappeared to her bedroom. As the closing credits for *Star Trek* gradually appeared on the screen, I sighed and switched it off again.

If only I could

I'd been standing in front of the confectionery counter of the 7–11 on Clapham High Street for over ten minutes trying to make up my mind. A number of people had come and gone purchasing fags, newspapers, condoms and bread, while I'd remained hunched over the counter silently gazing at the various bars of chocolate. My argument with Mel had turned my brain inside out. Nothing was as it should be. Not even chocolate. I knew that I didn't want a Wispa, Turkish Delight, Snickers, Star Bar, Twix, Toffee Crisp, Crunchie, Bounty, Aero, Lion bar, Yorkie, Caramel or KitKat. That was the easy part. The hard part came now that I'd narrowed down the selection to either a pack of Revels or a Mars bar. One was an intriguing collection of handy-sized chocolate coated thingies and the other was packed to the hilt with glucose energy. They satisfied two very different parts of me and together they made my life complete. Never one to resist an extended metaphor when there was one going, I picked up the packet of Revels in my right hand – *this is independence and excitement.* I picked up the Mars bar in my left hand – *this is Mel, the first woman in my life to convince me to fall in love with her.*

'Oi, mate!' bellowed the stocky unshaven youth behind the counter, interrupting my confectionery cogitation. 'Are you gonna buy those?'

'What?' I said, gradually returning to Planet Earth.

'You've been standing there for the last ten minutes staring at that chocolate in your hands,' he said, rapping several gold sovereign ringed fingers on the counter. 'Now are you buying 'em or weighing 'em?'

'I was just trying to work out which one I wanted,' I explained feebly. 'It's a hard decision to make, you know.'

'Not any more it isn't,' he said forcefully. 'Those chocolate bars have been in your hands so long now they'll have melted to mush. No, mate, you're not leaving this shop unless you buy 'em both.'

'If only I could,' I said under my breath. I handed him a pound coin, waited for the change and headed towards the door.

'Oi, mate!' he called after me. 'You've left your chocolate!'

'I know,' I sighed. 'You can keep them. I can't make my mind up, mate. So you know what? I think I'm just going to go home and have some toast instead.'

My journey up the Northern Line from Clapham Common to Highgate flew by, occupied as I was with thoughts about The Proposal. Mel and I had been together so long it was impossible for me to imagine life without her, but that was no excuse to tempt fate – to wave a metaphorical two fingers in the direction of erudition. *Like the saying goes*, I told myself, '*if it ain't broke don't fix it.*' But maybe things were broken and I just didn't see it. Mel had after all brought the subject of our living arrangements up more times than I could remember, and I'd always avoided it, reasoning that if we didn't live together we couldn't discover that we didn't like living together. Because it's usually when people discover they don't like living together that they split up, and

I didn't want us to do that. Granted it was a twisted kind of logic, but it was logic all the same. But maybe now was the time to give it some serious thought.

Most women would've given up on me years ago. I knew this and was under no illusions who this partnership would benefit most. Mel lived on her own in a big flat in a well-spoken part of Clapham, while I shared an all-right-if-you-don't-mind-damp-in-the-kitchen flat in Muswell Hill with my friend Dan. Mel had an excellent career in advertising sales while I'd been temping for what felt like forever while I waited patiently (some might say a little too patiently) for my career as a stand-up comedian to take off.

Sometimes I really felt sorry for Mel – her life would've been so much better if she'd fallen in love with someone normal. Instead she fell in love with me and had been paying for that mistake ever since. Occasionally when feeling my lowest I'd imagine what it was like when she met up with her friends for an after-work drink. They'd all be talking about their partners' promotions, increased salaries and company cars, while Mel's sole contribution would be that I'd once (eight months ago to be exact) been paid forty-two pounds for a sketch I'd written about Richard Branson's beard for a satirical comedy show on Radio 4. At this point I always saw Mel's imaginary friends throwing her pitying glances that said, 'Ah, Mel and her bad luck with men.'

Actually Mel never complained once about any of this. In all the time we'd been together she'd never even hinted about me getting a real job and giving up comedy. In fact in a weird sort of way she was proud of me for sticking it out.

'It's one of the reasons I love you so much,' she once told me after a particularly traumatic gig in Manchester in which a good eighty per cent of my material went over the heads of the audience attending the Crumpsall Pensioners'

Association annual dinner and dance. 'I know one day you're going to make it. I just know it. I have faith in you.' Then she added, grinning, 'And when you do, I want a Ferrari.'

Sometimes it was hard to have that kind of faith in myself. In my head I was about as likely to give Mel a Ferrari as I would be to give her the remote control for the TV. It was never going to happen.

It was crap being bottom of the pile, begging promoters to put me on, watching comedians who I knew weren't anywhere near as talented as me become successful. It was soul destroying. But it was the success stories that kept me hanging on: stand-ups who, after spending fifteen years on the dole, had all their blood, sweat and beers vindicated by winning the Perrier Comedy Award at Edinburgh.

There was another side of the coin of course – the ones who no one ever talked about – the comedians who tried and failed miserably and as time moved on joined the real world and became teachers, accountants, bank clerks and builders. That was my real fear – joining the real world. Me and my flatmate Dan, who was also a stand-up, set ourselves a deadline once, that by the time we were thirty we would either have made it or moved on. Originally it was by the time we were twenty-eight, but as we'd never expected time to move half as fast as it had done, we'd given ourselves an extension. I didn't know about Dan, but I just didn't have it in myself to become an accountant.

In the end it took me nearly an hour to get back from Mel's. Seconds after leaving Goodge Street the Tube driver told everyone on the train that there'd been an incident at Warren Street and that we'd be stuck in a tunnel until he got further information. 'Further information', as it happens, didn't arrive for another twenty minutes, seconds after which, we moved off. What with the delay, my row with Mel and a sudden realisation that thanks to The Proposal I'd missed out on the Thursday night Chinese takeaway, my general antipathy towards the world was at an all-time high.

It was ten past eleven by the time I reached home. The flat was empty. I headed straight for the kitchen where there was a note from Dan on the fridge door saying he'd gone for a drink with someone called Natalie. I made a pint glass of Ribena and grabbed a loaf of bread from the bread bin. It was time to make toast.

I love toast. I really do. Toast is just about the best food there is. You take a slice of humble white bread (never brown) and you put it in a toaster (What is it? It's a toaster! What does it do? It makes toast!) and a few minutes later you have a hot nutritious meal. You can put any foodstuff handy from the fridge on top of it and it will pretty much always taste fan-bloody-tastic. *Toast*, I thought, as two slices popped up, *makes a whole lot more sense than chocolate bars.*

Moving into the lounge with three hot slices of Flora'd toast, so hot the toast sweat build-up on the plate was threatening to dampen the crispness of the whole affair, I pressed play on the answerphone. There was only one message, from my mum, in which she rattled on about how much she hated answerphones, and how she especially hated leaving messages on ours because she didn't know who Robert De Niro was. Puzzled, I played back the outgoing message and sure enough there was Dan's voice telling callers they'd got through to Robert De Niro, and to leave a message after the beep.

Looking at my watch I wondered if it was too late to call my mum. I decided that it was, but I currently felt so sorry for myself that I was in danger of calling Mel, so I phoned Mum anyway.

'Hi, Mum, it's me. Did I wake you up?'

'No, not at all. I was just listening to the radio. How are you, Ben?' My mum was the only person in the world who still called me Ben. 'Are you okay?'

'Fine,' I lied. 'You know.'

'You don't sound fine.'

'I'm fine, Mum, honest.' It was nice to be fussed over like this. To know that there was someone in the world who, no matter whether you were a convicted homicidal maniac, a porn baron or crack addict, would love you unconditionally.

We chatted about her life for a while. Since she'd retired as a 'catering assistant' (or dinner lady as she still called it) at St Mary's RC comprehensive for girls in Leeds, she'd been spending more and more time with my mad aunt Margaret. Since her husband had died Aunt Margaret had discovered a new lease of life and was constantly dragging Mum away on out-of-season holidays to places like Corfu and Ibiza. According to my mum their next jaunt was going to be Lesbos, which Aunt Margaret had described as 'the island where ladies who liked ladies lived'. Quite what my mother and my aunt were going in search of I don't know, but their curiosity was sufficiently piqued for them to book two weeks there in the middle of May.

'You'll have a great time,' I said. 'You could do with a holiday.'

'If anyone could do with a holiday it's you and Mel,' replied Mum sternly. 'You two work too hard. You should try relaxing and enjoying yourself more, otherwise you'll become like all these London types who just work and work and don't do anything else. Take Mel on holiday, Ben – and that's an order.'

My mum thought Mel was the best thing that had ever happened to me and frequently told me so. The first time

I introduced them, five months after we'd started going out, they'd got on so well that I almost got jealous. They had this thing between them as if they could communicate with each other by means unknown to me. For the most part it didn't bother me, but occasionally I felt like I had my flies undone and that they'd noticed but weren't telling me.

'I don't think we'll be going on holiday,' I said.

'Whyever not?' said Mum. 'If it's the money, I'm sure I can give you some if you're a little bit short.'

'No, it's not the money,' I began. I suddenly felt the strange urge to do something I'd not done since I was at secondary school and was worried about a twenty-question geography test on the Norwegian leather industry – I wanted to share a problem with my mum. Actually, not just any problem – *the* problem.

'Mel wants us to get married,' I found myself saying. 'She proposed to me tonight and it's taken me a bit by surprise.'

'That's wonderful news!' exclaimed Mum. 'Mel's a lovely girl. I always said she was the one for you. To tell you the truth I can't believe it's taken the two of you this long to get it together.'

'But that's just it,' I said despondently. 'I'm not sure I want to get married. You're right, Mel is an incredible person, but I'm only twenty-eight. I'm not sure I'm ready for all that . . . you know . . . marriage stuff.'

'Don't be so silly,' she responded, gearing up into no-nonsense maternal mode. 'Of course you're ready. You love her; she loves you. You've been together four years as it is. What more do you need to know?'

I stopped and thought for a moment. It was a good question.

What more do I need to know?

'I haven't the faintest clue,' I said after some reflection. 'But whatever it is I can tell you now I don't know it.'

Mum refused to let the subject drop for the rest of the phone call in the hope that somehow I might just give in. Perhaps it hadn't been the best idea telling her about the ins and outs of my love life after all. I gave her five minutes to reprimand me and then I told her I had to go. She rounded things off with a reasonably chirpy, 'I'm not trying to organise your life, Ben. I just want you to be happy,' and we said our goodbyes.

Putting the phone down, I hunted for my toast. It was cold now and had gone soggy from toast sweat. While I munched on a slice I took a moment to consider my mum. She must hold the world record for being the world's most optimistic mother. How could one person be that happy after what she'd been through?

I'd never met my dad. He left us when I was six months old and Vernie was two and a half, and divorced my mum five years later. Mum rarely talked about the reasons why he left, and neither Vernie nor I ever asked because we knew it would upset her. All I'd managed to glean in twenty-eight years was that they hadn't been getting on, and that he left two years and ten months after they'd got married.

You would've thought that my mum of all people would be able to see that marriage was a ridiculous idea at the best of times, but she had gone totally the opposite way. She believed in marriage with a strength and a vigour that I've never seen equalled. When Vernie married her long-term boyfriend Charlie four years ago, Mum was overjoyed. I just didn't get it. My dad had promised to be with her for richer for poorer, in sickness and in health, and he'd still felt able to leave her with no money and two kids to raise. Yet here she was, after all this time, still believing it possible for two people to love each other for ever. Now that is what you call faith.

Cosmopolitan is a Ouija board

'Hi, Mel. It's me, Duffy. I left a message on your answerphone yesterday. And the day before that, and the day before that and the day before that and the day before that. I just wanted to say that I'm sorry. And that I'm stupid, but I suppose you already know that. 'Bye.'

It was now Tuesday and five days had gone by since I'd last seen Mel. She was refusing to acknowledge my existence via any of the methods of communication at her disposal – telephone/fax/mobile/carrier pigeon/e-mail/doorbell. My days at work were now spent moping around the office. I couldn't think straight at all and was so depressed that I was taking a toilet break every half hour, which when combined with fag breaks and the mid-afternoon snack runs I'd started volunteering for, meant I got little or nothing done. Not that anyone noticed of course. I'd been in this particular temping job, inputting data for DAB, a market research company, for over three years now. Admittedly, it was a long time for any one person to temp in any one job, but according to the powers that be, it made more sense financially for the personnel officer at DAB to reserve the right to drop me at a second's notice than to employ me full-time. This arrangement suited me fine because in return I reserved the right to tell them what to do with their ridiculously pointless job the moment I got enough stand-up work to make a decent living. Perfect symbiosis.

Having just left yet another message on Mel's home answerphone, I decided it was time to take a look at The Proposal from a different perspective. Sneaking past Bridget on reception (a woman who thought gossiping to management about the lives of temps was a fundamental human right), I escaped to the lift and descended into the bowels of the building, to the newsagent-cum-sandwich-shop in the basement. Bathed in the harsh white glare of strip lighting, I stood staring at the rows of glossy women's magazines, all with unfeasibly beautiful women on the cover airbrushed to perfection.

Mel read these sorts of magazines religiously. Within their pages was a world of wisdom and advice that was completely alien to me. Mel understood these magazines and they understood her. *I'm fed up with being on the outside looking in,* I thought, scanning the shelves. *I'm tired of not knowing what's going on with my own girlfriend.*

I picked up *New Woman* and flicked through it, and then I picked up *19* and then *Company* and continued plucking titles off the shelves until I'd amassed a pile on the counter that left me with twenty-nine pence change from a twenty-pound note. Sneaking past Checkpoint Bridget (thankfully she was on the phone discussing the previous night's *Coronation Street* so I didn't have to explain my reading material) I returned to my workstation and hid the magazines in the bottom drawer of my desk which I normally reserved for sandwiches, my ball of rubber bands and stapler collection.

As soon as the coast was clear I sneaked out the first of the magazines, *Cosmopolitan*, and began to execute my plan. With my tongue firmly lodged in my cheek I'd managed to convince myself that if I directly asked these magazines the questions that I wanted to know – like a Ouija board only more scary – they would somehow provide me with the answers I so longed for.

Checking the coast was clear of snoopers and eavesdroppers I closed my eyes, spread my palms over the magazine and its free astrological supplement and in a deep ominous voice whispered, 'Oh, mighty *Cosmopolitan*. You speak for young go-getting women the world over. I have some questions for you:

1) Why, after four years, does Mel suddenly want to get married?
2) Why does Mel insist on holding conversations in the middle of my favourite TV programmes?
3) What is this season's hem length going to be?'

I was chuckling so dementedly by the time I got to the third question that Scottish Helen, a fellow temp who sat in the workstation opposite me, stared at me open mouthed as if I'd well and truly lost my mind (which in a way I suppose I had). 'What are you doing?' she asked peering over her computer.

'*Cosmopolitan* is a Ouija board,' I deadpanned, 'and I'm asking it questions about women.'

'Oh, that's nice,' said Helen, who had, in the three months that I had known her, come to accept my erratic behaviour more or less without question. 'Can I borrow it when you're finished?'

'No problem,' I said. 'Just give me a moment.'

That 'moment' lasted an hour and a half. By the time I'd finished looking through it and the other magazines it was time to go home, so I put them on a neat pile on Helen's desk and left. Needless to say I didn't discover the answers to questions one or two, but what I didn't know about the current season's hem length really wasn't worth knowing.

With no answers forthcoming from the world of women's magazines, I decided it was time to get a little sisterly advice on the matter. Vernie was two and a bit years older than me and had always been the bossy one in our family. Growing up in a single-parent family, my sister took up the mantle of the man of the house as soon as she was able. Many a time at primary school, having smart-mouthed the school bully once too often, I'd be suffering painful torture at his hands only to have my sister bound across the playground and pummel my assailant within an inch of his life, earning herself the sobriquet Muhammad Duffy.

Years later little had changed. Vernie might not have physically assaulted anyone in the last two decades, but she could still administer the kind of tongue-lashing most people never forgot. Charlie, her husband, was a much mellower character. He was the Yin to her Yang and together they made each other normal. Charlie really was great. He was laidback in a way that made me envious, and yet wise in a way that wasn't obvious. Like me he enjoyed the simple things in life: the love of a good woman, evenings in the pub talking about nothing in particular, and football. So when Charlie and Vernie moved from Derby to London and ended up in a huge house in nearby Crouch End, it was only a matter of time before he became mine and Dan's top mate, drinking buddy and third musketeer.

'What's wrong?' said Vernie, as soon as she opened her front door. 'You look like a right misery.'

'I dunno,' I said, watching my breath rise up into the cold night sky. 'I know that's a bit lame but I really don't know what's wrong.'

'You'd better come in,' she said, and I followed her into the kitchen where she made a cup of tea and handed me a can of Lilt and a glass filled with ice cubes.

We moved into the lounge, and while she told me about her day at work in great detail (she was a system analyst for a large computing firm in the City), I sucked ice cubes noisily and looked out of the bay window wondering what Mel was doing right now. After some minutes of this, it became obvious to Vernie that I hadn't been listening to a single word she'd been saying.

'Okay, let's talk about you!' she said, throwing an embroidered cushion at my head in mock anger. 'That's what you're here for, isn't it? You're so self-obsessed sometimes it's frightening.' She paused and looked at me. 'It's Mel, isn't it?'

I nodded.

'You've had a row because she's fed up waiting for you to agree to move in together.'

'Nearly, but not quite.'

Vernie raised her eyebrows. 'She asked the big question?'

I nodded again. 'How do you know we've had a row? Have you spoken to her, then?'

'No.' Vernie rolled her eyes, signalling my dense stupidity. 'And I'm not psychic either. Duff, this has been on the cards for a long time.'

'That's what she said as well,' I said, kicking off my shoes.

'You don't sound convinced,' said Vernie.

'I don't get it,' I sighed. 'If even you know, how come it was news to me?'

Vernie shook her head and issued the universal sound for stupidity: 'Doh! It would be news to you, Duffy. And do you know why? Because everything is news to you.' Over the next fifteen minutes she gave me one of her many extended lectures on life, love and the stuff in between. This one was about how men didn't pay attention to the small things in life because they didn't think small things were important, when in truth small things are everything. She concluded her speech with the accusatory flourish: 'You bumble about in your own selfish worlds completely oblivious to the things that really upset us and then wonder what it is you've done wrong.'

I concluded from the length, pace and formidable sense of personal frustration in her speech, that Charlie had done something to wind her up and that her words were meant more for her absent partner than for me. Revealing an impeccable sense of timing, this was exactly the moment Charlie chose to come through the front door after his day working in the town planning department of Westminster Council.

'All right, mate?' he called out as he entered the room, dropping his briefcase on the floor and kicking off his shoes.

'Yeah. Not too bad,' I replied, looking at Vernie, who was in turn glowering at Charlie's recently abandoned shoes.

Charlie immediately picked up on the bad vibes that were issuing forth from his wife like a laser beam, tidied away his shoes and briefcase, walked over to the sofa and attempted to kiss Vernie hello. He failed. She glared at him, put her mug of tea down firmly on the coffee table that she never lets anyone put anything down on without a coaster, and in one smooth movement huffed her way out of the room slamming the door behind her.

Charlie tutted quietly to himself and sat down.

'What've you done?' I asked as Vernie banged her way loudly up the stairs. 'Murdered someone? Forgotten her birthday? Started wearing her underwear again?'

'Long story,' said Charlie, which was coded Charlie-speak

for 'Let's talk about something else.' He took off his suit jacket and slumped on to the sofa with his feet up on the coffee table. 'Just visiting, were you?'

'No,' I said flatly. 'Woman trouble.'

'Oh,' was Charlie's disdainful reply. 'You too. Which kind?'

'The kind where Mel wants to get married.'

'Oh.'

'Oh indeed.' I stopped and mulled over a thought for a minute. Here I was sitting with a married man. Someone from my team who had made The Big Decision and lived to tell the tale. Surely he could give me some advice. 'What was it that made you get married, Charlie?'

He frowned and loosened his tie. 'Hang on a sec.' He disappeared out of the room for a few moments and returned with a can of Coke. 'Where were we?'

'You were telling me why you got married.'

'You want the truth?'

'No,' I said. 'I was after complete and utter lies but the truth will do.'

He ignored my attempt at biting sarcasm and took a sip of his drink. 'I knew she was the one,' he said matter-of-factly, as if love was an equation to which he'd worked out the solution. The scientific edge to his voice I'm sure was for my benefit. 'Yes,' it said, 'we are talking about emotions but in a logical non-soppy way, so it doesn't count.' 'She was the right one for me. Simple as that.' He drained the can in four huge gulps and set it on the table next to Vernie's half drunk tea.

'Is that all it takes?'

'That's all it took for me. But you know. Different strokes and all that.'

'Yeah, I suppose,' I said despondently. 'Thing is . . .' I stopped and attempted to add Charlie's logical tone to my voice. 'Thing is I love Mel. I don't want anyone else. So why is this marriage thing freaking me out so much?'

Charlie shrugged his shoulders. 'Only you know that, mate.' He picked up the TV remote control from the coffee table and started browsing through the channels systematically – thirty seconds and then he'd move on.

'How did you ask Vernie to marry you?' I asked, as BBC2 was turning into ITV. 'Did you do something special or did you just come out with it?'

Charlie just raised his eyebrows warily as if his refusal to answer was down to the Official Secrets Act rather than embarrassment. 'I forget now. It was a long time ago.'

It was actually four years ago and Charlie hadn't forgotten, he just didn't want to tell me. Fortunately, I already knew and was just pulling his plonker for the sheer pleasure of it. The manner of his proposal was meant to be top secret, but I knew because Vernie had told Mel and Mel in turn had told me, saying, 'It's the most beautiful thing ever.' Apparently, Charlie had told Vernie he was taking her away for the weekend as a surprise. She was expecting somewhere like the Lake District at the very best, so she must have been ecstatic when they ended up in New York. On their first day in the Big Apple he took her to the top of the Empire State Building, and as she looked through the twenty-five cents telescope on to Central Park he put a piece of paper at the end of it with the words 'Will you marry me?' on it and she burst into tears and immediately said yes. At the time I was really surprised by this story, because anyone who knew Charlie well knew that big romantic gestures just weren't his thing.

'C'mon, Charlie,' I said smirking. 'I need some tips on what to do. Surely you can remember how you asked my sister to marry you?'

'I know you're trying to wind me up,' said Charlie, laughing, 'and it won't work. I'm not alone in my actions, because when it comes to stuff like this, every man has a poem in his heart.'

'It's a nice thought, but mine's bound to be more of a limerick,' I said, picking up my glass.

'Nah,' said Charlie, and for a moment I could've sworn that I saw a flash of his special brand of wisdom twinkle in his eyes. 'You've got a poem in your heart, mate. You've just got to find it. Okay, you get moments like this,' he glanced up at the ceiling pointedly, from where the sounds of Vernie stomping on the floorboards emanated. 'But you know . . . I wouldn't swap it for the world.'

I am not your mother!

It was late evening by the time I got back to the flat. The first thing I did was check the answerphone – no messages. The heartbreakingly pitiful message I'd left on Mel's answerphone had obviously failed to melt her heart. My flatmate Dan was lying across the sofa silently watching the *Nine o'Clock News*. 'All right mate?' I asked, sitting down in an armchair in the corner of the room.

'Yeah, I suppose,' he said despondently, his face half squashed into a cushion. 'Got something in the post today,' he pointed to an envelope on the floor in the middle of the room.

'What is it?'

'Read it and find out,' he said, his eyes still fixed on the television. 'Weirdness.'

I picked up the envelope. Inside was a wedding invitation on cream paper embossed with gold. I read it aloud. '"Meena Amos and Paul Midford would like to invite Daniel Carter and guest to their wedding . . ."' I stopped as it dawned on me what this all meant. 'Your ex-girlfriend is getting married?'

'Looks like it. I know him too. He was on my drama course at Manchester Uni. I've seen him on *The Bill* and *Casualty* a few times. Talentless git. Never liked him. Wouldn't know Ibsen from his arse, that one.'

'Why is Meena inviting you to her wedding?'

Dan shrugged and changed channels.

'I mean it's not exactly like you finished on anything vaguely like good terms is it?'

'Precisely,' said Dan. 'Like I said before, this is pure weirdness.'

'And anyway, isn't it a bit early to be sending out invitations, it says here she's not getting married until September.'

'I know. She always did like to plan ahead.

Meena was the last woman in Dan's life to have fitted the description of 'Girlfriend'. They'd met at university and up until a year ago had lived together in the flat which I now shared with Dan. Back then Meena used to terrify me every time I met her. She was a complete maniac when her back was up and towards the end of her and Dan's relationship her back was permanently in the arched position, teeth bared, claws out and hissing wildly. I couldn't blame her really. As far as I could work out, since they'd moved in together Dan had begun some sort of mission to see just how far he could push his luck. The day they split up was the day that he found out.

At the time Dan was working part-time as a security guard in between stand-up gigs while Meena worked as a set designer for a theatre in East London. On the day in question I'd been round at their flat with Dan, trying to think up less soul-destroying ways of making money than temp work. What I didn't know was that he'd promised Meena that very morning that he'd tidy up the flat because her parents were coming to stay. So when she came home early from work to discover a sink full of washing-up, me asleep on the sofa and Dan watching *Countdown*, she well and truly lost it.

Now Dan might be a lot of things, but he wasn't so stupid that he couldn't see this coming. Although he never admitted to it, it was my belief that this was his way of forcing the issue and letting Meena know that he didn't want to live with her any more. My guess was that he wanted his old life back and he wanted it back now. I think he was banking on my presence in the flat tempering Meena's outburst, thus making the transition from relationship to non-relationship as trauma free an experience as possible. Best-laid plans of mice and men and all that. It was not to be.

'It's not you, it's me,' explained Dan, after a five-minute dressing down in which Meena not only failed to hold back for fear of embarrassing me, but also revealed some information about Dan's sub-duvet activities that I think both of us wished she'd kept to herself.

'Of course it's you,' said Meena defiantly. 'There's only room for one selfish, self-centred, egotistical, monomaniac, commitment-phobic bath-dodger in this relationship, and that's you.'

'Bath dodger?'

'Bath dodger.'

'Who are you calling a bath-dodger?'

'You, you filthy dirty bath-dodger!'

'I had a bath,' protested Dan.

'When did you have a bath?' She reached into her handbag, took out her pocket diary and read from it. '"Tuesday fourteenth, Dan has not had a bath. Wednesday fifteenth, still no Dan bath." Do I need to carry on?'

'You've been keeping a note of how often I wash?' said Dan incredulously.

'Yes,' she snapped. 'I've also got documentary evidence to the fact that you haven't touched the vacuum cleaner in three months, you've not washed the bathroom sink in weeks and . . .' she checked her diary for this one . . . 'right now you're wearing a pair of boxer shorts that you've had on for two days in a row.'

'Two days?' Dan, much to his shame had no answer to this one. 'Time flies, eh?' And then he said something that took me completely by surprise. 'Listen, Meena,' he said, 'I'm sorry. I can change.'

'Pants or personality?'

'Personality,' he said sheepishly.

This was very un-Dan. Very uncool. He normally had his goodbye speeches down pat, a throwback to his days at drama college. He was wavering. I think he was unsure if he really did want to split up with Meena or whether now he'd finally realised that if he pushed hard enough Meena would eventually push back, he wanted her more than ever. But it was too late and he knew that.

'Dan, you'll never change,' spat Meena furiously. 'You are you and that's all there is to it. You leave everything to me and expect me to run around after you like you're some sort of naughty schoolboy. I am not your mother! We've been together since we left college six years ago. We've been living together for just five months of those six years and it seems to me that as soon as we moved in you gave up on us. You used to be so sweet, Dan, you used to try and impress me . . . you even used to take a shower every day when we first met! What happened? Why did you give up? I'll tell you why. You gave up because you're lazy and selfish and think that I was put on this earth to please you. Well, I wasn't, okay? It's over, Dan. We're finished.'

Dan didn't say a word. It was almost like he was in a trance, trapped in his subconscious weighing up the current situation on his internal scales of justice. On the one side was his pride, and on the other his love for Meena. Whatever the result, in the end he decided to bale out – to try and save what was left of his dignity.

'Hang on,' said Dan regaining his confidence. 'You're leaving me? I'm the one who said, "It's not you, it's me." I'm leaving you, okay?'

'You're damned right you're leaving me,' said Meena. 'I spent months looking for this flat to rent and I want you out of it now!'

'Now?'

'No, yesterday.' She pointed to the door. 'I want you to find yourself a time machine like Michael J. Fox in *Back To The Future*, I want you to climb into it, switch on the controls and erase yourself from my history.'

His newfound confidence began to falter. 'But where will I go?'

'I don't care, but whichever stone you crawl under, you can take that one with you!' She pointed at me. It was the first time Meena had addressed me directly in months. She usually refused to acknowledge my existence in the hope I'd somehow dissipate, like an embarrassing fart from an elderly relative.

'It's not enough that you assassinate my character, now you're having a go at my mates?' said Dan in my defence – although strictly speaking it wasn't in my defence, he was just trying to score points now. 'I thought you said you liked Duffy.'

'Is there no limit to your feeblemindedness?' she said, as if addressing a mischievous five-year-old. 'I can't stand Duffy. He eats our food. Watches our TV. Uses our telephone.' I momentarily contemplated some sort of financial offering to make amends for the phone abuse, but all I had in my pockets was a twenty pence piece and a Blockbusters video

Mike Gayle

card. 'I want you,' she pointed at me again, 'and I want you,' she pointed at him, 'out now!'

'Well, I'm not going.' Dan crossed his arms defiantly. 'This is my flat as much as it is yours. So if you want me out of your life so badly, you'd better start packing.'

That was then. Before I moved in Dan and I were just equally non-achieving mates from the comedy circuit, but after twelve months together we were so similar it was scary. We liked the same films, TV, music and sitcoms. The only thing we differed on was relationships. While I had the steadiest of steady girlfriends, after Meena, Dan became a subscriber to what he called the Doner Kebab Theory of Women – 'A nice idea on a post-pub Friday night but not the sort of thing you want on the pillow when you wake up next day.' I couldn't help but think that it was all an act to stop himself from getting hurt again, but as acts go it was remarkably convincing.

Dan didn't seem to want to talk about Meena for the minute, so leaving the wedding invitation open on top of the bookcase next to my seat I disappeared to the kitchen and emptied the remains of a three-day-old jar of Ragu over a bowl of cold pasta and shoved it into the microwave. I watched impatiently as the bowl rotated in the oven, and thought about the wedding invitation. Meena was clearly rubbing it in – letting him know that she'd moved on and he hadn't. Hell indeed had no fury like a woman scorned.

Scratching his stomach absentmindedly Dan came into the kitchen, opened the fridge door and peered in. 'There's nothing to eat,' he said, rooting about. 'Can I have that cheese you bought last week?'

'No problem.' I threw a packet of cream crackers at him.

'Have these as well.' I returned to staring at the microwave waiting for the ping. 'Does it bother you that Meena's getting married?'

'No,' said Dan a little too quickly and then changed subjects. 'What kind of cheese is this?'

'Dunno,' I said. 'Cheddar I think.' Dan didn't want to talk about Meena and her impending nuptials when there were clearly more pressing topics to discuss like cheese. I didn't blame him. He wasn't made of stone, but it was pointless talking about something that he had no control over. He'd do his grieving in private and if he needed me to accompany him on an evening of Drinking and Forgetting down our local, the Haversham Arms, then accompany him I would.

After what felt like a decade the microwave pinged and I made my way back to the living room with my steaming bowl of pasta. As Dan flicked between the weather report on BBC1 and a documentary on Channel Four about burglars in Leeds, I wondered if I should collect his opinion on The Proposal to add to those of Vernie, Charlie and my mother.

'So that's why you've been moping round the flat like a lovesick teenager,' he said after I filled him in on the details of The Proposal. 'You told me she'd gone on a course for work.'

'Yeah, well, I lied,' I confessed. 'The thing is, what do I do now?'

'I'll tell you what to do,' he said, switching channels with the remote. '*Do* nothing. Take it from me, there's no way she's going to dump you just because you don't want to get married. You've been with her what . . . three years?'

'Four years,' I admitted.

'Four years! You're practically Mr and Mrs anyway. My advice – keep your head down and wait for it all to blow over.'

I liked the sound of that. 'Pretend it didn't happen?'

'Exactly. Head in the sand, mate. It was most likely just one of those moments that's best forgotten. She's probably embarrassed she even mentioned it to you. I bet you that's why she hasn't called.'

I gave his advice the consideration it deserved. Ignoring this whole thing in the hope that it might go away was an extremely attractive proposition – neither of us had to lose face and we could go on with life as it was before.

'Are you sure?' I asked.

'Of course I'm sure,' he said confidently. 'Listen, Duffy, it's like this: Mel's invested three—'

'Four,' I corrected.

'All right, four years of her life with you. She's got you pretty much well trained. Think how long it would take her to get another bloke to your level of obedience.'

'So you're saying she's not going to dump me because she's too lazy to train someone else?'

'Sort of.'

'Thing is . . .' I began.

'Don't tell me that you're actually considering getting married.' Dan shook his head in disbelief. 'Have I taught you nothing? Did I not teach you The Ways of The Bachelor? And now you want to go over to the dark side? I can't believe you. I forgave you for that regular girlfriend thing because, well, it was quaint. But getting married? This is definitely one of your worst ideas. It'll be the end of life as you know it. Everything changes.' He looked over at Meena's invitation on the bookcase. 'Me and Meena would've ended up getting married. Now what kind of mistake would that have been?'

Dan was depressing me beyond belief. 'Cheers, Yoda,' I said curtly. 'I'll sort it out myself.'

I stood up, picked up the remote control from the arm

of the sofa Dan was sitting on, and returned to my seat, flicking through the channels erratically while I shovelled huge forkfuls of my now cold pasta dinner into my mouth.

This was the closest Dan and I had ever come to an argument. He must have felt bad about it too, because he left the room and returned minutes later with a maxi pack of Skips and two cans of Red Stripe as a peace offering. Tearing open the bag he placed it carefully on the carpet between us and handed me a Red Stripe while he searched for the video remote control. 'Forget the crappy pasta and forget Mel for the minute. Eat Skips, drink beer, watch telly and stop thinking,' he said sagely. 'Thinking isn't good for either of us.'

Even Nosferatu seemed to be smiling

It was now nine days since I'd last seen or heard from Mel. The advice of my mum, sister, brother-in-law and flatmate had been rattling around my head for days without having any effect on me other than giving me a headache. I couldn't escape the feeling that at the age of twenty-eight the answer to my predicament really should've come from inside me and not from friends and relatives. Which is why, I decided, that even though I still wasn't sure how I felt about marriage, it was time for Mel and me to talk and come up with a solution that we could both live with.

'Oh, it's you.'

It was Julie who answered the door to Mel's flat. She was the only person in the world who could make 'Oh, it's you' sound like 'Burn in hell, you unfortunate bag of crap.' It was a bad sign that she'd taken over door-answering duties, because it meant without question that she'd been spending every second since The Proposal at Mel's, rubbishing my good name.

Julie – whom I referred to in private as Nosferatu, Princess of Darkness, for no other reason than it made me laugh – was Mel's best friend and my arch enemy. The first time I met her I was incredibly nervous, because Mel had told me that if I could pass the Julie Test, then meeting her parents would be a piece of cake. Over poached oysters with iceberg butter sauce at Julie's house, I watched her mentally ticking off the points against me as I revealed I was a temp (-4), had dropped out of university (-2), was constantly broke (-6), considered amusing people in the back room of a pub was a smart career move (-4) and was doing little to rectify any of my point-minusing situations (-10).

At the end of the evening it was clear to both me and Mel that I'd failed the Julie Test with a record-breakingly bad score. I remember thinking, *If my performance tonight is anything to go by, Mel's parents are really going to hate me*. Julie, however, loved Mel just like Thelma loved Louise, although without the lesbian subtext, and so for her sake she tolerated me as if I was a bad habit – like nailbiting or not washing your hands after you've used the toilet – that Mel just couldn't break.

Julie lived with and was engaged to Mark, who I quite liked but for the fact I was totally intimidated by his success. He made music videos for hideously famous bands, was always travelling to glamorous places, and to top it all was two years younger than me – which galled me immensely. Mark was one of life's doers. While I'd been drinking cider in the park and chasing girls who didn't know better, as a teenager he'd been writing and shooting short films on a Super 8 camera. We had no common ground whatsoever. Occasionally when we all went out together he'd try and draw me into a conversation about high-performance sports cars, trekking holidays in China or his latest music video, and every time without fail I'd just look at him vacantly, desperately hoping that at some point he would ask me what was going on in *EastEnders* so that I'd have something to contribute to the conversation.

Together, Mark and Julie were couple perfection at its Dyson-owning-two-newspapers-on-a-Sunday-his-'n'-hers-

Birkenstocks-three-foreign-holidays-a-year-and-smug-about-it worst. But there was no escaping them because we 'double coupled' all the time, usually at Julie's insistence. I never understood why she stipulated that we did so many things together. It was as if because she and Mark were a couple they were only allowed to socialise with other couples for fear of catching single-people disease.

'All right, Jules?' I said chirpily. Julie loathed being called Jules more than anything. 'Are you going to let me in or what?'

Guardedly Julie opened the door to the communal hallway of the house and let me in, but I could tell she was in two minds about whether to do so. 'What do *you* want?'

'I've just popped round to hear what you think's wrong with me this week.'

'How long have you got?' she snorted, flicking a stray strand of strawberry blonde hair out of her eyes.

'As long as you want,' I said grimacing.

She let me in and we squared up to each other in the hallway like two gunfighters at the OK Corral. As I stared deeply into her defiant pale blue eyes. I was reminded of something I'd read once in a magazine. Apparently when two animals hold each other's direct gaze for longer than a minute, the laws of nature state they will either tear each other to pieces or copulate. The thought of having carnal knowledge of Julie unsettled me so much that I began to smile nervously.

'Well, for starters,' said Julie, ignoring the grin fixed to my face, 'you're a selfish pig. You have no respect for Mel or her feelings.'

'And?'

'You're inconsiderate.'

'And?'

'You do that hateful thing where you roll your eyes.'

'And?'

'You put everything else that's in your life before Mel.'

'Errrrrrrrr!' I made the annoying quiz-buzzer-type noise from *Just a Minute* on Radio 4. 'Repetition. I think you'll find putting everything that's in my life before Mel is the same as being selfish.'

Julie scowled threateningly. She was officially angry now, which in an incredibly petty sort of way made me happy. 'You *would* say that you—'

'You don't know anything about me, Julie,' I interrupted. 'You just think you do. I do respect Mel and her feelings, I don't put everything that's in my life before her . . .' I paused briefly. 'But I admit I do occasionally leave the toilet seat up, which might be interpreted as inconsiderate, and I definitely do that thing when I roll my eyes, but that doesn't exactly make me Darth Vader in a pair of Levis, does it?'

Julie screwed up her face angrily like a bulldog chewing a wasp. 'I don't know what she ever saw in you . . .' she began furiously, but then her voice trailed off. *Pants*, I thought nervously. *If she's not going to tear me to pieces maybe she is going to have sex with me after all.* Fortunately I soon discovered what had stopped her outburst so abruptly. It was Mel.

'Oh, please, you two,' sighed Mel. 'Can't you ever just give it a rest?'

Like a petulant child Julie threw a thunderous 'It was all his fault' glance in my direction while I cranked my ever-so-angelic smile up in the hope it would make Julie melt, or combust, or whatever it is that vampires do when they've been defeated.

Mel was wearing her it's-Saturday-therefore-I-shop clothes – jeans, white T-shirt and a long thick woollen hooded top.

She'd had a haircut, too, and it made her face look that little bit more beautiful. I resisted a genuine compulsion to tell her that she looked stunning, because I knew she'd only think I was trying to flatter her. So instead I smiled warmly, hoping that the upward curling of the corners of my lips would somehow convey my keen appreciation. Mel didn't return my smile, though. Her expression revealed neither approval nor disapproval of my appearance in her hallway, although the manner in which she sat wearily on the bottom stair was a strong indicator that I was far from being back in favour.

'How are you?' she said abruptly.

'Okay,' I mumbled. 'How are you?'

Silence.

'How's work?'

Silence.

I hated arguments like this. I wanted her to stop being angry with me. 'I love you, you know,' I said, kneeling down in front of her.

'So you say.' She took off her jacket. 'Is that all you came to tell me?'

I looked into her eyes, trying to find the real her. The Mel sitting in front of me was Hard Mel, an alter ego she sometimes utilised to stop herself from forgiving me when she knew she really shouldn't. It was true that she was too forgiving and perhaps I did deserve the harsh treatment I was receiving, but even so, I thought this was a bit much. The offence of Not Knowing When To Marry Your Long-term Girlfriend was new legislation and I felt quite strongly that the marathon begging, shuffling and scraping I'd done in the past week was more than recompense.

So I waited, saying nothing. The silence was so uncomfortable even Julie felt the need to disappear upstairs to Mel's flat on the pretext of getting a glass of water. The longer I said nothing, the more Hard Mel stared through me like I didn't exist. Soon whatever regret I had about the way I'd treated Mel was swallowed up whole by resentment. What I'd done wrong was no longer the point. It wasn't about apology, making up or explanation. All that counted now was winning.

'This is pointless,' I sighed. 'You're not in the right mood to talk. Okay. I'll come back later.'

1–0

In a single swoop I'd claimed the moral high ground, belittled her feelings and made myself out to be the last remaining reasonable person left on Planet Earth.

'You can't stand being wrong, can you?' retorted Mel. 'You're not man enough to admit when you've made a mistake.'

1–1

The moral high ground that I craved so highly was all Mel's. She'd pinpointed my insecurities and cast slurs upon my masculinity. I was in great danger of looking stupid.

'Whatever,' I sighed exasperatedly, *2–1* argument shorthand for 'I'm pretending that I can't be bothered to argue with you.' *I'm bound to win now*, I thought spitefully, and then Mel started to cry.

Game over.

This wasn't fair at all. 'Whatever' wasn't a phrase worthy of tears. Mel had cheated by using the crying card when I hadn't even provoked it. Most of our big arguments ended with tears. She'd say something horrible. I'd say something equally horrible. She'd cry. And I'd feel guilty. Tears were the secret weapon from which I had no defence. *One day*, I decided, *I'm going to get into an argument with Mel and burst into tears before she does, just so she can see how it feels.*

I hated seeing her cry. Absolutely hated it. I wanted to put my arms around her and tell her I was sorry, but I knew she'd just reject my peace offering. So instead, brushing past Julie – who had returned to watch the intriguing spectacle of two people not talking – I shook my head in her direction in a high-minded 'I pity you' manner, and opened the door.

I was – mentally speaking – already huffing my way down Clapham High Street, moaning to myself about how I was never going to understand women and their strange ways, when Mel shouted out after me, 'What *did* you come round here for anyway, Duffy? Just to show me how much I can't stand you?'

I searched for something equally horrible to say, but the genuine hurt I heard in her voice thankfully brought me to my senses, so that the worst thing I could find in the deep well of regret into which I was currently sinking was, 'I came to tell you, yes, I want to marry you.'

This was actually a bit of a lie.

Well, not a lie, but not exactly the truth.

Kind of ninety-seven per cent truth and three per cent total fabrication.

I did want to marry her – just not now – not yet. The words I'd said instead, however, had sort of leaped from my lips and now they were out I was almost proud of them. I'd never quite understood how people came to make decisions of this magnitude: 'Let's have a baby'; 'Let's get married'; 'Let's commit suicide.' These are all monumental life-changing decisions from which there is no return. I'd always believed it would take a certain type of strength from a certain type of person to say, 'Let's get married,' so I was pleased that even I, a metaphorical seven stone weakling in a world crammed full of emotional heavyweights, had been able to cut it with the big boys.

Hard Mel disappeared instantly, as did my incarnation as

'Stupid Boy'. In their places were the Mel whom I knew and loved so much, and the good old me who thought Mel was the best thing since toast. She raced towards me and wrapped her arms around me tightly, making me feel like more of a man than I'd felt in a long time. As she kissed me fervently again, and again I realised I'd just made all her dreams come true. *If only it was always this easy to make people you love happy*, I thought. Sometimes I felt like my whole reason for being was to fill the lives of those I loved with disappointment – it was a nice change to do the opposite.

I was happy.

Mel was happy.

Even Nosferatu seemed to be smiling.

Everything was going to be all right.

The Six-million-dollar Man

The reactions to the news of my forthcoming nuptials were strange to say the least. My mum burst into tears. 'I'm so happy,' she said through her joy-filled sobs. 'I'm just so happy for the two of you.' She dropped the phone about a million times, and made me tell her the details over and over again as if she couldn't believe it the first time.

I went round to Vernie's to tell her, and her initial comment was a terse, 'About time too,' which made me laugh because I knew deep down her excitement was on a par with my mother's. Charlie congratulated me with a hearty handshake and said he thought my getting married was the best news he'd heard in ages.

Dan, needless to say, thought my getting married was a bad idea but didn't say so because he knew that wasn't what I wanted to hear. So he gave me a kind of backslappy hug, cracked a joke about advertising in *Penthouse* for a new flatmate and promised to arrange a celebratory drink on Friday night. As Mel had arranged a quick 'I'm-engaged-isn't-it-great?' drink on the same night, Dan's plans fitted in perfectly with the weekend schedule Mel and I had prepared for ourselves, now that we'd been upgraded into the serious-couple club.

Sitting in the Haversham on Friday night, Dan and Charlie

decided unanimously that the whole evening's entertain-
ment would be at my expense, despite my having been
an engaged man for only six days. For the next few hours
I was the butt of their jokes, jibes and mockery, which was
actually quite reassuring in its own way – laughter was the
perfect antidote to any apprehension I was feeling about marriage. The evening's conversation went a little something like
this . . .

8.23 p.m.
'What is it about weddings that women like so much?' asked
Dan.
   'The dresses?' suggested Charlie.
   'You could have a point there,' said Dan. 'What have all
weddings got in common apart from the bride and groom?'
   'A posh dress!' replied Charlie.
   I tried my hardest not to become tainted by the sheer ludi-
crousness of their conversation but I couldn't help myself.
'You're not seriously trying to tell me that women the world
over have been getting married just so they can get a new
frock? What about Elizabeth Taylor? Married more times than
I can remember and she can afford as many posh frocks as
she likes.'
   'Ahhh,' exclaimed Dan astutely, 'but the wedding means
she's always got somewhere nice to wear it.'

9.28 p.m.
Charlie played question master. 'Why do you think blokes
are so scared of commitment?'
   'Simple,' answered Dan. 'It's the Daisy Duke principle.'
With the utterance of those words Dan had our attention
in full. For everyone around the table and probably any
member of our generation, Daisy Duke – of *The Dukes*

of Hazard fame – was a byword for truth, beauty and cheek-revealing denim hotpants. 'In our formative years we're exposed to a huge number of amazingly beautiful women,' continued Dan. 'We men become conditioned to seek out perfection and spend our lives in pursuit of the ultimate babe. Of course this search will prove fruitless because perfection doesn't exist. But that won't stop us wandering through life nomadically, refusing to put down roots until our quest is over.'

'We are to be pitied not chided,' chipped in Charlie. 'Ours is a thankless task.'

'When you think about it,' said Dan, 'finding the perfect partner is a bit like a game of pontoon. I mean, you get your cards and you make your decision. Do you stick or twist? Do you play safe and settle for nineteen or do you go all out for twenty-one, even if you might end up bust?'

'On a good day Vernie's a twenty-one,' Charlie laughed. 'Although I reckon she thinks I'm an eighteen. What do you reckon, Dan? Ever had a twenty-one?

'Let's think,' he said, mulling it over. 'There was Cerys in college, she was a fourteen. Then there was Louise after that who was probably a seventeen, but I think the closest I've ever come was with Meena.' He hesitated for a moment and took a sip of his beer. 'She was definitely a twenty, but you know me, just like Kenny Rogers I'm a gambler. I had to go for the twenty-one. Didn't seem right not to.'

'Mel's my twenty-one,' I said, more to my pint than to my assembled friends. 'She is the perfect hand.'

10.05 p.m.

It was Dan's turn to pontificate. 'Your conventional modern action hero doesn't need a full-time woman, because they get in the way and reduce his ability to catch the bad guys and save the world from certain disaster. That's why none of fiction's greatest heroes are happily hitched. Discuss.'

I attempted to think of a betrothed hero and found it more difficult than I'd anticipated. 'James Bond,' I said triumphantly after a few moments of deep thought. 'He was married.'

'*Was* married,' said Dan. 'In *On Her Majesty's Secret Service*, to be exact. He gets married but his wife gets killed near the end of the film by a bullet meant for JB. The subtext is obvious: James Bond cannot save the world and be an icon for young men the world over with a bird in tow. Plus, if you take the meaningless sex with all manner of exotic kung fu/spy/killer beauties out of James Bond, what have you got? Nothing but a middle-aged man acting like a teenager.'

'He's right,' said Charlie. 'Think about it, Duff. *Starsky and Hutch*, *Magnum PI*, Dean Martin in *Matt Helm*, *Batman*, *Shaft*, Han Solo in *Star Wars* . . . Han *Solo*, I ask you.'

'All the guys in *The A Team*,' added Dan.

'*The Six-million-dollar Man*,' I contributed reluctantly.

'Charlie from *Charlie's Angels*,' added Charlie. Simultaneously Dan and I turned to him for an explanation.

'I'm pretty sure he was married,' I said. 'Bosley was single I'll give you that but I reckon Charlie was definitely married.'

'He's right you know,' said Dan. 'Charlie from *Charlie's Angels* is married. I think they even mentioned it in one show.'

Charlie refused to be convinced. 'As the only person here who has a wife let me tell you. Any bloke who employs three of the Eighties hottest women to fight crime isn't going to be married. There's no way his wife would let him get away with it. Could you imagine Vernie letting me go off to weekend conferences with Sabrina, Kris and Kelly. I don't think so!'

'You could have a point there mate,' said Dan. 'It would be asking for trouble. But anyway, we're digressing. All of these heroes – bachelor men the lot of them,' said Dan. 'It has to be the way for real men to exist. No ties. No hassle. Just fighting crime and babes on tap.'

'Okay,' I countered. I'd been racking my brains trying to find married fictional heroes. 'What about Bruce Willis in the *Die Hard* films? He's married.'

'You're kidding,' said Dan, laughing. 'How long's a marriage going to last when your husband keeps getting himself into the kind of scrapes where he loses his shoes and has to run around upstate New York wearing nothing but a vest?'

11.15 p.m. (Time ladies and gentlemen please!)

'I'm a pretty amazing bloke,' said Dan, adopting a pompous tone of voice. 'I'm a big hit with the ladies, I look the business – in short I am the bee's knees. But . . .' he paused thoughtfully . . . 'if you were to look through a selection of photographs of me when I was seventeen you'd say to yourself, "Why upon my life, cool Dan is in fact nothing but a geek! Look at that haircut, his dodgy Iron Maiden T-shirt, his pitiful attempt to grow a moustache!"'

'So what's your point?' I sighed, as if I hadn't already guessed.

'Marriage is a lot like a photograph. The person you get hitched to is a snapshot of who you are at the time. Granted, you might think she's the best thing ever, but think about it . . . imagine if you got married to the first girl you fell in love with.'

'What?' said Charlie.

'Imagine her. There you are seventeen years old. You're in love. You think it's never going to end. But imagine meeting her now with her big hair, marble-washed jeans and her Amnesty International membership card. Would you want to be married to that?'

I tutted despondently. 'You're presuming that she's stayed the same. You don't know that. If you've changed, then she's bound to have changed too.'

'Of course,' said Dan. 'But into what?'

11.31 p.m. Inside the Archway Fish and Chip Bar across the road from the Haversham

'I'll tell you what's wrong with living together,' said Dan as we waited for our chips and curry sauce. 'It's the root of all evil in every relationship: you take each other for granted. You assume she's always going to be there, so you stop putting in the effort. She assumes you're never going to change and you go out of your way to prove her right. You start treating each other like furniture – and what's worse, not even furniture that you actually like.'

The phone was ringing. I looked at the glow-in-the-dark alarm clock Mel had given me for my twenty-sixth birthday, only to discover it was 2.57 a.m. I attempted to go back to sleep, but the beer, chips and curry sauce churning in my stomach, combined with the madperson at the end of the telephone who clearly refused to believe we were asleep, made resting impossible. Eyes half closed I got up and walked along the hallway, throwing a menacing squint in the direction of Dan's bedroom as I passed. *I bet he's unplugged the answerphone so he could use the toaster in the living room again*, I thought, scowling. I was right. There next to the phone was the toaster with a piece of cold toast in it. I picked up the toast, took a bite and answered the phone, still chewing.

'Hello?' I said about to take another bite of my toast.

'Isssh meee,' slurred an unquestionably inebriated Mel.

'What's wrong?' I asked, as if I didn't know the answer.

'Aaaallcoooohol,' she said desperately. 'Too much . . . think am going to die . . . come round please . . . now.'

'But it's three o'clock in the morning,' I protested. 'I'm knackered. I've only been asleep a few hours.'

'Oh, please come, Duff,' she whined. 'I think I'm going to be sick.'

'You're not going to be sick,' I reassured her. 'Just take a couple of paracetamols, go to bed and I'll see you in the morning. Okay?'

'Okay,' she said, repeating my instructions with a childlike innocence. 'Take a couple of paracetamols, go back to bed and . . . bleuuuurghhh!' The sentence ended abruptly with the unmistakable sound of projectile vomit hitting the telephone mouthpiece.

It was a quarter to four in the morning by the time the taxi pulled up outside Mel's. I got out, handed the driver twenty pounds and told him to keep the change. I didn't usually tip but I was grateful that he hadn't made any comment on my Man United football shirt and paisley dressing gown. Too ill to open the door when I rang the buzzer, Mel hurled the front doorkey out of the upstairs bedroom window and I let myself in.

She was lying on the sofa, still dressed in her work clothes, with a washing-up bowl next to her head and a look of sheer biliousness across her features. 'Oh, Duffy!' she said, employing the quiet self-pitying whiny voice of the repentant drunkard. 'I'm going to die, aren't I?'

'Of course not,' I comforted, glancing at the carrot-based contents of the washing-up bowl. I kissed her lightly on the cheek and removed the bowl to the kitchen. I returned with a glass of water, which I made her sip while I stroked her forehead. While I attempted to scrub a spot of sick off the carpet with a dishcloth, she laid her head back on a cushion and made small murmuring noises.

'How did you get like this?' I said, and sat down beside her.

With her eyes closed quite firmly she began her sorry tale. 'It was only going to be a quick one after work. Just to celebrate our engagement . . .' she whimpered. 'And then Julie told me about a new bar in Poland Street and then everyone thought we should go there and so we did and they kept buying me drinks and I couldn't refuse, could I?' She opened her eyes. 'I couldn't, honestly, Duff.'

'I know, babe,' I said nodding. 'What were you drinking?'

'Vuuurkahanoorraaahhh,' she mumbled.

'What?'

'Vodka and orange,' she repeated guiltily.

'Oh, Mel,' I chided gently. 'You should know better.' Everyone has a loopy juice, a lethal alcoholic cocktail that releases the beast within. For me it was Cinzano and lemonade, for Dan it was cider and black, but for Mel it was vodka and orange. At various times in the past under its influence she had ruined a dress from Ghost trying to climb a fence, lost a purse containing at least fifty quid, and told me for the very first time that she loved me. They were an amusing but volatile double act. 'You said never again after last time,' I reminded her. The last time being Dan's birthday six months ago when after a large number of vodka and oranges, she'd got up on a table in the Soho All Bar One and started dancing in a provocative manner to Shirley Bassey's 'Hey Big Spender'.

'I know,' she said. Her voice was even more pitiful than before. 'I'm sorry.'

I kissed her forehead. 'You did have a proper meal before you started drinking didn't you?'

'Dry roasted peanuts,' she said sorrowfully. 'It was all I could find.' I had to laugh. With a stomach packed with nothing more substantial than peanuts, and seven hours' worth of vodka and orange juice, it was a wonder her brain hadn't melted, let alone her stomach regurgitated its contents. 'I think I'm going to be sick again,' she whimpered.

I looked around for the washing-up bowl but I'd left it in the kitchen. 'Are you sure?'

She nodded.

'Can you walk?'

She shook her head.

'Right, I'll have to carry you then.' Picking her up in my arms, I carried her to the bathroom and placed her on the floor. On her knees she crawled to the toilet, lifted up the seat and threw up while I held her hair out of her face, then collapsed in a heap on the floor.

'I feel much better now,' she groaned mournfully and promptly fell asleep.

I carried her to the bedroom, where I undressed her and put her pyjamas on. I tucked her into bed and then fell asleep beside her.

'Duffy, are you awake?'

It was the day after the night before and I'd been awake for some time staring at the ceiling and thinking about nothing in particular. 'What time is it?' I asked.

Mel looked at her bedside clock. 'Just coming up to two

o'clock in the afternoon.' She pulled herself up close to me. 'Duff,' she said quietly, 'you do know I'm sorry about last night, don't you?'

'There's nothing to be sorry about,' I said, rolling over to face her properly.

'But I got you out of bed at three o'clock in the morning and dragged you halfway across London to look after me.' She sat up, pulling me up with her. 'I love you, you know. Not many men would have done what you did.'

I shrugged my shoulders, embarrassed by her gratitude. 'It wasn't that special.' I paused, lost for words. 'Anyway, you'd do the same for me.'

'That's not the point,' she said, looking so deeply into my eyes I thought she was going to cry.

'What is the point?' I asked, more than a little confused by her behaviour.

'The point is this: I don't think that I've ever loved you more than I do right now.' And then she kissed me.

Because if you are I will be forced to kill you while you're asleep and plead diminished responsibility

It was a sunny Sunday afternoon, one of those freak flashes of summer that now often occur in spring, thanks to global warming. I'd been engaged for a month and was still getting used to the idea of marriage, but with the help of Mel it no longer seemed like such a formidable proposition. Mel, Charlie, Vernie and I had all been for lunch at the Haversham, and as we headed for Highgate Woods we all donned our sunglasses with pride – *Reservoir Dogs* let loose in Muswell Hill.

Our plan for the afternoon revolved around us finding a patch of grass to sit on, earnestly reading the various sections of Charlie's Sunday newspaper and then discussing any current events that caught our eye – just like we'd always imagined proper adults did. In reality, however, I knew we wouldn't do any of these things, because it was such a beautiful day and all we really wanted to do was lie down on the warm grass, stare at the sky and drink the bottle of wine we'd brought with us.

Walking through the iron gates of the park, Charlie and Vernie decided to race each other to the benches in the open space in the middle of the woods. Laughing maniacally, they grabbed at each other's clothing as they tried to stop each other from getting ahead. Mel and I, still digesting our pub lunch, opted to follow them at a far gentler pace.

There was a new seriousness about the two of us, as if the people we had been before our engagement were becoming more and more like distant relatives. Family and friends' responses to us had changed almost overnight – suddenly I was an adult; I was respectable. In recent weeks we'd driven to Southampton to see Mel's mum and dad and taken them out for dinner; my mum had come down to London specifically to see us both and had stayed the whole weekend at Mel's; and we'd seen more of Mark and Julie than ever. Without fail everyone would mention our 'wonderful new life together' as if our old life together had been a complete waste of time. It was hard not to feel nostalgic for the old days when we just 'were'.

As we ambled along, we were drawn to the sounds coming from the adventure playground in the middle of the woods. We stood by the wire fence looking in. The climbing frames, swings and slides – in vibrant shades of red, yellow and blue – were a heaving, screaming mass of kids, like ants crawling over lollypop sticks in summer. Their parents watched enthralled at how much fun these small people could have without the aid of artificial stimulants. The noise was incredible, their Lilliputian voices communicating overwhelming joy and on occasion individual sorrow. A small boy in red dungarees tripped over whilst racing his friends to the slide and immediately burst into tears. Like a one man ER his dad scooped him up into his arms and gave him a huge hug. Within seconds the tragedy was over and the boy was back with his friends again racing towards the slide. The whole scene reminded me of when I was small and my mum would take me and Vernie to the park. I'd always insist that Mum play football with me, and to her credit she did. She was terrible of course – it's impossible to be a good goalkeeper in high heels – but at least she tried.

Mel nudged me gently on the shoulder, rousing me from my reminiscences. She took my hand and squeezed it gently. 'Duffy?'

'Yeah,' I said breezily.

'You were somewhere else.'

'I know,' I said and kissed her.

Reaching up she put a warm hand on either side of my face, pulled me towards her and placed her lips firmly on mine. 'We're getting married,' she said excitedly.

'Yeah, we are.' Holding her hand in my own I absentmindedly rotated the engagement ring I'd bought her. It was a white gold band with a single sapphire. It wasn't particularly expensive compared to the meteorite-sized rock arrangement Mark had commissioned for his engagement ring to Julie, but Mel seemed genuinely to love it.

'Do you think we know enough about each other?' she asked wistfully.

'Yeah, of course,' I replied. 'What I don't know about you I could write on the back of a stamp. I'd need very small handwriting, mind you.'

She punched me in the arm playfully. 'Are you saying that just to shut me up?'

'No.'

'Are you sure?'

'Yeah.'

She took a moment to collect her thoughts. 'So we agree on all the important things that future husbands and wives should agree on?'

'What like?' I said, sitting down on a patch of grass and pulling her down after me. 'Who's going to do the cooking? Who's going to do the washing up?'

She shuffled herself round on her bum so that she could rest her head on my lap. 'Yeah, I suppose.'

'I'll do the cooking. You do the washing up. I'm a dab hand with the microwave, as you know. But as for DIY jobs around the flat – I think we'll get a man in.' I looked across to the playground to watch the kids again. A little girl, roughly six years old, was sauntering aimlessly, arms outstretched in front of her with a yellow plastic bucket on her head.

I looked down at Mel under the cover of my sunglasses. An expression of deepest deliberation animated her face. She was waiting for me to ask what was on her mind. I let the silence live a little longer. She sighed heavily to get my attention. I kissed her. 'You've got something on your mind, haven't you?'

'No,' she said, shaking her head playfully. She took off her sunglasses and lay them on the grass next to her.

'Okay, then,' I returned to playground watching. Another little girl wearing what must have been the brightest orange tights that have ever existed was racing around the edge of the playground shouting out how many laps she'd done every time she passed her dad.

Mel sighed again heavily. 'Do you ever think about . . . oh . . . forget it.'

I lifted my sunglasses on top of my head and made eye contact with her briefly. 'What is it that you want me to think about?'

'Come on we're going for a walk,' said Mel, standing up. I stood up and she put her arm through mine and led me on a walk around the playground. 'Duffy, do you ever think about . . . you know . . .'

'Watching TV uninterrupted? I dream about that . . .'

'No.'

'Why I'm marrying a mad woman?'

'Don't push it.'

'What is it that you want me to think about? C'mon, just spit it out. It can't be that bad.'

She came to a halt, her face half hidden by the shade of an oak tree. 'Children,' she said firmly.

'Children?' I repeated needlessly.

'Yes, children. Do you ever think about us having children?'

'No,' I said almost under my breath. Suddenly all the kids in the playground became sinister and creepy – they still had the same bodies, but all the boys looked like me and all the girls like Mel. Little people with big people's heads on. It was very disturbing.

'Don't you ever think about kids?'

I refused to look at her while we were having this conversation. I knew that if I locked eyes with her she'd suck me into yet another debate in which I'd come off worse. 'I think about kids about as often as I think about how nice it would be to set fire to all my savings, scratch my furniture, wear patches of sick on my suits as a fashion statement and invite unemployed psychopathic dwarves to share my life.'

'That's exactly the sort of thing that Charlie said,' replied Mel.

I finally looked at her and smiled. 'You've been talking about having kids with Charlie?'

'No.' Mel said impatiently. 'Vernie and Charlie have been talking about having kids for the past few months. Or rather in the case of Charlie – not talking about having kids.'

'How do you know all this?'

'Vernie told me.'

'How come I don't know this?'

'Because all you and Charlie ever talk about is TV and sport. You never talk about anything that's even vaguely important.'

'Now hang on,' I protested. 'That's not true. Why, over lunch we talked about . . .' I mentally flicked through the list of topics: yesterday's football results, ten reasons why Roger Moore was a better Bond than Sean Connery (we only came up with eight) and the various pros and cons of Dan's new haircut (pro: it made him look younger; con: it made him look stupid). I changed subjects. 'Vernie wants kids? What for?'

'You say "what for" as if children shouldn't exist unless there's a logical reason for it, like . . . I don't know, you needed someone to wash the car for free.'

'I'll grant you that's a reason . . .' I smiled. 'What did Charlie say, then?'

'Vernie keeps bringing up the subject and he continually changes it. He says he's not ready, but I think he's just being really selfish.'

'He's not being selfish,' I said, defending Charlie's integrity. 'He's just thinking things through logically. That's what we men do. We think, we ponder, we mull and then we think and ponder and mull some more and then—'

'They've been together seven years!' interrupted Mel. 'They've been married for four of those . . .'

'Exactly,' I countered. 'So why change a winning formula?'

Right at that moment Mel and I simultaneously turned to the adventure playground and watched as a small boy handed his mother a bunch of dandelions. I wasn't sure, but it looked as though this tiny gesture of love had moved his mother to tears.

Mel was momentarily silent. 'So you don't want kids either.'

A sudden nausea came over me as I put two and two together and made five. 'Are you trying to tell me something?'

'You must be joking!' exclaimed Mel, horrified. 'Of course not.'

'Okay,' I said, breathing a sigh of relief. 'It's not like I don't want kids. It's just that I'm sure they'd be a good idea one day, but not right now.' I squeezed her arm affectionately. 'You've got your career. I've got my stand-up. There's plenty of time for that sort of thing.'

'I wasn't talking about right now,' said Mel emphatically.

'Good,' I replied, hoping to put a full stop to the conversation. I tried to change subjects. 'What do you fancy doing tonight?'

She ignored me. She wasn't going to let it lie. 'So when?'

'When?'

'When.'

'When?'

'Are you just going to keep repeating everything I say? Because if you are I will be forced to kill you while you're asleep and plead diminished responsibility. Twelve months on probation for manslaughter and I'll be a free woman, and you won't be so annoyingly smug.'

'Smug?'

'Go on, say it one more time, I dare you!'

'I dunno,' I said disdainfully. 'Four years? Five years? It's hard to say. It's a big enough step getting . . .' My words trailed off as I realised a little bit too late that finishing my sentence wouldn't be the smartest move in the world. 'Let's drop it, eh?'

'Carry on,' she said indignantly. 'It's a big enough step getting . . .'

'Okay,' I said, no longer able to put up resistance. 'When did you have them in mind?'

Mel wouldn't say at first, but I coaxed her gently to tell me, even though I didn't really want to know. I just wanted us to get on well together. I didn't want to have an argument or talk about children we couldn't afford and that fifty per cent of us weren't in favour of. It was the expression on her face that gave the game away. She looked embarrassed and uncomfortable. Together with her silence this was a bad sign. A terrible sign. The sign of the devil. In Mel's facial lexicon this meant 'I've been thinking about babies for a while and I think I'd like them quite soon but I'm embarrassed because I don't want you to think that I'm behaving like "a woman".'

'Oh, Mel,' I said mournfully.

'Don't you "oh, Mel" me! Since Vernie's been going on about babies morning, noon and night these past months, they've been on my mind. It's not about hormones. It's not about feeling maternal. It's about me and what I want from life. It's not a crime to think about the future, Duffy. I know to you it's the biggest crime in the world, but I've got a news flash for you – real people think about the future every day. I'm thinking about my future and your future – our future, to be exact. I'm not talking about having them right now. I'm just talking about them, okay?'

'What's it called?' I countered.

This time she avoided my gaze. She pretended not to know what I was talking about, but it was my turn not to let it lie. 'Okay,' she said resignedly, 'so I did imagine our baby. That's not a crime either. We called her Ella. After Ella Fitzgerald.'

'Ella's a nice name,' I said. 'We'll have a baby one day. But not yet. And when we do we'll call it Ella. Okay?'

'Okay.'

With this sorted, Mel fell strangely silent, and so I gave her a hug because I think we both saw that this one was a draw, and we made our way to join Charlie and Vernie.

Later, having lain in the sun all afternoon, using the various sections of Sunday newspaper for nothing other than shading our heads, the four of us walked back through the woods. Vernie and Mel peeled off after a few minutes, hastened by the need to go to the loo, leaving me and Charlie to lag behind and talk about the sort of stuff Mel accused us of not talking about.

'Mel says that Vernie wants kids.'

'Oh, yeah, who with?' Charlie laughed. His smile soon evaporated, to be replaced with a kind of philosophical grimace. 'Yeah, it's true,' he shrugged. 'She's been on about it for ages. I don't know how I'm going to get out of this one.'

'You never know,' I said encouragingly, 'you might have a low sperm count.'

'I'd be surprised if any of the little fellas could count,' said Charlie feebly. 'Although they're bound to be reasonably intelligent, if their manufacturer is anything to go by.'

'Mel was asking me about kids too,' I said. 'I don't think she was serious, though. Merely speculating, if you get my meaning. I don't quite understand why me and her have got to talk about babies just because you and Vernie are in discussions.'

'Women like doing things in pairs, don't they?' said Charlie, only half joking. 'Going to the loo in nightclubs, supermarket shopping, buying shoes—'

'No,' I interrupted. 'Mel always buys her shoes on her own. Too many opinions cloud her thought processes apparently. That said, she still buys shoes that are a half a size too small in the hope that she'll be able to squeeze into them, but at least they're always the right colour and style.'

Mike Gayle

'Well, you get my drift.'

We stopped and stood out of the way while a jogger holding a tangle of dog leads raced past us down the hill followed by three Highland Terriers.

'Do you think you'll give in?' I said, once the last of the dogs had passed.

'I don't know,' said Charlie. 'I mean, it's not like I don't want to have kids: a little girl to play footie with, a little boy to hate me when he's a teenager, but you know . . .' His answer trailed off. I nodded sympathetically. 'Thing is, the minute we have kids that'll be it – everything will change. Nothing will be the same. No more just the two of us. No more throwing a couple of bags into the back of the car and clearing off somewhere for the weekend. No more sitting in the Haversham with you and Dan. No more . . . I don't know . . . no more fun. It'll be nappies and feeding times . . . and breast pumps . . . and bright green baby poo . . . and getting up in the middle of the night . . . and baby seats . . . and my mum and dad coming to see us every other weekend . . . and pushchairs . . . and then one day she'll want another baby because one's never enough.'

'I see what you mean,' I said weakly, still somewhat shaken by the thought of bright green baby poo.

'Do you?' said Charlie sceptically. 'Because I'm not sure I do. I think they're just a big bunch of excuses. I think at the end of the day if I'm truthful I have to say that I'm just absolutely terrified by the thought of being a dad. I'm not ready.'

'I suppose it's a bit like how sometimes I don't feel I'm ready to be a husband,' I added helpfully. I thought about Dan and his denial over Meena and the wedding invitation. 'And not altogether dissimilar to how Dan isn't ready to be a dad, a husband or even a boyfriend.'

70

'When do you think we'll be ready?' said Charlie.

Simultaneously we looked at each other, shrugged a simple 'Dunno' and ran up the hill to catch up with Mel and Vernie.

For days after my conversation with Charlie I couldn't shake the feeling that he, Dan and I were some sort of metaphor for every malaise that had ever affected the modern male. It would only be a matter of time before the women in our lives swapped our real names for American Indian ones: He-whose-sperm-is-his-own; He-who-must-be-single; and He-who-loves-his-girlfriend-but-is-scared-of-marriage.

It really was only a matter of time.

Nice use of light

It was the following weekend and I was just coming to the end of a fifteen-minute set at the Giggle Club – aka the downstairs bar of the Amber Tavern in Islington. Even though I'd only been the second comedian on that evening, the crowd had liked my regular material enough for me to experiment with some new stuff that I'd written on the way over on the bus that night. *This*, I thought, as I thanked the crowd for being a wonderful audience and walked off stage, *has been a very good night*.

As the compère came on and announced a ten-minute interval I sat down at the back of the room and caught up on the comedy circuit gossip with Steve and Alison, the Giggle Club's promoters, and Craig, Lisa and Jim, the other comedians on tonight's bill. Still buzzing from the response of the audience, I very nobly offered to get a round in for everyone. Big mistake. They all said yes. So I took their orders, tried not to cry at the thought of how much this was all going to cost me and disappeared to the upstairs bar. Just as I was about to order the first drink, someone tapped me lightly on the shoulder.

'Ben Duffy?' I turned around to see a woman standing behind me. 'I just wanted to tell you how much I enjoyed your set. You were brilliant.'

Even at this incredibly low level of comedy, it was possible to get the occasional groupie. Not that I'd ever had one. There was no way, however, even in my wildest dreams, that this woman was a groupie. Behind her black oval spectacles – the type hideously beautiful people wear to tone down the effect their visage has on mere mortals – was a pair of deep brown perfectly proportioned eyes. Her waves of thick black hair were tied back from a face so flawlessly perfect it felt rude not to stare. She was dressed casually in jeans, trainers, a cream skinnyrib polo neck and denim jacket. The whole look made her stand out a mile from the pub's mixture of students and professional Islingtonians. It said, 'I know who I am – I am beautiful.'

'Thanks for the compliment,' I said, offering my hand. 'I'm glad you enjoyed it.'

'I'm Alexa Wells,' she said, as if it was a name I should know. 'I kind of know the music video director, Mark Basset, and his fiancée Julie Watson.'

'Do you really?' I asked, balking at the fact that Mark had become so successful that he'd joined that selective band of people whose job title preceded their name.

'I mentioned to Mark last time I went round to theirs for dinner that the programme I work on was looking for a comedian. He told me about you and gave me a video of your act a couple of weeks ago. I only got round to watching it yesterday but I really loved it. *Really, really* loved it.' She floundered momentarily, embarrassed by her own enthusiasm. 'Erm . . . anyway, when I saw in *Time Out* that you were on the bill here tonight I just grabbed a bunch of the researchers and the assistant producer . . .' she pointed at a group of unfeasibly trendy twenty-somethings, their faces obscured in a haze of Marlboro Light smoke . . . 'and dragged them here to see you. And I have to say it was worth it. You were brilliant tonight. So relaxed and confident.'

'Cheers,' I said diffidently. I could feel my forehead furrowing apprehensively – partly because I always got embarrassed by compliments but mainly because I hadn't the faintest clue how Mark had got hold of a tape of one of my gigs. He had mentioned to me several weeks ago that a friend of his who worked in TV was looking for a comedian. He'd even given me the address to send the tape to. It was still on the kitchen cork noticeboard back at the flat.

'What are you up to now?' asked Alexa, lighting up a cigarette and squinting in an outrageously sexy manner as the smoke got into her eyes. She noticed me staring at her. 'Oh, I'm sorry, did you want one?'

I shook my head nervously. 'Not at the minute.'

Silence.

'So?'

I looked at her, bewildered.

'What are you doing now?'

'Right now?'

She nodded.

What am I doing right now?

'Nothing,' I said a little too late for it not to be totally obvious that I'd been trying to think of an excuse why I couldn't talk to her. 'Why? What do you want to do?'

She laughed loudly, unfazed by my lack of social skills. 'You go find a seat,' she said patiently. 'I'll get us a drink and we'll have a quick chat.'

I chose a seat as far away from the bar as possible. My friends downstairs were so Scrooge-like they were bound to send out a search party for their drinks. With my head hidden behind a large cardboard lunchtime menu, I watched as Alexa hovered in the middle of the room looking for me, seemingly unaware that nearly all the pub's male clientele were watching her every move. I waved cautiously. As I stood up to give her a hand with the drinks, I imagined the whole pub sigh collectively as the same thought occurred to all of them: 'What is *she* doing with *him*?'

'So,' I said sitting down, 'what exactly is it you do? All Mark said was that you work in TV. What are you, a runner, researcher or a producer?'

'None of the above,' said Alexa, laughing knowingly. 'I used to present a cable TV music programme about five months ago, but now I co-present *The Hot Pop Show*.'

'I watch that!' I exclaimed a little too excitedly. I wasn't lying either. Since Dan and I had been living together, watching Saturday morning kids' TV had become one of the highlights of our weekend survival ritual. 'I watch it every week. I'm a huge fan.' I paused. 'How come I don't remember seeing you on it?'

'You might be a huge fan,' she smiled and took a sip of her Beck's, 'but you must have been busy for the last few weekends because I'm the show's latest presenter.'

She was right. I had been busy on Saturday mornings lately. Busy doing engaged-couple things with Mel.

'Come to think of it, I might have read something about you,' I said. 'In one of those men's mags that always have about a zillion pages of car and clothing ads.'

She smiled and delved into her shoulder bag on the floor and pulled out a magazine. 'Page fifty-six and fifty-seven,' she said succinctly as she handed it to me.

There in full colour was the woman sitting across the table from me, wearing what could only be described as La Perla-type underwear and a big grin. Across the picture ran the headline: 'TV's Hottest Totty!'

'Nice use of light,' I said, examining the picture carefully.

'Yeah,' she smiled. 'That's what they all say.'

'Do you always show men you've just met pictures of yourself in your underwear?'

She shook her head and smiled. 'Only the nice ones.'

We talked for quite a while. She told me about how she'd finished drama college two years ago, gone travelling in Thailand, come back to England expecting to end up on the dole and instead found herself at an audition for a presenter on a cable TV music programme and got the job. She stayed there for about a year before she was poached to front *The Hot Pop Show*.

'That must be amazing,' I said as she finished her story. 'You have the coolest job on earth. What are you doing talking to me? I'm not worthy.'

Although I was joking, there was a degree of truth to what I'd said. I couldn't help but think, *What does a woman like this want with me?*

'I'm talking to you for two reasons. Firstly, like I said before, we're looking for a comedian for the show. Just to do little sketches and gags and all that. I have to be truthful: the powers that be are auditioning quite a few people, but I'd really love it if you came down and gave it a try. What do you think?'

'Yeah, why not?' I said casually, as if it was every day that I was asked to do a television audition. 'Sounds okay.'

'Right then,' she smiled. 'I'll be in touch.' She looked at her watch – a huge, chunky plastic affair with about eight million buttons. 'It's bedtime for me. I'm shooting a piece about urban rock climbing at six a.m. tomorrow morning.'

I smiled and nodded knowledgeably, as if I well understood the rigours of early morning shoots.

She stood up and we shook hands. 'It was nice to meet you.'

'It was nice to meet you too,' I replied imaginatively.

Mike Gayle

She handed me a business card. 'It's got my work number on it and my mobile . . . so you can get me when you want to.'

'Cheers,' I said, placing the card in the back pocket of my jeans. 'I'll see you around maybe,' I added, although I was pretty sure that the places we chose to be 'around' weren't exactly going to coincide. I watched as she turned, walked halfway across the room, stopped and came back again.

'I was just wondering . . . are you doing anything tomorrow night?' she said, toying with the mobile phone in her jacket pocket. 'I've got tickets for a preview screening of some new Hollywood blockbuster. Lots of explosions, crashes and bullets – a boys' film basically. Do you fancy coming to see it?'

'With you?'

'Yes.'

'Just the two of us?'

'Uh huh.'

I thought about her invitation very hard in the few seconds allotted to me, and then as casually as I could, which probably wasn't all that casual given that for some reason I was unable to use the personal pronoun I said, 'Can't. Staying in with girlfriend.' And if that wasn't bad enough, I managed to spit the word 'girlfriend' at her like it was a bulb of garlic and she was the Bride of Dracula.

'That's a shame,' she said as if she truly meant it. 'Maybe another time.'

'Just one more thing,' I enquired carefully. 'You said that you were talking to me tonight for two reasons. What was the other one?'

She smiled cryptically and said, 'I'll tell you all about it another time.'

*   *   *

It's not a big deal.

It's not even a medium-sized deal.

If it's any sort of deal at all, it's a teeny weeny teeny tiny one.

All I'd done was have a drink and a chat with a female kids' TV presenter for half an hour tops. All she'd done was have a drink with me, look fabulous and ask me out to a film preview.

She couldn't have fancied me, I thought as I left the pub.

Women like that don't fancy men like me, I convinced myself on the bus on the way home.

So, if she didn't fancy me, there's no reason to tell Mel about the bit where I thought she fancied me, ran my thought processes through my sleepless night.

Nice try, said my conscience next morning, *but you know as well as I do that you're guilty as a guilty thing.*

I laughed so hard milk came out of my nose

Propelled by guilt I decided it was time to spend more quality time with Mel. So the next evening, a Friday night, as Dan had an overnight gig in Northampton, I invited her round to the flat so that we could spend some time on our own. I tidied up in anticipation of her arrival and actually considered cooking a meal, but thought better of it and sorted out a Chinese takeaway instead.

Together we consumed a couple of bottles of wine, ate king prawns in black bean sauce, watched TV and chatted about nothing in particular. She lay on the sofa with her head on my lap, and as I stroked the hair at the back of her neck with my fingertips I suddenly became aware that this cosy domestic scene might just be a snapshot of the future. *This is nice*, I thought. *It feels . . . comfortable*. Then it occurred to me that although I liked comfortable, I needed to be honest with Mel even more.

Though some twenty-fours hours had passed since my encounter with Alexa, I was still feeling guilty. While there was a slim possibility that if I told Mel what had happened she'd see the whole thing my way, I had to accept that my small deal ran the chance of being a big deal to her. Massive. Gargantuan. Even so, I still I felt the need to confess everything.

81

Up until this point in my life I'd worked on the basis that what Mel didn't know about couldn't hurt her, and without much trouble I'd managed to gather together a nice collection of so-called skeletons in the cupboard. They didn't rattle too much and gave me absolutely no trouble at all, but since The Proposal Mel had, unbeknownst to me, managed to instil in me something approaching a conscience, and I now couldn't rest. I wondered whether now was the time to get those skeletons out. A few sprang to mind immediately, and just for my own amusement, while Mel dozed, I took them out of store in my head and had another look at them.

The Crossover Skeleton

There was a slight crossover period of two weeks between the end of my last girlfriend and the beginning of Mel. I didn't count this as a particularly big skeleton because its existence was due to the fact that I was terrible at dumping girlfriends. Her name was Amanda. She was a comedian I met at a gig at the Edinburgh festival. As she lived in Manchester we only ever saw each other at weekends, which was handy because although she was fun, she certainly wasn't proper girlfriend material.

When the time came, I tried to tell her it was over between us in the only way I could – I didn't phone, I was sullen and surly whenever she came to London to visit, but she thought I was just being enigmatic. I even told her, 'Look, Amanda, I'm sorry but it's over. I'm going out with someone else,' but in her mind that only served to make me even more alluring in a 'he's a challenge' sort of way.

Eventually I had to call upon Dan's master dumping skills to assist me. Which was of course a bad move. A very bad move. He told her that I was dead. She turned up one day at my old flat in Wood Green, and Dan, after having spotted her out of my living-room window, answered the door with tapwater dripping from his eyes. Employing his very best acting skills he sobbed, 'Amanda! Haven't you heard? Duffy was killed last week in a terrible accident. Workmen were repairing Lambeth Town Hall, and as he was walking past, some loose masonry fell and killed him. Instantly.' She believed him, as you would do (who's going to make up something like that?), and even wanted to come to the funeral, but Dan told her it was for close family only.

It should've been perfect. Immortalised in Amanda's head as the Difficult Dead Boyfriend. She would've forgotten all the bad bits about me, and remembered only the good times. But me being me, I had to go and bump into her three weeks later at a club in Hoxton Square when I was out with Mel. She didn't say a single word to me, but her menacing Mancunian scowl spoke volumes.

Mel noticed Amanda's looks of hatred immediately and asked me who she was, so I told her the first thing that came into my head: 'She's a stalker. Comedians get them sometimes.'

In my defence for the overlap, I didn't count it as cheating on Mel because I really was trying to do The Right Thing.

The Naked Skeleton

Last year I kind of semi-lied to Mel and told her I was going with Dan to the Prince Charles to see a rerun of *Get Carter*, when in fact the two of us went to a topless bar called the Rising Moon in the West End. It was all Dan's idea. He'd become obsessed with an article he'd read in a men's magazine, '101 things you must do before you're thirty. Of the 101, Dan was pleased to discover he'd done ninety-two of them. Of the ones that remained, two were illegal, one he decided was definitely immoral, and with his limited finances he wasn't in a position to do any of the others, with the exception of attending a lapdancing club. We both agreed that lapdancing clubs were both morally reprehensible and ludicrously expensive, so we compromised and settled for a topless bar.

As neither of us had ever been to a place like this before, we weren't entirely sure what to do when we got inside. So taking a table in the darkest corner possible, we sat for ages making the tiniest of small talk, pretending that this whole thing wasn't really happening. Eventually a G-string-clad young woman, profoundly gifted in the chest area, sauntered over to us to take our order. Embarrassed beyond belief, I couldn't bring myself to look at her breasts and was too ashamed to look her in the eyes, so I conducted the entire conversation focusing on her nose. Our topless waitress looked about our age. In fact she reminded me of a girl I went to college with called Karen Braithwaite. She had blonde hair and the same puffy forehead that Karen had, but she had a much nicer body, although technically speaking I'd never seen Karen Braithwaite in a G-string. I thought about asking her if she was Karen, but then it occurred to me that if she was the same person this wasn't really going to be the right moment for us to talk over old times. I ordered two bottled beers and she disappeared, leaving Dan and me to gape around the room.

The bar was full of solitary businessmen, tattooed fat blokes with their tattooed fat bloke mates, and large groups of young men on stag nights. This depressing sight brought me to my senses as I was suddenly struck by three things:

1) it was depressing to discover I had anything in common with these people;

2) I'd never felt more embarrassed in my life;

3) none of this was giving me any pleasure whatsoever.

As Dan and I sipped our beers in silence, I thought about being there and I tried to remember the last time I had thought about anyone but Mel. And I couldn't. It was a key moment for me. Like being handed the meaning of life on a plate. Mel was all that I wanted.

The Artistic Butcher Skeleton

About two and a half years ago Mel and I split up. We just weren't getting on very well. So she called an end to it. Depressed beyond belief I met a girl at a gig who mistook my melancholy for sensitivity. I suppose we had a common cause: we both hated our day jobs (she worked in a butcher's but by night painted abstract images in her Clerkenwell studio) and we'd both been recently dumped. I tried to put her off; I told her about my ex-girlfriend and how wonderful she was, but she said, 'You can't have been that serious if you weren't even living together.' I didn't really have an answer for that one. I told her I didn't want anything to happen and I also told her I certainly didn't want a relationship; we could be mates and nothing more.

One evening, we met up for a drink after work. She tried to kiss me and failed; then later I tried to kiss her and failed too; then some time around midnight we both tried to kiss each other and succeeded and I ended up staying the night at hers. I don't know why I did it. I didn't even like her. I especially don't know why I called her the next day and left a message on her answerphone asking if she wanted to go to the cinema. Guilt, I suppose. I thought I owed her something. But whatever it was I owed her, she obviously didn't want it because she never called back.

Mel and I got back together a week later.

End of skeletons

*   *   *

'Is anybody home?'

At the sound of Mel's voice I shook my head clear of the cobwebs of deep thought. I'd been reflecting so intensely on my skeletons that I hadn't noticed her awaken from her nap. Now she was staring up at me intently and probably had been for quite a while.

'What were you thinking about?' she said, curious.

'Oh nothing,' I said dismissively. 'What's on telly?'

Mel sat up and looped her arm through mine squeezing herself closer to me. 'Don't tell me "nothing", Mr Benjamin Duffy. What were you thinking about? Come on, I can tell when there's something wrong.'

It was true. Mel had an amazing ability to monitor my emotional landscape – evidently even when asleep. My mulling over the skeletons must have alerted her sleeping body to my troubled psyche. Resistance would be futile.

'Tell me,' she demanded finally.

I deliberated over her request and decided against it. We'd been together four years. We were planning to get married. Now wasn't the right time for either of us to start telling The Truth.

'Look it's nothing,' I said testily. 'I'm okay.'

'Tell me,' she cajouled, narrowing her eyes at me.

I reviewed my position. I wasn't really giving her a chance. It was unfair to act like she was a walking bundle of unreasonability waiting for an excuse to explode.

I took a deep breath. 'You know I had a gig last night?'

'You said it went really well.'

'Yeah, it did. It's just that . . . well, afterwards this girl . . . well, woman, I suppose . . . the one who Mark knows, who

needed a comedian for her TV show . . . well, she was there.
Turns out she's a TV presenter.'

'Oh, yeah?' said Mel inquisitively. 'What did she want?'

'She said she liked my act and invited me to audition for
the TV show she works for.'

'And?'

I weighed up Mel's 'and' in my head. It would've been much
easier if there hadn't been room for an 'and'. I didn't want
this to be one of those situations where five minutes later
I'd be wishing I'd chosen the 'LEAVE WELL ALONE' option.
But I wanted to be honest. In fact I had a deep-seated need
to be honest.

'Well, I don't know if it was just in my head, but I think she
might have been flirting with me.'

'Flirting with you?'

'And she asked me out,' I blurted.

'And?'

'And nothing,' I said confidently. I was pleased with myself.
I'd come up trumps.

'So why are you telling me all this?'

'No reason.'

'But you never tell me anything like that unless I drag it
out of you. What's so special about this woman? Apart from
the fact that she's on TV, of course.'

'Nothing,' I said, endeavouring to disguise the worry creep-
ing into my voice as masculine indifference. 'There's nothing
special about her. I was just making conversation.'

'Why does she fancy you? She hardly knows you.'

'I don't know.'

'Did you tell her about me?'

'Yes.' I nodded.

'So why did she ask you out?'

'I dunno,' I said, shrugging my innocence.

'Did you make her laugh?'

'No . . . yes . . . a little bit.'

'How many times?'

'I don't remember.'

'Is she pretty?'

I had to be deadly careful here. Too attractive and Mel would be jealous. Too ugly and Mel would think that I was lying to cover up the fact that she was TV's Hottest Totty. 'Average really. She was all right, I suppose, if you like that kind of thing.'

'She can't have been that plain if you're telling me about her. You're feeling guilty, Duffy. So what else are you hiding?'

'Nothing.' I wavered. I was seconds away from confessing to anything just to stop this torture. 'I was only making conversation!' I protested. 'Telling you all the stuff that happens in my life that you say I never tell you. But if you're going to accuse me of things every time I tell you what I've been doing, then we won't get very far, will we?'

Mel started giggling wildly. 'Good grief! I'm only pulling your plonker, Duff! I know all about Alexa. Her card is marked, I can tell you.'

'You know?'

'Everything,' she said, leaning over the side of the sofa and rummaging about in her bag. 'Still, you did leave out one small fact.'

'What?' I said warily.

'That she's TV's Hottest Totty!' she said brandishing the men's magazine Alexa had posed for. 'Apparently she described you as "cute in a little-boy-lost kind of way", but you turned her down because you said you were staying in with me, your girlfriend, which I might add was the right response.'

'How do you know all this?' I said, trying desperately not to show any hint of joy at being described as 'cute' by someone as fabulously gorgeous as Alexa.

Mel pecked me on the cheek and giggled. 'I have eyes everywhere!' she laughed. 'The boring answer is that Alexa called Mark and then Mark called Julie at work and told her and then Julie called me about a millisecond after and probably added a bit more to the story to make it more juicy.'

'So she didn't fancy me?' I said, trying to sound relieved.

'Oh yes she did,' said Mel knowingly. 'Julie wouldn't embellish *that* kind of detail.'

'So if you knew all the time why did you put me through all this?'

'I've been waiting all evening for you to tell me. I thought I was going to explode with excitement.' She stopped talking and carefully examined the two-dimensional Alexa in the magazine. 'Granted she's got a pretty face and a nice pair of bazookas, but her teeth are crooked, her bum's much bigger than mine, and green lingerie really doesn't suit her!' She creased up into a ball of laughter. 'My boyfriend chatted up by TV's Hottest Totty!' she tittered, failing to regain her composure. 'I quite like the idea of having to fight for you. Makes you seem more . . . I don't know . . . interesting!' She kissed me and then added, 'It almost makes you seem sexy.'

'Almost?'

'Nearly,' she purred.

'So you're not annoyed, then?'

'Of course not. I trust you completely.'

I hugged her and kissed her firmly. Staring over her shoulder, once again I began to ponder the other skeletons in my mental cupboard, but decided to save them for some other time.

Later that night, still lying on the sofa with the TV on in the background, I looked down at Mel, who was lying next to me with her eyes closed. I whispered her name quietly to see if she was asleep. She wasn't.

She opened her eyes. 'You can turn over and watch *Frasier*,' she said, yawning.

'That's not what I wanted,' I said quietly. 'I still don't understand. How did Mark come to have a tape of my stand-up to give to Alexa?'

'I gave it to him,' confessed Mel sheepishly. 'I knew you'd never get round to sending it off yourself. I'm sorry, Duff. I'm an interfering old cow.'

'Don't be silly,' I said. 'You're right: I should've got round to sending the tape ages ago. I dunno what's wrong with me sometimes.'

'You just got a little bit scared, that's all.' She kissed me sleepily. 'I want to do everything I can to help you. You think that I take what you do for granted, but I don't. I know you sometimes think that I don't think you're funny, but you are. You make me laugh all the time – although not always intentionally. Just promise me even when we're old and grey that you'll keep making me laugh until milk comes out of my nose.'

I looked at her puzzled.

'You don't remember, do you? Last summer. We were round at my flat and I was feeling really down about work. You were trying your best to cheer me up and it wasn't working because I was being a miserable old bag, and then just as I began drinking a glass of milk you leaped up and down on the sofa like a chimpanzee, singing "New York, New York". I laughed so hard milk came out of my nose.'

'I'll try my best.' I paused. 'Mel, thanks for . . . you know . . . everything you've done.' Words seemed to fail me.

'Don't thank me,' she smiled. 'Just get me that Ferrari!'

This isn't about wardrobes

The alarm clock in Mel's bedroom went off at 7.30 a.m. I took a long hard squint at it before entombing it beneath a large pile of clothes. *It's Saturday morning,* I thought groggily, *no one should be up this early on a Saturday.* Out of the only eye I was willing to open this early in the morning, I observed an already up-and-out-of-bed Mel keenly.

'Time to get up,' she said, coyly beckoning me out of bed. She was wearing a long misshapen Snoopy T-shirt and nothing else. She looked crumpled and yet strangely alluring, so much so that I was half tempted to leap up and chase her around the room Benny Hill style. Unfortunately, given how early it was I lacked the strength of will to execute my plan, so instead, as my libido faded to black I resolved not to reply, closing my eyes instead in a bid to feign sleep. *Maybe now she'll leave me in peace,* I thought, turning over.

She didn't. Instead, her counter measure was to wrench the kingsized duckdown duvet off the bed, exposing my body to the cold of the room, and in a move carefully calculated to wind me up shouted, 'Time to get up!' again in a chirpy singsong voice, whilst dancing coquettishly just out of reach. Without saying another word, I made my way to the bathroom and took a shower.

My rude awakening was based on the fact that it was now March and six weeks had passed since we'd become engaged. It was time for us to plan the wedding. We'd already settled on a date in October the following year and her parents' local parish church. My only suggestion for the big day – that we had a disco for the evening do – was shot down by Mel for being 'tacky above and beyond the call of duty'. I couldn't believe it. As far as I was concerned, a wedding reception without a mobile DJ playing the Commodores' 'Three Times a Lady' and Dexy's Midnight Runners' 'Come On, Eileen' just wasn't a wedding reception. Mel, however, wanted something more tasteful, like a string quartet or a band, and wasn't going to budge. Thus began a minor argument which concluded in a win for her corner, when I gave up after ten minutes of going backwards and forwards having realised *The Simpsons* was on TV and I'd already missed five minutes.

These minor wedding decisions were only the beginning. There were the catering, flower arranging, photographers, wedding video, hotel and honeymoon booking, reception-room scouting *and* booking, car hire and cakemakers all to be organised and paid for. Mel had a thick loose-leaf folder with the words 'Wedding Planner' emblazoned across it in swirling gold lettering – a present from my mum. Weekends – once a time to relax and renew one's batteries after a week of work – were now more toilsome than days in the office. Weekends were now officially Duffy and Mel days – devoted to the pursuit of marital harmony.

'Where are we going today?' I asked Mel sulkily, having showered, shaved and sufficiently warmed up my personality.

'We talked about it last night.'

'We did?' I tried to remember the previous night. All I managed to recall was eating a Chinese and falling asleep in front of the telly.

'Yes. While we were watching the news. I told you we needed to go there to put things on our wedding list and your reply was, "Whatever you want."'

'Oh yeah,' I said, bluffing total recall. 'We're going to . . .'

'IKEA.'

I'd never been inside an IKEA before. I'd been as far as the car park on a couple of occasions, but I'd always preferred to wait in the car as though repelled by an invisible forcefield. I didn't understand the concept of shopping for home furnishings at all. To me a chair was a chair. A table was a table. Curtains were curtains. But to Mel these things took on a mysterious significance which I couldn't begin to comprehend. To her a chair wasn't a chair unless it was a set of six and matched the napkins. A table wasn't a table unless it was large enough to seat six to eight people at a dinner party. Curtains weren't just curtains, they were the critical focal point of a room. 'Make a mistake with your curtains,' she once informed Nosferatu, 'and you might as well give up altogether.'

My heart sank the moment we arrived at IKEA. Such was the allure of home furnishings, that like salmon in search of their spawning ground, teeming multitudes of Proper Couples had felt the mysterious urge to come here. We queued for ten minutes just to get into the car park. After that we had to drive around like buzzards circling wounded antelope in search of the last parking space in the western hemisphere. Still, there were brief moments of satisfaction to be had. I spotted a parking space only seconds before a couple in a Vauxhall Tigra; the race was on but even in Mel's 2CV there was no way they could beat me. As I eased into the space and checked the rearview mirror to gloat, I was just in time to see the male driver of the Vauxhall Tigra being harangued by his other half for not being quick enough off the mark.

'What are we doing here, Mel?' I whined miserably, as we came through the electronic doors and she put one of those huge shapeless yellow bags on her shoulder. I'd meant the question metaphysically rather than literally.

'Shopping, stupid,' joked Mel, choosing to take my words at face value.

This one sentence said more about the gap in under-standing between Mel and me than anything else in our lives. This was different. This was innate. Shopping to her wasn't a means to an end – it was an end in itself. She was on a spiritual journey, searching for that elusive something or somethings that would help her to make sense of the world and her place in it. Why she needed me to join her on this journey I failed to understand, but I *was* there, and we *were* getting married so I opted to make the most of it.

Within minutes Mel had a look of post-coital bliss over her face as she glided from sofa to armchair to futon and back again, casually stroking their material as if they were fondly remembered lovers.

'So what do you think?'

She was now pointing to a beige object of roughly the same dimensions as the lifts we had at work. By the look on her face I gathered she'd been in conversation with me about this item of furniture for some time. To have admitted my folly would've been, well, sheer folly. So I bluffed.

'It's nice.'

She gave me The Look.

'What have I said?'

Silence.

'What have I said?'

'You know,' she said barely moving her lips.

'What?'

Silence.

'What?'

'Saying it's "nice" like that. I'm not stupid, Duffy. If you didn't want to come why are you here? Can't you just make the effort this one time?'

'What's wrong with it being a "nice" wardrobe? It is a "nice" wardrobe. It's pleasant, agreeable, congenial and pleasing to the eye.' I stepped forward and ran my fingers along its surface, attempting to empathise. 'Smooth.'

A smile gradually cracked across her face, which eventually manifested itself into a toothy grin. I'd won her back from the edge of an argument, which was no mean feat. I gave myself a pat on the back as if I'd just defused the timer on six tonnes of plastic explosive.

'I think it would look great in our bedroom,' said Mel, still examining the wardrobe. Mel had been talking about 'our' bedroom for a while now. She wanted to hand in her notice on her Clapham flat and move in with me and Dan so we could save up enough money for a deposit on a place of our own. While it was true that my flat was cheaper, it was also true that Mel would hate living with me and Dan. Mel was allergic to slovenliness at the best of times and, well, the flat Dan and I inhabited was pretty much the shelter of the slovenly. She'd be fighting a losing battle that would eventually drive her insane.

I looked at the wardrobe again. In Mel's bedroom it would've looked fine with her antique-pine dressing table, framed Hopper prints and lilac walls. But in my bedroom it would've looked crap because it would never go with my off-white walls, Incredible Hulk poster and bookshelves littered with CDs, records, video console games and my ever-growing collection of comedy videos. I had no concept of what 'our' bedroom would look like, but there was little doubt in my mind it wouldn't look like *my* bedroom. Not if Mel had anything to do with it.

Out of curiosity I read the label on the wardrobe and was horrified. 'We can't buy it anyway. It's a flatpack wardrobe. Remember the flatpack chest of drawers we tried to assemble that one Bank Holiday? It took us three days just to find the screws and another three days to give up and chuck it underneath your bed!'

It was a joke of sorts, although to be truthful neither of us had the time or patience for flatpack furniture. Mel, however, didn't laugh. Instead she fell into the kind of silence you'd imagine fills the air before a volcano erupts. I was scared.

'I'm sorry, babe, it's just that—'

I didn't get the chance to finish my sentence. Mel turned and walked briskly away, and I chased after her berating myself for not choosing the option marked 'LEAVE WELL ALONE.'

IKEA was now overspilling with examples from the entire couple rainbow. Ones in matching jumpers, ones with matching kids, odd ones, young ones, old ones – and they were *all* in my way. I lost sight of Mel whilst trying to get round an Indian couple wheeling their children along in two of IKEA's pushchairs. By the time I'd apologised my way through them she'd disappeared. I raced frantically through Beds, Office Furniture and Storage Units before I caught sight of her in Dining Rooms.

'Mel!' I called out after her but she refused to acknowledge me. 'Mel wait!' I shouted.

A blond man wearing a herringbone jacket and jeans, with a small boy on his shoulders and his heavily pregnant significant other by his side, tapped Mel on the arm and pointed to me. She stood still but the flow of couples was coming too fast for her to remain stationary for long. She stepped out of the couple slipstream wearily and sat down on a dining-room chair that was part of one of the displays. It was a sleek modern-look dining room with a frosted-glass table. A perforated metallic black lampshade hung above it; Swedish novels lined the 'Billy' bookcase; a large sign pointed out the wooden-effect flooring was from the Tundra range at £15.00 a square metre.

I pulled up a chair opposite her. 'Look, I'm sorry,' I whispered – we were now attracting a considerable amount of attention from passing couples. 'It was a stupid thing to say. Of course we can get the wardrobe. Please.'

'This isn't about wardrobes!' said Mel through clenched teeth, her voice increasing in volume and anger with each syllable. 'It's about *you* and *your* attitude. All I want is a bit of support. Some reassurance. Is that too much to ask?'

Out of the corner of my eye, I noticed that a stout couple were watching us as though we were some sort of avant garde amateur dramatic society. This was my idea of hell. I hated rows in public. I hated them more than anything in the world. 'Of course it's not too much to ask,' I apologised. 'You're right. I'm wrong. Let's leave it at that okay?'

Mel's face contorted in outrage. 'You're not listening to me!' she screamed. Angry tears streamed down her face. 'You haven't listened to a single word I've said, have you?' Out of the corner of my eye I noted that the stout couple had been joined by a matching jumpered couple and a short couple in wax coats with their baby. I was now the recipient of an increasing number of sympathetic glances from the men and condemnatory glares from the women, as if Mel and I were the sex war writ large. I tried to remind myself I was twenty-eight and not ten. That I was a man not an errant schoolboy. But I couldn't help feeling small. And wrong.

I tuned back to my dressing down, ignoring the flourishing crowds of people no longer struggling to hear what Mel was saying because she was now 'talking' with such volume that eavesdroppers could've easily swapped their position in the eaves for somewhere more comfortable, like Sweden, and still have heard every word. 'Look, Mel. I understand that you're upset, but do you have to be so loud? Can't you just . . .' I made the mistake of issuing a small shushing noise.

'Are you shushing me?' she retorted.

'No.'

'You are, aren't you?'

'No.'

'Don't you shush me!'

'He is shushing,' spat the woman from the stout couple menacingly. 'I know a shush when I hear one!'

'I'm not shushing!' I exclaimed in her direction.

Mel sighed heavily, and the exhaled air seemed to take her volume with it. 'You're not being fair, Duffy. It's time you grew up and realised you're not a kid any more. You can't keep on acting like you're a teenager.'

'Listen, Mel, I'm sorry. Okay? I'm sorry.'

'It's too late, Duffy. It's over.'

Suddenly the world and everything in it seemed to slow down, as if we'd all been submerged under water. 'What?' I said, rubbing the back of my neck nervously. 'What are you talking about?'

'This isn't working, is it?' she said quietly. She refused to look at me. 'You don't really want to get married, Duff. I know you don't. You want your life to carry on just the same.' She began crying, her teardrops exploding on the glass tabletop like miniature water bombs. 'It's not your fault, it's just the way you are – it's part of the reason I love you. I love you because you are so carefree. I love you because you take things as they come. But I need more. I deserve more and you can't give it to me.'

I could barely believe what I was hearing. It was like Mel was having a conversation with me without my uttering a single word. The world had gone all wrong. Wrong and weird. *I have to make everything all right again*. 'What's going on here, babe? What's brought this on? Everything's fine.' I reached out and held her hand. 'Everything's going to be okay.'

'Duffy, I know everything about you,' she said accusingly.

'What are you talking about?' I protested. 'Things are getting out of hand. Let's just calm down and everything will be all right.'

She looked up at me at last. 'Look me in the eyes and answer this question: do you really, well and truly with your whole heart, want to get married?'

I met her gaze briefly and looked away.

'There's my answer,' she said, sniffing back her tears. 'I'd guessed there was something wrong but I wasn't sure until now.'

I wanted desperately to be able to lie. To say, 'Yes, I do want to get married,' but I couldn't. My newly installed conscience wouldn't let me. I loved her. I wanted to be with her. But I did not want to be married. At least not now. Not yet.

'We'll be all right, Mel,' I said, still holding her hand. 'We're going to be okay.' She didn't speak. We sat in silence while her unspoken reply made its way to my brain. It didn't quite get there. 'We're going to be all right, Mel. We can get over this.'

Silence.

'We don't need to split up,' I said desperately. 'We don't. I can learn.' I was grasping at straws now. 'I'll buy you the wardrobe.'

Still crying, she gently rotated her engagement ring off her finger and pressed it into the palm of my hand and closed my fingers over it. 'It was a nice try, Duffy . . .' she leaned across the table and kissed me softly . . . 'but it wasn't enough.'

'I want to do the right thing,' I said, fighting back the tears. She didn't hear me, though – she'd already stood up and walked away. I tried to follow her but she was too far ahead for me to catch up with her, so I watched as she manoeuvred her way through Bathrooms, Rugs and Flooring towards the checkout where finally she was swallowed up into the crowds of happy couples.

I can change

It was early Sunday morning, the day after the IKEA episode and I was on my way round to Mel's, determined to sort out this whole sorry mess. As far as I was concerned, all that had happened was that we'd had a stupid row which had blown up out of all proportion. All we needed to do was sit down and sort everything out and we'd be back to normal. The ten-minute walk from Clapham Common Tube to Mel's flat flew by as I imagined us realising that our row was nothing more than a silly quarrel brought on by pre-wedding jitters. The important thing was that we loved each other. That was all that mattered.

I pressed the buzzer for Mel's flat. After the fourth or fifth ring I heard footsteps on the stairs and seconds later a blurry Mel-shaped figure appeared through the frosted stained glass and opened the door.

'I'm sorry,' I said, not even giving her the chance to open her mouth to say hello. 'Yesterday was all my fault. I was being stupid. I'm sorry.'

Mel said nothing.

While I hadn't exactly expected a round of applause and a standing ovation, neither had I anticipated the short uncomfortable smile she gave me or the silence that accompanied it. I followed her up the stairs to her flat wondering what was going on.

Her living room was abnormally tidy. As a rule Mel was tidy but not obsessive – today, however, the entire room looked as if it had been cleaned from top to bottom by my mum, a woman for whom a thrice weekly removal of dust had taken on an almost religious significance. The flat's pristine condition didn't surprise me too much. It was Mel's way when she was unhappy to clean – to make sense of her environment by completing tasks that were completable. The room seemed to echo her thoughts: 'If only life were cleanable. If only it was a question of time and effort before life took on some semblance of peace and order.'

'I'm just going to make a cup of tea,' called out Mel from the kitchen. 'Do you want an orange juice?'

'Yeah,' I said, watching her movements through the open kitchen door. 'That would be great.'

I sat down in the armchair that Mel's gran had given her when she'd moved into a nursing home. Under normal circumstances it was my favourite seat in the flat but as soon as I sat there I knew I should've sat on the sofa so that Mel could sit next to me. Now there was this huge physical distance between us as well as the emotional gap we were trying to bridge. Just as I was about to swap seats however she entered the room with the drinks and sat on the sofa opposite. The coffee table lay between us like a latterday Berlin wall. We sat sipping and not speaking, listening carefully to the sort of sounds we normally never heard: the ticking of the clock on the wall; the sound of Cliff Richard on Radio 2 emanating from the house across the road; the sound of two people sipping in silence.

I knew I had to say something but I didn't want to mention anything more about our row. I felt that if we didn't talk about the problem directly then it didn't exist. It was ridiculously optimistic of me, but I couldn't escape the feeling that if I could just drum up enough normal conversation with her, through some miracle of amnesia she'd completely forget that less then twenty-four hours earlier she'd broken off our engagement. But what do you talk about when there really is only one thing to talk about? I looked out of the window for inspiration.

'Looks like it might rain later,' I lied. The sky was perfectly blue and cloudless. Clutching at straws? I was grasping at fresh air.

'Does it?' said Mel, gazing out of the window to join me in my meteorological studies.

Silence.

I looked inside the room for inspiration. 'The flat's really tidy.'

Mel took a sip of her tea. 'Thanks.'

Silence.

'This afternoon's *EastEnders* omnibus looks good.'

More silence.

So much for the weather.

So much for tidy flat observations.

So much for soap operas.

So much for sticking my head in the sand hoping it would all go away.

If I don't say something soon we'll still be here on the sofa having monosyllabic I-spy-with-my-little-eye conversations this time tomorrow, I thought nervously. Taking a deep breath to steel my nerves I decided to come out into the open. 'Are you okay?' I asked tentatively. 'I was worried about you.'

'Yeah, I'm fine,' she said lifelessly.

'I'm sorry. About yesterday. I'm really sorry. I was stupid and selfish and I'm sorry. But that stuff you said about us being . . .' I didn't want to spell it out, but the impassive look on Mel's face was scaring me into it. 'It wasn't true, was it? It was just you getting angry with me, wasn't it?' I smiled. I didn't want it to be an accusation – I wanted it to be light and airy.

Mel shook her head. 'We are over – you must know that, Duff, after yesterday.'

I opened my mouth to say something in my defence but she held her hand up to stop me.

'I know that you're going to tell me that you do love me and that you do want to get married after all, and that's really sweet but it's only half true. You don't want to get married, do you, Duff?' The saucer in her left hand was shaking ever so slightly. 'When I asked you yesterday if you really, truly wanted to get married, you didn't answer me. You confirmed what I knew already but was too scared to admit to myself: you love me but you don't want to get married.'

She put the cup and saucer down on the table and looked out of the window. 'I think I knew you felt that way even on the day that you finally said yes. But I was so happy . . . so relieved, that I put it to the back of my mind. I threw myself into making wedding plans, trying to sort things out, celebrating us being together. Looking back at it now, I can see that all I was doing was trying to block out the thought that you might not feel the same way about us being together as I do. I was hoping that somehow you'd catch me up, that this would excite you as much as it did me.' She hesitated slightly and looked right into my eyes. 'Then yesterday as we argued it struck me, just as if someone had slapped me across the face, that your heart wasn't in it – that you were marrying me because it was what I wanted, not because it was what you wanted. All you wanted to do was the right thing. The thing is, Duffy, I don't want you to think of us spending the rest of our lives together as some sort of sacrifice you've got to make. I don't want you to turn round to me one day and tell me I forced you into it. I'd hate it. Absolutely hate it.'

'That's not true,' I said quietly.

'It is, and you know it. If you want proof I'll give you proof.'

I raised my eyebrows sharply, as if she was about to spring a surprise expert witness on me. Who would it be? My mum? My sister? My conscience?

'It's just the small things really,' she continued. 'Like the last time we went to Mark and Julie's – all night you were miserable and I could see it was because they were talking about the wedding. Or when we chose the engagement ring. The look on your face when the jeweller handed it to you – it was only fleeting but I saw it all the same – it was a look of doubt, a look that said: 'Am I doing the right thing? But the real evidence is us. Four years together and the longest we've spent living under the same roof was three weeks in Goa last summer.'

She paused. 'It isn't right that you've made me wait this long. It's not fair that I've not held back anything from you, and this one thing . . . this one thing you can't give me. Well, I can't wait any longer. I have a life too and I can't afford to waste any more of it on you.'

She was right of course. Right about everything. That was the thing about Mel. She had this uncanny sense of seeing things the way they were instead of the way you'd want them to be, of knowing me better than I knew myself. She could sniff out the truth even if it hurt.

I couldn't think of a single thing to say that would stop what was happening, so instead we sat in silence digesting the magnitude of our conversation. Mel was crushing her thumb into her fist agitatedly, something she only ever did when nervous or angry.

I stared out of the window hoping that one of us would say something that would make this all go away, and while I waited for this miracle to occur I tried to list all the couples we knew in my head. *Beth and Mikey, Chris and Jane, Rekah and Veejay, Richard and Liz, Lara and Irvine, Kathy and Alex, Bella and Ian, Jess and Stuart, Mark and Nga, Fran and Eric . . . Mark and Julie.*

It wasn't an exhaustive list by any means, but it did the job. These couples were exhibit A: the evidence that had slowly but surely condemned Mel and me to a permanent parting. Because compared to them, with their perfect his 'n' hers lifestyles and complete togetherness Mel and I looked, well, sort of crap really. Within ten minutes of meeting up with them for lunch or a drink we'd experience the irrational feeling of envy and ineptitude that comes over insecure couples like me and Mel when they feel as if they're being left behind by their contemporaries. The solution to this problem was of course to try and befriend couples more dysfunctional and less secure than ourselves. But then again maybe that was why we were so popular on the dinner party circuit.

The thought leaked out into the real world.

'It's because we're not Mark and Julie, isn't it?'

'What do you mean?'

'It's because we're not perfect like them. You know, *perfect.*' I made the word sound hard and unpleasant. 'You know, stripping floorboards, installing Victorian fireplaces and all that. I thought we were above all that. You and me against the world type of thing. We were a cool uncouply sort of couple. We could do our own things separately as well as doing our thing together. We had our own space. I don't want us to be Mark and Julie.'

'Mark and Julie love each other, which is why they live together and why they're getting married,' replied Mel. 'It isn't unnatural. People fall in love and move in together all the time.'

'But it never stops there, does it? People move in together and just end up on the couple treadmill. Trying to keep up with the Joneses – or in this case the Mark and Julies.'

Mel shook her head in disagreement. 'You know we wouldn't have done that.'

'Yes we would,' I countered. 'Because everybody else does. Name me a single couple you know who own their own flat or house who haven't got a Victorian fireplace.'

Mel thought hard. 'Rachel and Paul.'

'Not good enough,' I said, shaking my head. 'You're right, Rachel and Paul haven't got a Victorian fireplace. That's because, if you remember, their interior decorator friend told them that Italian marble fireplaces were going to be all the rage.'

Mel shrugged her shoulders as if to say 'So what?'

'Can't you see what I'm saying? All these couples are going round trying desperately to improve everything in their lives because they want to be perfect. They want to have a perfect house, go to perfect restaurants and have the perfect relationship. But nothing's perfect, so they'll never be happy because they're not focusing on what they've got, only on what comes next. I love you, Mel. We'll be all right. We will. I know we're not perfect but we're so much better together than the alternative.'

'We'll have to agree to disagree on this one,' said Mel coolly. 'But nothing you've said changes the fact that *you* don't want to live with *me*. I could wait around for ever hoping that you'll change your mind but I'm not going to. Four years is more than enough. So I need you to go, Duffy. I need you to go right now. It's for the best. Please, please don't try and call me. At least not for a while.'

On the doorstep we kissed briefly. 'It's the saddest thing in the world, Duff,' she said, as tears welled up in her eyes. 'The saddest thing ever, because I know without question that you love me. And that we'd be so good together. But you're terrified of commitment, and whatever it is holding you back, this is something you've got to sort out on your own.'

Anyone see that Lassie film last night?

Outside W.H. Smith, half an hour after I'd left Mel's, walked all the way to Clapham Junction in the rain and caught the train to Waterloo station. I had a copy of *What Hi-Fi?* in one hand (the pages of which I was trying desperately to escape into) and in the other a maxi-pack of Revels (from which I'd already frantically located and eaten all of the orange ones). Refusing to think about, confront or admit to myself what had just happened, I made my way to the Tube and jumped on the Northern Line. I sat flicking through the pages of my magazine, poring over any picture or technical specifications that caught my eye. My plan was simple. I was going to go to one of the many hi-fi shops on Tottenham Court Road, hand over my credit card, point at a picture in *What Hi-Fi?* and say, 'Give me that.' For approximately twenty-six minutes – roughly how long it took me to get to my destination – I was happy again.

Even though it was a rain-sodden Sunday afternoon, Tottenham Court Road was busy with shoppers and tourists. I made my way through the crowds and the drizzle to the doors of the first hi-fi shop I saw, called Now Electronics. Walking into the shop, leaving the rain behind, I immediately felt at home. Dotted around the shopfloor were young men like me, exhilarated to be in a secure environment like this where we could stand and admire the latest and the best, and spend money we knew we couldn't afford because we'd managed to provide ourselves with perfectly structured arguments as to why this purchase was, more so than food, light or shelter, not only necessary but essential to our quality of life.

I stood in front of a pair of speakers that had received a five star rating in *What Hi-Fi?* and gazed at them longingly. A sales assistant, roughly my age, approached me, wearing a crumpled grey suit, ill-fitting shirt and really bad shoes. It was as if he didn't care about how he looked because there were so many other more important things in life than clothes. Like hi-fi equipment.

'Nice speakers,' he said reverentially. 'Really nice speakers.'

The people who run these kinds of shops were no fools. They employed people who thought like me to sell to people like me. This sales assistant knew exactly what to say, which buttons to press. It was like being seduced by the most beautiful woman in the world – with the worst dress sense in history. I was powerless to resist his charms.

'Yeah,' I said, acknowledging his point. 'They are.'

'They came in late yesterday afternoon. We've been so busy I haven't even had a chance to listen to them myself.'

'Really?'

He nodded. 'What system have you got at home?'

I hadn't got a 'system'. What I had was a massive, matt black all-in-one thing that I'd bought off Charlie years ago; I wasn't going to tell him that, though. Instead I lied and said I couldn't remember, and then added casually, as if possessed by the spirit of a high-rolling playboy, 'I might as well get a new CD player and amplifier while I'm here.'

'How much are you looking to spend?' he asked.

I shrugged and gave him a figure off the top of my head that in no way bore any resemblance to anything I could afford.

'Right,' he said, barely able to contain his excitement. 'Hang on a sec, and I'll make sure the listening room is vacant and then I'll wire up the speakers to the perfect CD player and amplifier. You'll love it.' He returned moments later carrying a bundle of wires and beckoned me to the glass-walled room at the back of the shop. It had a large worn brown leather sofa in the middle of it, perfectly positioned to optimise the acoustics of the room (apparently). While he matched up the wires with the sockets he gave me a rundown on the entire system. It was beautiful. There are few things in life more enticing than the sound of men talking hi-fi specifications. It put my world into perspective. The real world was a bad place where crappy things happened to me all the time, but this sales assistant was offering a way out, to a world of perfection, a place where every woofer, tweeter and bass note made sense. We both listened and spoke with awe when talking about the equipment. I didn't know as much as he did, but he wasn't condescending – he just wanted to share. The assumed knowledge. The attention to detail. It all brought us closer.

Once the speakers were wired up he asked me if there was anything in particular I wanted to listen to so that we could really put the speakers through their paces. It was then that I disappointed him. Refusing all manner of dance tracks, classic rock, soul, hiphop, jazz, guitar rock or pop, I handed him a compilation CD from the box on the floor, entitled *For Lovers Only*. It had a black and white picture of a preposterously attractive couple kissing in the rain.

'Track seven,' I said desperately. 'Play track seven.'

He looked at me incredulously. 'Are you sure, mate? I've got some banging techno that will sound brilliant through these.'

'Yes,' I nodded, no longer caring about what he thought of

me. 'I know it's cheesy but it was my . . . it was my . . . a friend of mine wasn't going to have it played at her wedding.'

'You're the boss,' he said, raising his eyebrows. He placed the shiny silver disc carefully in the drawer, pushed it shut and pressed 'Play'. Out of the speakers, crystal clear, as if the legendary ensemble were playing live right in front of me, came the rich vocal tones of the Commodores singing 'Three Times a Lady'.

Trudging through the pouring rain, weighed down by my brand new speakers, amplifier and CD player, I was already losing any sense of wellbeing my purchases had given me. I needed help. I needed my friends. I called Charlie on his mobile. He and Dan were holed up in the Shakespeare in Covent Garden watching the football because the TV in the Haversham had broken down. As I put down the phone, my spirits picked up from their downward spiral. Charlie and Dan were just what I needed. Why? Because they were my people.

People who talked about anything as long as it wasn't serious.

People who weren't constantly asking what I was thinking.

People who followed the rules of logic.

People who didn't talk when the TV was on unless it was to shout imaginative abuse at it.

People who thought red satin underwear looked great on the opposite sex.

'Anyone see that Lassie film last night?' said Charlie, absentmindedly dismantling a beermat. 'I think it was *Lassie Come Home*.'

The match had long since finished, a 0–0 draw and a typically dull performance from both teams, epitomising just about everything that was wrong with modern football. It had been such a tedious game that instead of discussing the highlights we were reduced to talking about what we'd got up to the night before. Well, as I'd spent Saturday night in my darkened bedroom ruminating on the IKEA episode, I lied and told everyone I'd gone to bed early because I was knackered. Dan announced that he'd spent his evening in the company of Lana, a rather attractive heckler who'd harangued him for most of his set at the Happy House in New Cross; and Charlie, rather bizarrely, had apparently spent his evening watching *Lassie Come Home.*

'They're all the same,' said Dan, dismissing the entire Lassie genre glibly. 'Small kid finds dog. Oh, Dad, can we keep dog? No. Please. No. Please. All right, go on, then. Small kid finds himself in danger. Lassie to the rescue. Happy ending.' He clapped his hands and shrugged like a cross between an East End barrow boy and a New York Jewish intellectual. 'All variations on a theme, mate.'

I didn't join in the banter because something about Charlie's evening activities didn't add up. 'Weren't you supposed to be out with Vernie last night? She said she'd booked you a table at some hideously expensive restaurant in Hampstead.'

'Yeah, she did,' said Charlie dejectedly. From the way he spoke it was obvious that their posh night out had been something of a disaster. 'We had a great time,' he added flatly.

'So how come you got to watch Lassie?' I asked.

'I taped it,' he said defensively. The tone of his voice defying us to mock him, which we of course did anyway.

'Do you know how sad that is, Charlie?' I said, laughing. 'I can't believe you taped a Lassie film. What kind of a depraved pervert does something like that in the privacy of his own home?'

Relaxing visibly, now that the topic of his night out with Vernie had been left behind, he bowed his head in mock shame. 'They were classics of their time,' he protested. 'One day they'll be up there with *The Godfather Part II, Les Enfants du Paradis* and *Digby The Biggest Dog in The World* as the greatest films ever made.' He paused, chuckling into his beer. 'Now, what I was going to say before I was so rudely interrupted? Oh yeah, in all the Lassie films, he always has to save a child from being mauled to death by some sort of vicious cougar-type animal . . .'

'Don't you mean she?' I prompted. 'Lassie was a bird.'

Charlie threw a puzzled glance at me, unsure if I was making this up. 'Lassie was a bloke, wasn't he?'

'Of course Lassie was a she,' chipped in Dan. 'Otherwise they'd be called Laddie films.'

'Good point,' said Charlie, nodding. 'All right, then. Well, in Lassie films *she* always has to save a child from being mauled to death by a cougar or something.' Dan and I nodded, wondering where this was going. 'Well how did they do that? Surely they didn't use real dogs to fight cougars?'

'Yeah,' said Dan. 'I once read in a magazine that they went through about eight stunt Lassies per film trying to get those cougar fights right.'

My mind was obviously somewhere else because I was just about to say how outrageous this was and shouldn't the anti-animal cruelty societies have done something, when Dan nearly choked himself to death with laughter. 'They took the cougar's teeth out,' he said, semi-convulsed. 'I found out all about it on a documentary on the Discovery Channel.'

I loved it – what I was experiencing at that very second. To me it was what life was all about; having a laugh and hanging out with my mates. It was the easy life incarnate. It was the way things were meant to be.

As late afternoon turned into early evening our inanity knew no bounds. Between us there was a degree in Drama and English (Dan's), an MA in Town Planning (Charlie's) and an inordinate amount of 'A' levels (some of which were mine) and yet this was the furthest you could get from intelligent dialogue. But the subjects we spoke about felt important. More important than anything else in our lives. Inspired by Lassie, topics of conversation covered the following, which despite long and often heated arguments boiled down to the following basic questions and answers:

Q: Could Batman beat Spiderman in a straight fight?
A: Not really. Spiderman has superhuman strength whereas Batman is just a bloke in a romper suit with some gadgets.
For the record: Charlie wanted it noted that he thought Batman would win because the likelihood of someone actually being bitten by a radioactive spider in real life was extremely small, whereas the odds of a bloke dressing up as a bat armed with a variety of crimebusting gadgets were slightly more realistic.

Q: Who weighs the most?
A: Me: 13 st. 5, Charlie: 14 st. 2, Dan: 12 st. 4.
For the record: Charlie insisted that it wasn't about weight per se, as about 'muscle to fat ratio'.

Q: Woody Allen's best film is . . . ?
A: *Manhattan* (two votes: Charlie and me), *Shadows and Fog* (one vote: Dan).
For the record: Dan refused to accept the judgement and insisted we institute a points system (ie. three points for our favourite, two for the next one, etc.) and demanded we all voted again.

Overall winner under new system: *Annie Hall*.

I disappeared to the gent's at the back of the pub and as I took a leak, checked my watch. It was eight o'clock. Thanks to our concentrated drinking efforts and the eight million packets of crisps I'd consumed as a replacement for Sunday lunch I was inebriated enough not to try and work out how long it had been since I'd last seen Mel but sober enough not to fall into the urinal.

Returning from the toilet I recalled a good anecdote that would embarrass Dan. It was the story of how he'd once confessed to having a bizarre crush on Elizabeth from *The Waltons*. Walking back to the table, desperately troubled by TV trivia ('Just what was the name of the actress who played Ginger Elizabeth?') I noticed that an extra person was sitting at our table talking to Dan and Charlie. It was only when he turned and waved to me that I realised it was Greg Bennet, a mate of mine and Dan's who was also a stand-up comic.

Greg wasn't really part of our inner circle – he was actually more of an associate, someone to drink with when there wasn't anyone else, and an alternative source of comedy-circuit gossip. The thing was, none of us really liked him. He was the sort of person who would make inflammatory comments in the name of humour – usually about women, but animals, asylum seekers and religious groups were often thrown into the bargain – in the hope that his 'on the edge' wit would impress us. What he failed to realise was that in his case, opposing 'the overbearing arm of political correctness' and just being a git were one and the same thing. He was, however, harmless in an odd sort of way and we tolerated him for this reason and this reason only.

'Guess what?' said Greg to all of us as I reached the table and sat down.

For a laugh we all had a guess at Greg's expense. Mine was, 'You've decided to admit that "high foreheadedness" and "balding" are one and the same thing.'

Charlie's was, 'You've discovered that you're not funny.'

Dan, however, got it right first time: 'You're getting married.'

'Yeah,' said Greg with a perplexed look on his face. 'How did you guess?'

I looked at Dan and could see that the news quite saddened him, as it had me. Dan had been on the same drama course at college with Greg's girlfriend – 'the lovely Anne' as we called her – and had nearly got it together with her, but for one reason or another it never worked out and she'd ended up with Greg. Dan always said she was the kind of woman he could've fallen in love with because she was an incredibly genuine person whose only flaw, it seemed, was that she couldn't see how much of a tosser Greg really was.

'It's like that joke,' Dan replied languidly. 'Why did the monkey fall out of the tree?'

'Dunno,' said Greg.

'Because it was dead.' He paused for a moment, letting the punchline soak in. 'Why did the second monkey fall out of the tree?'

'Dunno,' repeated Greg self-consciously.

'Because he thought it was a new game and didn't want to be left out.'

'And your point is?' said Greg, the only one of us not laughing.

'Well, this one here's already married.' Dan pointed to Charlie. 'This one here's getting married.' He pointed to me. 'It was only going to be a matter of time before another monkey thought it was a good idea, and it's not exactly going to be me, is it?'

'Are you calling me a monkey?' said Greg, working himself up to a point beyond indignation but just outside anger.

'No, Greg. I'm not,' said Dan, deflating a potentially combative situation. He'd drunk too much and Greg's presence was bringing out the more antagonistic side of his nature. He offered his hand in congratulation. 'I'm pleased for you, mate.'

'Cheers,' said Greg, shaking Dan's hand warily.

'Married, eh?' said Charlie, offering Greg a handful of dry-roasted peanuts. 'When did you ask her?'

'Last night,' said Greg, accepting the peanuts. 'I'd been thinking about it for a while now and I just thought why not?' He turned to me. 'How about a double wedding, then? You and me, Anne and Mel. It'll cut costs in half!'

I didn't laugh. I didn't grin. I didn't even shrug my shoulders. I didn't do any of the things I was supposed to do. Instead I cried. Big fat tears by the bucketload. Everybody has a few really embarrassing moments in their lives. Well, I decided to have all mine and somebody else's right there in the pub. I honestly couldn't remember the last time I'd cried. Mel used to joke that I'd had my tear ducts removed, but the truth is, I think I just forgot how to. And now she had reminded me.

No one spoke. Instead they stared emptily into their pints. I think even the jukebox stopped playing, although that could've been my overactive imagination. I'd let myself down. Badly. There was a time and place for emotions and this wasn't either of them. Not here in a bar, with my mates watching me like I was some sort of freak show, and not now over Mel. All my tears did was point out the obvious – that whatever I did to avoid or escape it, real life would ultimately rear its ugly head. Everyone around the table knew real life existed – we also knew that was why after Stone Age man invented the wheel, the very next thing he did was invent the pub.

After some moments of awkward silence so painful that I strongly believe they'll scar me for my duration on this planet I reasoned that perhaps I owed my friends an explanation, which would perhaps make me feel better but would without a doubt only serve to make the situation worse. 'Mel and I have split up,' I confessed. 'She said I wasn't sure about getting married. Which is true. But that doesn't mean that I don't love her . . .' overcome with emotion I failed to finish the sentence. The heavy sense of despair that had been bearing down on my shoulders since this morning finally crushed me. 'My life has turned to arse. Somebody, anybody tell me how to be sure.'

There was a huge silence. A tall, wiry-looking bar man with spiky blond hair came over and collected our empty glasses. I wiped my eyes and attempted to clear the snot from my sinuses. Still no one uttered a single word.

A few moments passed and then as if he'd just woken up Charlie said quietly, 'Vernie's pregnant. She told me yesterday at that restaurant she took me to. I knew something was up. We never go out for posh meals without a reason . . . I thought I was ready . . . I thought I'd get used to the idea but I haven't and now it's happened I . . . I don't want to be a dad.'

Silence.

Dan coughed loudly and we all looked at him. 'You all know about Meena's wedding invitation. Well, last night, as I sat chatting up that girl I met after my gig even though I knew my heart wasn't in it, it dawned on me that I made the biggest mistake of my life splitting up with Meena. I think she was . . . you know . . . The One.'

We all exchanged glances and then stared at our pints and then at our laps and nobody said a word.

After a few minutes of contemplative silence, Greg sniffed nervously, lit up a Silk Cut and offered them round the table. We all took one, waiting to hear whether he too had had a shock revelation that would gain him membership to the inaugural meeting of Emotional Losers Anonymous.

'Right,' he said, settling down in his seat and lighting his cigarette nervously, 'did anyone see that Lassie film last night?'

I am committed to non-commitment.

—Federico Fellini

Exchange emotional CVs

In the beginning there was her and there was me and an awful lot of happiness. We were in love. Totally, utterly and incontrovertibly. People, usually women, would comment on Mel and me at parties saying things like 'I can't believe how well you two get on together,' 'You look so in love,' and my favourite, 'You really are each other's best friend.' Which was true. I'd never met a woman like her in my life. She was beautiful, compassionate and intelligent. She constantly made me laugh, drank like a fish, and like me enjoyed nothing more than shouting words of advice at the TV for the benefit of the characters in *EastEnders*. She was some sort of miracle. Some sort of angel from above. The funny thing is, when I first met her I genuinely didn't think I stood a chance.

I was twenty-four, and back then I'd just started a two month block temping in the administration department of a magazine publishing house just off Leicester Square. I spotted Mel on my first lunch break. She was in front of me in the queue in the Italian sandwich shop around the corner from my office building. I walked slowly behind her as she left the shop to see where she went and was immensely pleased when she disappeared into the rotating doors of the Mentorn House, the building where I worked. My joy continued as we shared a wordless journey in the same lift, and nearly exploded when she got out of the lift on my floor and disappeared in the direction of ad sales.

I stood, open mouthed, watching her, as I attempted to define in my head what it was about this woman that stopped me in my tracks. After a few moments, in which I was told off by a senior member of management for blocking the lift exit, I worked it out. It wasn't her face or body that attracted me – although both were pretty hard to fault – it was her walk. She had the most hypnotic walk I'd even seen. It was strident, sexy, and that rarest of qualities, sassy. A living, breathing, moving version of Chrissie Hynde singing 'Brass in Pocket'.

In the next fortnight I discovered the following facts about my dream woman: her name was Mel Benson, she was twenty-four and had gone to university in Edinburgh. She liked chicken and avocado sandwiches, hated her aerobics teacher, did 'something' in the advertising sales department, wasn't married, and looked brilliant in black. It was a further week, however, before I actually managed to have a conversation with her.

Every Friday lunchtime the ad sales department went to the George, a pub just across the road from the office. Realising this could be a way in, I shamelessly ingratiated myself with Tony, a middle-aged ad executive whose sole reason for living was cricket, and within a week he had invited me to the Friday pub session. I ruthlessly abandoned him at the first opportunity and manoeuvred myself into position next to Mel.

We got chatting almost immediately and I asked her what she did. Her answer 'I'm a media planner' left me none the wiser. When she returned the question I admitted to my temp status but told her I was a stand-up comedian too. The usual response I got when I revealed this information was, 'Tell us a joke,' which I hated, because I wasn't a performing seal. Mel, however, just said, 'It's nice to meet someone with dreams,' and left it at that. I was impressed. In the twenty-seven minutes that remained of lunch I made her laugh a total of twenty-three times. A personal best.

I did the same thing the following week and the week after. It soon got to the stage where on a Monday we'd ask about the quality of each other's weekends and on a Friday we'd ask what each other had planned for our time off. Of all the love crusades I've waged in my life, this was by far my longest and most concerted effort.

On the Friday of the fourth week of my campaign I finally made my move. Mel was standing next to the lift, tapping the pale blue plastic bottle of the water fountain with a biro. 'I'll name that tune in three,' I said smiling.

A huge grin spread across her face, so wide it revealed for the first time her teeth, small, perfect and glistening. 'Why are you always making me laugh?' she asked as if I was part of some sort of conspiracy to make her happy.

'I don't know. Maybe you have a low humour threshold.'

'Could be. But maybe it's because you're a funny guy.'

Not bothering to work out whether she meant 'funny' as in 'ha ha' or 'funny' as in 'Stop following me, you weirdo,' I decided this was it. The opportunity. I didn't need to be told twice. 'Do you fancy going for a drink after work tonight?'

'Are you asking me out?' she said matter-of-factly.

I searched around for the correct answer. I'd tried to make my invitation sound as casual as possible, giving her the option to brush me off without smashing my ego to pieces, but here she was asking me to define one of two things you should never, ever define, not even if threatened with death.

'Er, no . . . well, I suppose . . . yes.'

'I thought so,' she said smiling. 'Thanks very much. I'm flattered but I'm afraid the answer's no.'

I hadn't even included rejection on my list of possible reactions. I know I should've just left it at that and walked away, and on behalf of my mouth I'd like to apologise to my ego for not having done so. Instead, throwing caution to the wind, I asked, 'Why not?' the question any man with a modicum of self-respect would never ask because it's tantamount to begging.

'It's just one of those things, I'm afraid,' she said, wringing her hands nervously. 'You've caught me at the worst possible time.'

I scuttled back to my desk to lick my wounds and throw myself into my work in a manner I'd never done before. My survival plan was simple: I was going to avoid Mel for the rest of my life. With this in mind I skulked around the office, dodging her in the corridors, by the water fountain and in the George. On the last day of my contract, however, fate had it that I should bump into her in the lift as I was on my way home.

'You're avoiding me, aren't you?' she said, as the doors closed and she pressed the button for the ground floor.

Once again I searched around for the correct answer. I'd tried to make my avoidance of her as casual as possible, giving her the option to stay well away from me, but here she was, asking me to define the other thing you should never, ever define, not even if threatened with death. 'No . . . well, I suppose . . . yes.'

'I thought so,' she said smiling. 'I've been hoping I'd bump into you.'

'Why?'

'You've changed my mind,' she said shyly. I noted her curious choice of words but refused to let her say any more. Additional conversation would only confuse the matter. If I could change her mind without knowing it, I could just as

easily change it back again by accident. So we descended the
fifteen floors to the lobby in silence. When the doors opened
she took out a biro from her bag, grabbed my hand, scribbled
her phone number across my palm and walked away.

We arranged to meet in a bar called Freud that same evening.
Mel arrived at a quarter to nine – fifteen minutes late – an
ideal length of time for me to reach the wet-palm stage of
nervousness and for her to appear more enigmatic than
I thought humanly possible. She was wearing dark blue
jeans, trainers, a white T-shirt and a jacket. She'd dressed
down, which was good. Dressing down called for the kind
of self-confidence I admired in a woman.

'Can we get one thing straight?' she said, sitting down at
the table. I looked at her blankly. 'I don't want a . . . you
know . . . a relationship.' I put on my Blank Face. 'We'll just
be friends.' My Blank Face went into overtime. 'Don't take
this personally but relationships are too complicated and I
could do with the easy life right now. Don't get me wrong,
you're a nice guy, but this is a case of wrong place, wrong
time, wrong girl, wrong planet.' She paused as if sensing my
disquiet. 'Well, aren't you going to say anything?'

It was at this point in the proceedings that I took a chance,
the like of which I'd never taken before or since. I kissed her
– contravening not just one but two of the rules of snogging
people you don't know very well:

Rule one: always drink too much.
Rule two: always wait for The Moment.

In my hand was a glass of lime cordial and soda water (the
cheapest drink in the house), and as for The Moment, I can
only assume it was subject to delays due to leaves on the

track. It was just as I was contemplating where this impulse might have had its origin when she kissed me back. We came up for air three breathless minutes later, somewhat flushed and distinctly hot under the collar.

'I can't believe I've just done that,' she said, avoiding all eye contact.

'Neither can I,' I replied, looking at my shoes. 'But we have.'

We spent the rest of the evening drinking and talking – totally enthralled with each other. Later, we became hungry and Mel suggested we get something to eat. The last of my money had long since disappeared, forcing me to explain my poverty-stricken situation to her. She didn't seem to mind at all, in fact she thought it was funny, and so at her expense we ate at a nearby Italian restaurant. In the middle of a mouthful of pasta, I noticed she was staring at me not saying anything. She clearly had something on her mind.

'What?' I said, narrowing my eyes suspiciously. 'I've got tomato sauce on my chin, haven't I?' I wiped my hand across my mouth.

'No, it's nothing,' she replied in a manner that clearly meant the complete opposite. I shovelled in another mouthful of pasta just as 'nothing' was metamorphosing into 'some-thing'. 'We've kissed each other. We barely know each other. Don't you think we ought to do that background thing?'

'Exchange emotional CVs?'

Mel smiled winsomely. 'Swap relationship resumés.'

'Yeah,' I said, 'but you first.'

She told me she'd recently split up with a man she'd been with for two years who she thought might be The One. Unfortunately he thought she definitely was The One and wanted her to move in with him, but she didn't feel the same. She took two hours to tell me this information. Her narrative was all over the place and massive amounts of useless information came with it, huge chunks at a time.

I discovered that when she was six years old she fell over and cut her knee and now had a scar that looks like a smile. I discovered that three years ago she'd bought an Ella Fitzgerald album at a car boot sale which she claimed was her most treasured possession. I discovered that she had always wanted a cat but now she was single it seemed a bit of a cliché. It was all utterly endearing but confusing at the same time.

The record of my own romances took all of five minutes to reveal. Reluctant to go into the whole Amanda crossover skeleton thing for obvious reasons, I concluded the ups and many downs of my love life with the one before her, Rebecca, whose last words to me were, 'I'm leaving the country. Don't try and follow me.' I thought that was quite funny but Mel didn't seem to want to laugh.

'Is that it?'

'What?'

'Your love life?'

'Yeah.'

'Where are your details? I need details.'

'I've told you everything.'

'You told me nothing. I told you everything.'

I gave her my Bewildered Face – a slight variation on the Blank Face.

'What is it with men? Why can't they talk? Do you learn this at some strange boy school? Do you have your vocal cords removed at birth?'

'No,' I said. Thankfully she laughed this time. So I told her more about my past even though I felt incredibly uncomfortable doing it. I knew it was a good sign – that she was interested in me – but I couldn't help thinking all this talk of failed relationships was somehow tempting fate.

'I think it's time for us to go,' she said, licking the back of her dessert spoon and looking around the restaurant. When we'd come in the room was full; now it was empty and the waiters were dropping the heaviest of hints that we were the only thing preventing them from going home.

'I enjoyed tonight,' I said, as hand in hand we made our way through the crowds emptying from a nearby theatre on Shaftesbury Avenue. 'It was . . . interesting.'

'Me too,' she said as we quickly crossed into the road, narrowly avoiding being struck down by a homicidal bus driver. 'But you know this isn't going to work out, don't you?'

I stopped and looked at her, unsure whether it was her insecurity speaking or whether she was trying to let me down gently. 'Why?'

'Because.' She took a step closer to me as traffic whizzed by on both sides. 'For one thing, I'm trying to concentrate on my career at the moment . . .'

'And for the other?'

'And for the other . . . I've just come out of a long-term relationship. Which would mean you're the rebound. Which means one of us is going to hurt the other, and I already like you too much for it to be me.'

'So don't.'

'What?'

'Like me. Don't like me. I'm not your perfect partner. I'm not the man of your dreams. I constantly forget important dates – birthdays, anniversaries *and* bank holidays – my intentions towards you are totally dishonourable and I spend too long in the bathroom.'

'How long?'

'Half an hour.'

'Practically makes you an honorary girl.'

'But on the other hand, for as long as it lasts we can have a good time. It'll be a laugh. Like a holiday romance without being on holiday. And I promise no postcards or long-distance phone calls when it's all over.'

'A holiday romance,' she said wistfully. 'I like the sound of that.' We kissed, and as a passing taxi beeped its horn at us, drawing us back to reality, Mel stood on the tips of her toes and whispered into my ear, 'Bring on the sangria!'

That was then.

My favourite dress

It was my mum who took the news of my split with Mel the worst. She was devastated, especially when I told her the reason was all my fault. 'Can't you do anything about the way you feel?' she'd asked me, like it was breaking her heart. I tried to explain to her my way of thinking but she wasn't convinced. Vernie wasn't much happier. In no uncertain terms she told me that I was a fool if I thought there was something out there better than Mel. It was clear that with the exception of Dan and Charlie, my friends and family all thought it was my fault.

The whole of April went by in a blur as in response to such criticism I threw myself into my comedy, travelling to crappily attended gigs in places like Norwich, Chichester and Northampton. I threw myself into an awful lot of alcohol (a strangely romantic feeling, conjuring up the sophistication of *A Lost Weekend* and apparently very surreal turns behind the mic), and such was my state of mind that I even threw myself into my temping job.

The only blip on my fast-track attempt to forget Mel came near the start of April, when I woke up on the fifth and realised it was her twenty-ninth birthday. I'd wanted to call her more than anything in the world. Not just because it was her birthday, but also because I missed her. She hadn't even collected her things. Her designated space in my bedroom chest of drawers still contained a jumper, a bra, two pairs of pants, a box of tampons and a pair of tights. The tattered Nike trainers she used for aerobics were still underneath my bed. The freezer still contained the massive bag of broccoli she'd bought after reading a magazine article that said it helped prevent cancer. *What am I going to do with three tonnes of sodding broccoli?* I'd asked myself when I discovered it behind a box of fish fingers. In the end I chucked it in the bin – it was too painful a reminder. But now a month had gone by since I'd last seen her, and as far as I was concerned I'd respected her wishes by not calling – now it was time for her to respect mine.

In the past, like most people, I'd used the phrase 'Let's be friends' as shorthand for 'Please don't put my photo on a dartboard,' but as I thought about calling Mel I really meant it. Pre-Mel girlfriends had always been functional creatures – designed to fulfil their destiny as 'girlfriends' and little else. But this was different. This was Mel. What we had couldn't be scrapped without some attempt to salvage a friendship from the wreckage.

I called her at work at the beginning of the week. 'Hi, Mel, it's me,' I said brightly.

'How are you?' she said eventually.

'Okay. How are you?'

'Okay. Not too bad.'

'How was your birthday?'

'Good.'

'What did you do?'

'Went for a drink with some friends.'

Silence.

'How's work?'

'Okay. How's the comedy?'

'Okay.'

Yet more silence.

It quickly became apparent that without day-to-day inter-action our smalltalking abilities had wasted away. *This is what time apart does to you*, I thought angrily. *Leaves you unable to talk about the small stuff with your ex-boyfriend*. I attempted to get to the point of my call before the repertoire of our relationship disintegrated any further.

'I know it's over between us, Mel, and I know that you'd rather we didn't see each other, but I want . . . I need us to be friends. I know it would be a lot easier just to get on with our new lives alone, clean breaks, and all that. But I don't want a clean break. I want you and me to be part of each other's lives no matter how difficult it is.'

I'd like to think my big speech was a sign of newfound maturity, and I think that's how Mel interpreted it, because she actually agreed to meet up with me that Thursday. If I'm really truthful, though, I'd have to admit that there was the slightest possibility that it had less to do with maturity than it did with me wanting to hang on to any scrap of my ex-girlfriend that I could get.

It was the day that we'd arranged to meet. I left work ten minutes early, cunningly sneaking past Checkpoint Bridge. Once out of the office I avoided any form of transport that might cause me to be late and instead opted to race through central London on foot to my destination.

At Mel's suggestion we had arranged to meet in the base-ment bar of a vaguely trendy Thai restaurant in Soho. I'd never been there before and to the best of my knowledge she hadn't either. I remember at the time thinking that she'd done this on purpose – selecting somewhere unfamiliar to us both so that it would be free of associations. It was a smart move on her part because the suggestion on the tip of my tongue had been the bar, Freud, where it all began.

Mel had called me briefly at work in the afternoon to remind me that she could only meet me for an hour because she had other plans for later on in the evening. I'd said it wasn't a problem even though it was. My confidence was running high now that she was meeting me, and I'd convinced myself that if I played my cards right, any plans she'd made for the night would be cancelled to make room for a whole bunch of my own.

I arrived at the Paradise out of breath but with plenty of time to spare and so I headed downstairs to the bar, perched myself on a ridiculously high stool, bought a bottle of Michelob and sat staring up at the metal staircase expectantly.

When Mel arrived (fifteen minutes late), it was her legs that I saw first. She was wearing her short black sleeveless dress, my favourite dress, the one I'd always thought made her look perfect.

She greeted me with a kiss and sat down. 'Hi, Duff.'

'Hi,' I said sheepishly, returning her kiss with a peck on the cheek followed by a hug to balance the lack of intimacy of the kiss. These were all delicate manoeuvres that required a deftness of touch I wasn't sure I possessed.

'You look great,' I said warmly.

'Thanks,' she smiled. 'You look a bit sweaty.'

I examined myself in the mirror behind the bar. Mel was right. I couldn't have looked sweatier if I'd been in a sauna. All that running to get here on time had taken its toll on a body as unaccustomed to exercise as mine. I attempted to make myself look a little less flustered while she spoke to the barman. She ordered another beer for me and paused carefully before ordering a vodka and orange for herself.

Our conversation was nowhere near as stilted as it had been on the phone. In fact after a while it was almost possible to forget that we weren't a couple. We updated each other on the small but important details of our lives (I told her about work, recent gigs and last night's *EastEnders*, while she told me about work, her flat and new bars and restaurants she'd been out to).

Mel really was pleased when I told her the news of Vernie's pregnancy, and made me give her all the details that I knew. I told her she should go and see Vernie, but she smiled awkwardly and said she didn't think she'd have the time because of work. It was a real shame that our not being together had to mean that she and Vernie couldn't be friends. She asked me to send her love to Vernie and Charlie and made a note in her diary to send them both a card. She asked me about Dan, too, and I told her he was okay. I considered telling her about the wedding invitation from Meena, but reasoned it was a subject too close to home for us to be comfortable with. In the end, though, it cropped up in the conversation all by itself.

'I had a letter from Meena,' said Mel. 'You know, Dan's ex-girlfriend. You'll never believe this, but she's getting married.'

'I know,' I said warily. 'She sent an invitation to Dan.'

'Oh,' she said ominously. 'I suppose she has her reasons.' She paused. 'Meena sent me an invitation, too, along with the letter. Well, actually it's addressed to you and me. She didn't know about us—'

'I think it must just be for you,' I interjected quickly, stopping her from finishing the sentence. 'Meena was never exactly my biggest fan.'

'No,' she said, handing me the invitation. 'You take it. It's ages since I've seen Meena. I'll just send a present or something in the post.'

I handed the invitation back to her. 'Look, she's inviting

you because she likes you. My name's only on the invitation because she's being polite. Anyway, if Dan's not going – which he isn't – then I don't think I should go either. Why don't you and Julie go or something? You know how you love a good wedding—' I stopped, glaringly aware of my own stupidity. 'I'm sorry . . . you know what I mean.'

'Don't worry,' she said. 'I know what you mean.'

The bar was beginning to fill up with after-work drinkers, so to help create a 'groovy' ambience the barman dropped a tape into the cassette deck behind the bar. I was hoping it would be something inspirational to lift my mood, but instead through the speakers came one of those songs you recognise immediately because it's played every thirty seconds on daytime radio.

'Mel,' I said, as the song reached its annoyingly catchy chorus, 'it really means a lot to me that you could come today. I kept thinking that you must hate me and want me dead and all that. I just want you to know that I still love you – it wasn't anything to do with you. What I mean is . . . it's not that I couldn't marry you. I couldn't marry anyone . . .'

'Thanks,' she said bitterly. I desperately wished I'd left well alone.

'I don't understand. Why are you taking this the wrong way? I want us to be friends. I need us to be friends.'

Mel emptied the contents of her glass in one smooth movement. 'This is so typical of you, Duffy. Sometimes you're so caught up in yourself that you don't see anyone else's needs. What about what I need? What makes you think that I'd want to be friends with you? Every meeting, every phone call a reminder that you'd rather live in . . .' she flicked through her internal phrase book for the perfect putdown . . . 'the kennel of the unkempt with Dan than with me! I waited four years for you and I've got nothing to show for it. This isn't a meeting of equals: it was *you* who didn't want to marry *me*.'

I didn't have a leg to stand on. It didn't take any great insight to see that she was right. If the tables had been turned, there would be no way that I'd be sitting in some poncy bar that played terrible music, listening to Mel give me excuses why, although she loved me, she didn't want to be with me until death did us part.

'I've done this all wrong,' I said.

'Yeah, you've got that right,' she sighed, and ordered another beer for me and another vodka and orange for herself.

I tried to get us back on to safer ground by asking how Mark and Julie were getting on.

'They're fine,' said Mel, sipping her drink slowly. 'Mark's been busy at work as usual. Julie's busy, too, but she's somehow managed to take up pottery classes after work. So far all she's made are ashtrays. Well, they start out as vases and then end up as ashtrays. I've got five of the things!' she laughed, seeming to relax a little. 'Do you want one?'

'A Watson original?' I said laughing. 'I'd love one.' *This is good*, I thought. *This is what we are about*. 'Any other Mark and Julie news?'

She paused, sipped, and thought the question over. 'They've decided that they're definitely moving somewhere bigger next year. Hopefully in time for their wedding.' Mark and Julie were obsessed with moving house. In the time I'd known them they'd bought and renovated three houses. I think the plan was that as soon as prices in their corner of Shepherd's Bush reached critical mass, they'd sell up and finally move to their spiritual homeland, Notting Hill Gate. 'Oh, and they're going to rent a villa in Tuscany at the start of August with a few friends. They've invited me along. I told them I didn't fancy it, but Julie's twisted my arm, so I just might take up the offer after all.'

She checked her watch. 'It's seven o'clock, Duff. I'm going to have to go.'

'Okay,' I said, sliding off the stool. I was disappointed that she hadn't changed her mind, but I was sure it didn't mean that I wasn't in with a chance. The bar was now completely packed. We worked our way across the room and up the stairs, stepping out through the door into early evening sunshine.

'Okay then, Duff,' said Mel abruptly. 'I'll have to say good-bye now.'

'Off anywhere nice?'

'Just out with some friends,' she replied. 'Which way are you going?'

'Leicester Square,' I said, having duly noted that her friends were now nameless.

'Listen,' said Mel, 'I'm sorry I was horrible to you just now, about this being friends thing.'

'No. No, you weren't,' I apologised. 'It was nothing less than I deserved. Really.'

She smiled patiently. 'This is still hard to deal with but I'm glad that you want us to be friends, because we are, aren't we? I don't want us just to drift apart, okay?'

This is it, I thought. *The Moment.*

She kissed me on the cheek and I gave her a hug and returned her kiss briefly. On the lips. It wasn't a peck either. It was a full-on, pressure-filled 'give-me-a-few-more-seconds-and-I'll-be-playing-tennis-with-your-tonsils' snog. It was wrong of me, shallow and contemptible. My title was that of ex-boyfriend, and as such my kissing location was restricted to the cheek. Cheeks were for ex-boyfriends, acquaintances and relatives. Lips were for current boyfriends, close friends and stuffed animals. Those were the rules and I'd broken them.

Mel's glare put me right within seconds. She pulled away awkwardly, opened her mouth about to share her thoughts with me on my behaviour, but obviously thought better of it. Instead, she sighed as if I'd managed to disappoint her more than even she'd thought possible, and walked away.

Burdened with guilt I made my way down Wardour Street towards Leicester Square Tube, but something – you could call it a sixth sense but I prefer to label it my sense of tragedy – made me look back just in time to see a black Saab convertible with the licence plate ROB 1 pull up next to Mel. The car's casually attired driver got out, greeted Mel, put his hands on either side of her waist and kissed her.

On the lips.

He wasn't a close friend, otherwise I'd know him.

And he certainly wasn't a sodding stuffed animal.

So there really was only one option left.

Thinking back on it, as I walked to the Tube with a black hole in the place my heart used to be, it occurred to me that it wasn't so much the kiss that bothered me. It was his hands on her dress. My favourite dress.

You need to get out more

Mel's mysterious, lip-kissing, personal-number-plated new 'friend' completely threw my world off course. If I was the earth, then Rob 1 was a huge meteorite knocking me off my axis, thus heralding in a new ice age.

I'd never have believed Mel would want to find a replacement me this soon, only a month after we'd broken up, let alone one so solvent, good looking and upwardly mobile. Whatever happened to grieving periods? *That's the problem with modern women*, I decided. *No bloody sense of decorum*. The thing that really hurt was that it hadn't even occurred to me that I might even need a replacement Mel. *That's how stupid I am.*

I wondered whether it was just me being unreasonable. What did 'real' people consider a decent mourning period following the death of a four-year relationship? I conducted a (fairly) scientific straw poll of family, friends and associates to find out.

Results from the Duffy Institute of Relationship Statistics as follows:

Dan: 'For a woman like Mel? Three months minimum. You've obviously made some mistake, mate. This guy's got to be her brother. What, as far as you know she hasn't got a brother? Even better, mate, he's got to be her *long-lost* brother.'

Charlie: 'I have difficulty even recalling the existence of any woman before Vernie but I pretty much agree that for a relationship like yours three months would seem to be the industry standard.'

Greg: 'For women to get over a relationship of that length, anything from six months to never. But for us men pretty much as and when we feel like it – the sooner the better, though. It's not sexist, it's genetics: women want a long term provider while blokes just want to have a good time. It's the way of the world.'

Vernie: 'Even though I'm a pregnant woman and there-fore a cauldron of unreasonability, I have to say this: women can do whatever they like when they like because all men are stupid.'

My mum: 'Enough time to heal the hurt but not so much that you drown yourself in depression.'

With the exception of my sister's answer (and needless to say Greg's), I interpreted the results of the survey to conclude that Mel should still have been in mourning. She'd obviously made a mistake in her calculations and was gallivanting around town with her new man when she was still, accord-ing to conservative estimates, some six weeks away from recovery.

It's only the beginning of May, woman! You're meant to be in mourning! You're not supposed to get over me until at least August!

Up until this stage of events I'd been coping reasonably well with life without Mel – it was as if she'd gone on holiday and was taking a long time to come back – but seeing her with Rob 1 made everything more real than it needed to be

– and now it hurt more than anything I'd ever experienced in my life. When I'd split up with girlfriends in the past, I'd dropped out of their lives so completely that it was easy to imagine that they'd stopped existing altogether. But with this stupid let's-be-friends thing still at the forefront of my mind, I had to come to terms with the fact that the never-ending ache in my heart was bound to get a lot worse before the passing of time would make it any better.

It made no sense to be the only one of us grieving. But grieve I had to. So I let myself go wild for a while. I called in sick at work, cancelled all my gigs for the coming week and ate bag after bag of Butterkist toffee popcorn whilst watching bad daytime TV. I even adopted the uniform of dressing gown and blue Marks & Spencer pyjamas my mum had bought me for Christmas. I told her at the time that I wouldn't need them because I slept naked, and I remember quite clearly that she said, 'Take them. In case of an emergency.' Now I knew what she meant.

During that week I fell apart. Every few days Dan, Charlie and Vernie would try to drag me out of my melancholy, but I always refused, explaining to them that this was only a temporary measure I needed to go through in order to come out the other side.

Two o'clock Saturday afternoon – approximately eight days since I'd gone into mourning – I did just that. It wasn't like I'd stopped hurting – I still felt the Pain as keenly as ever – I think it was more a case that through my grieving I'd learned to live with it.

I let LadyBic razor and chin meet for the first time in over a week (sweet justice indeed. Mel was forever telling me off for using her leg razors to shave with), I moulted my mourning clothes straight into the washing machine, and naked, strode into the shower where I symbolically washed the sadness from me. It was then, as I rubbed a large hand-ful of Mel's abandoned Laboratoires Garnier frequent-use fortifying shampoo into my scalp, that I made a decision. The decision to change. To become a bachelor boy like Dan – a superstud of seduction, a he-who-will-never-again-come-off-worse-with-the-chicks, a righteous dude committed to anything but commitment.

What I needed to start me off in my new role as a superstud of seduction was a dead cert. Someone to break me in gently. I flicked through my address books looking for past liaisons that might have fallen into that category. A–Z and back again. Twice. None of them had been dead certs when I had met them – and it would have taken an outlandish brand of optimism to make me believe that things had changed that drastically in my four years out of the game.

When I came across Alexa's card with her phone number I thought long and hard about making contact. 'Didn't she describe you as "cute in a little-boy-lost manner"?' said my ego eagerly. 'She's TV's Hottest Totty, you know.' Alexa was precisely what my ego needed to get over the Rob1 blow, but I needed practice, a few jogs around the block before I'd be in any shape to tackle a New York marathon like her.

Over mid-afternoon toast and beer (Dan's idea of a welcome-back-to-the-land-of-the-living feast), we discussed the prob-lem at hand and together arrived at the perfect solution not just to my own predicament but Charlie's and Dan's too. Now all we had to do was persuade Charlie.

'I'm not going to a nightclub!'

It was later that same day and Dan and I were round at Charlie's listening to him reject our master plan. He sat on the edge of their huge sofa looking at me and Dan as if we'd lost our minds on the short journey from Muswell Hill to Crouch End. It was at times like this that the age gap between Charlie and ourselves became most apparent. At thirty-four he felt he'd served his time doing pointless youthful activities, and was one of the few people of his years who took comfort in the idea of middle age.

'Nightclub?' goaded Dan. 'Have you just beamed in from 1962, Grandad? "Nightclubs", as you so quaintly call them, lost their "not daylight" prefix a long time ago. You need to get out more.'

'All right, then,' said Charlie, 'I am not going . . .' he faltered as if the word alone was making him feel nauseous . . . 'clubbing.' He paused to see what effect it'd had on him. 'I can't believe you made me say that. What kind of worthless tosser uses words like "clubbing"? It's like "pubbing". Are you coming pubbing on Saturday? No, I'm afraid I can't. I'm going clubbing. After which I'm doner-kebabbing and then cabbing home. I hate progress. Suddenly every noun has been turned into a verb.'

Dan and I exchanged glances as if Charlie was going off on one.

'Sorry, lads. I'm too old for this. I am. Look at me.' We did. Although Charlie had a youthful face, his body let him down. The contentedness of married life had increased his girth like the passing of time adds rings to a tree trunk. But somewhere deep inside him we were convinced there was a teenager who wanted to party. We just had to find a way to let him out.

'Don't stress it,' reassured Dan. 'We've got everything planned out. A boys' night out will take your mind off the baby, Duffy's mind off the whole Mel saga and, fingers crossed, my mind off Meena and her stupid wedding invitation.'

'A boys' night out,' I said encouragingly. 'It'll be just what the doctor ordered.'

Getting ready for our night out brought back a flood of memories. Memories of before Mel. In fact before the girl before that and the one before her too, right back to when I was seventeen and every Saturday night had the potential to be *the* best Saturday night of my life. The ritual was exactly the same every week:

1) Watch *Blind Date*.
2) During the ad break one of my more organised friends would call with a suggestion of where we could go.
3) Me and Vernie would get into a fight over who was next in the bathroom. I'd lose and have to wait an hour for her to finish, only to discover she'd used all the hot water. While I had a lukewarm bath, another mate would call and leave a message with my mum saying who was going, where and when to meet.
4) A whole gang of us would arrive at the Hollybush – just around the corner from our sixth form college – half an hour later than we'd arranged, wearing clothes we thought made us look eighteen and reeking of Paco Rabane.
5) After a few drinks, loud conversations and several rebuttals from the convent school girls who frequented the pub at the weekend, we'd get the bus into town and head off to a club, knowing full well that three quarters of us wouldn't get in.

That was what Saturday nights were supposed to be about: friendship, dressing up and boundless optimism.

*   *   *

Dan and I met up with Charlie in the Haversham at 9 p.m. half an hour later than arranged. I could tell by the look on Charlie's face that despite his earlier reluctance he was just as excited as me. Even Dan, whose Saturday nights had never been all that mundane, had something about him that bit sharper tonight. It was as if we'd all agreed to pretend that the last ten years hadn't happened to us. For the next few hours we were seventeen again and up for it. It felt great. Such were our good moods that we even invited Greg, who'd dropped into the Haversham by chance, to join us. He was so enthusiastic about the idea that he took a taxi home, showered, and was back in the pub in under half an hour. All present and correct. We were ready to go.

I love this!

The club, just off Leicester Square, was called in predictably kitsch fashion 'Boogie Nights'. The decision to go Seventies had been unanimous. We'd briefly considered trying to get into one of the capital's trendier clubs, but the feeling amongst the super studs of seduction (i.e. me and Dan) was that the women in clubs like those tended to be of the choosier variety. So, for a night of guaranteed good times with the kind of girls whose expectations were as low as our own, the Seventies night was ideal.

Walking through the double doors into the main room of the club was like stepping straight into 1978. Here was a world where the Bee Gees were groovy, John Travolta was an icon for disaffected youth, and bellbottoms were so hip it hurt. As we strode determinedly across the scarlet carpet to the bar, the strobe lighting making us look like we were walking in slow motion, I just knew the night was going to be one to remember.

'What are you drinking?' bellowed Greg in my direction.

I scrutinised the optics for inspiration and found none. 'I'll have a Stella,' I replied.

'Me too,' said Dan, checking his reflection in the mirror behind the bar.

'I'll join you in that,' said Charlie, edging out of the way of a gang of women dancing a drunken conga. He let out a yelp of surprise as they passed.

'What's wrong?' I asked, turning to Charlie.

'One of them just pinched my bum!' he said incredulously.

Hearing this, Dan turned round and gave Charlie a playful wink. 'What can I say, mate? You, my son, are dynamite!'

Dan went off in search of a fag machine and Charlie disappeared to the toilets, leaving me alone with Greg, who was now unashamedly scanning the room for 'talent'.

'Look at the arse on that,' he said, pointing in the direction of a group of attractive girls who had just walked in. I smiled weakly so that he didn't feel totally stupid, but refused to indulge him any further. While I was all for the appraisal of the feminine form, Greg's tabloid manner lacked any subtlety or grace at all. When Dan and I went on the prowl, we'd never say a single word to each other, we just knew – it was a mixture of Jedi mind tricks combined with a unique sense of timing. Greg's coarseness made me feel as far removed from the purpose of coming out tonight as possible. Now I really did miss Mel.

While Greg disappeared to the toilet, leaving me to stand guard over the four pints of Stella on the bar, I thought about Mel, or more accurately Mel and her new man, Rob1.

They're bound to be together tonight. I can picture them perfectly: Rob1's being really attentive, telling her amusing stories, making her feel special – doing all the things I used to do when I first met her. Mel's looking into his eyes, hanging on to his every word, wallowing in that buzz of excitement that comes from anticipating the unknown.

I stopped thinking and felt lower than ever.

By midnight we'd all run out of steam. Charlie had spent the last hour looking at his watch, moaning that he'd served his time in nightclubs and wanted to be in bed with his wife like any normal thirty-four-year-old married man. Next to him, a very disgruntled Dan sat on the arm of a sofa, occasionally sipping his beer. He'd spent most of the night scowling in the general direction of Greg, who was on the dancefloor in hot pursuit of some helpless girl. The irony wasn't lost on Dan and me that Greg – the only one of us who was engaged – was also the only one to have spoken to a member of the opposite sex all evening. Even Charlie – a married man – had had his bum pinched. So much for the superstuds of seduction.

'I can see it a mile off,' said Dan irritably. 'Greg's going to get off with that girl. It's amazing. Why can't women smell a loser when one whiffs by?'

'Depressing, isn't it?' I said in agreement. 'Here's us, two young, free, single guys, and there's him, not so young, certainly not so good looking, and engaged to be married. I dunno what the lovely Anne sees in him.'

'That's women for you,' pronounced Dan. I could feel one of his this-is-how-the-world-is speeches coming on. 'They believe that inside every heartless bastard is a small boy yearning to be loved. But their theory falls short . . .' he glared over at Greg again . . . 'because what they don't understand is that there are certain types of heartless bastard who if hacked in two would only be found to contain yet more heartless bastard.'

As if taking his cue from Dan, the DJ played Gloria Gaynor's aptly titled 'I Will Survive' and the place erupted in unison. A studenty girl wearing a neon-blue Afro wig approached the sofa of doom, and without saying anything, grabbed my hand and pulled me on to the dancefloor. It was a split-second decision: resist and show a modicum of self-respect or surrender and let everyone know how desperate I was. In the end I surrendered, because desperate or not, in spite of the wig I could tell that she was far from ugly.

She grinned at me dementedly and began gyrating as if her life depended on her performance. She knew all the words to the song and was even clicking her fingers in time to the music. It was as if the concept of embarrassment was completely unknown to her. Her confidence was infectious and within seconds I'd lost all my inhibitions as I strutted, boogied and generally got down with my bad self in time to the music.

'What's your name?' yelled Blue Afro Girl, over the music.

'Duffy!' I shouted back. 'What's yours?'

'Emma!' She held out her hand for me to shake. 'Emma Anderson. Nice to meet you, Duffy!'

As we continued dancing I noticed that not only had she got the most beautiful greeny-grey eyes I'd ever seen, but in addition to this she was using them to draw me into her funky world. I tried desperately to remember what I was supposed to do in this sort of situation. The procedure for pulling a member of the opposite sex was supposed to be like riding a bike – something you never forgot – but somehow I'd managed it.

As the song finished I turned to escape, but she grabbed my shirt sleeve and refused to let go. I looked over despairingly at Dan and Charlie, who were clearly enjoying the floor show. Greg, still dancing with the same girl, smiled smugly over her shoulder as if to say, 'Wa-hey! We've both pulled!'

Just as I was convinced that things could get no worse, the Village People's 'YMCA' came on – my all-time least favourite record. For her tenth birthday, my auntie Kathleen had given Vernie a double compilation album of disco hits called *Boogie's Greatest Hits Vol. 2.* For the next few months my sister constantly played 'YMCA' whilst pretending to be *The Kids From Fame.* Every time, she got to be Coco while I had to be Leeroy or else suffer the harshest of Chinese burns.

It wasn't fair. I knew Coco was a girl, but she was just so much more exciting than bloody Leeroy. This was why I hated the Village People. Looking around the club, I realised I was in a minority. Like a clarion call to the inebriated, the record's opening trumpets drew the merry throngs from the bar, the toilets and the sofas to the dancefloor.

'I love this!' screamed Emma excitedly.

'Me too!' I shrieked back. 'Me too!'

My sweat-soaked shirt was clinging tightly to my armpits and back by the time the song came to a close. Emma dragged me determinedly by the hand to an empty sofa at the edge of the dancefloor, lodging herself as close to me as possible without sitting on my lap. 'It's hot, isn't it?' she said feverishly. She peeled off her Afro wig and ruffled her cropped sandy-brown hair. 'I bet you thought I really had blue hair!' A wide smile lit up her elfin face. 'What kind of a name's Duffy, then?'

'Duffy's my surname,' I admitted timidly. 'My first name's Ben but I don't like it. Sounds too much like the name you'd give a Yorkshire Terrier.' Out of the corner of my eye I spotted Dan surreptitiously walking past. Seeing him brought me to my senses. This just didn't feel right. Sitting here with a strange, slightly mad girl who wasn't Mel. It was time to admit to myself that I was no superstud of seduction.

'Listen,' I explained. 'My friends and I have to go soon.'

'Anywhere interesting?'

I shook my head vigorously. 'Home.' She raised her eyebrows suggestively. 'Work in the morning, you see,' I added quickly, and then for some unknown reason mimed digging actions.

'So you're a labourer?'

'Yes. Amongst other things.'

'What sort of labouring do you do?'

'Oh, you know . . . a bit of moving heavy stuff here, a bit of moving heavy stuff there. The work of a labourer revolves around shifting heavy stuff.'

She licked her lips provocatively and squeezed my right arm tightly. 'Hmmm. That must be where you get this wonderful physique from.'

Realising that I was now officially out of my depth and unable to tread water, I made a move to escape before I drowned. Her hands, however, were firmly gripped around my arm and she was using all her weight to keep me anchored to the sofa. 'I haven't finished with you yet,' she said slyly. 'And you're not going anywhere until I have.'

Surely things haven't changed this much since I last went out on the pull? I told myself. *Surely I was the hunter and she the hunted?* In an attempt to calm myself down I considered my options:

a) I could escape her advances (and no doubt regret it the next day);

b) I could succumb to her advances (and no doubt regret it the next day);

c) I could defer her advances (and work out what to do the next day).

It had to be 'c'.

'I really am going to have to go,' I said firmly, 'but do you fancy meeting up for a drink next week?'

'Yeah, brilliant,' she said, nodding enthusiastically. 'Whereabouts do you live?'

'Muswell Hill,' I replied. I couldn't believe it. My first real live date in four years, without even trying! Maybe I was a superstud of seduction after all. 'How about you?'

'Hornsey,' she replied, stroking the hair on her Afro wig playfully. 'Do you know the Kingfisher in Crouch End? It's nice in there.'

'I don't, but I can find it. Sounds great. How about this Tuesday?'

'No can do,' she said, shaking her head.

'Wednesday?'

She shook her head again. 'And before you say it I can't do Thursday either.'

'Busy with university exams?' I asked, hoping that she hadn't changed her mind about fancying me.

'Not exactly,' she said coyly. 'It's just that my parents will go mental if I start going out on school nights again.'

If it had been possible for the earth to have opened up and swallowed me in my entirety, there would've been nothing that could have made me happier. I'd given this life thing a good try, but this time fate had gone too far; now I was reduced to chatting up a girl for whom Seventies nights weren't just an evening of kitsch fun but a lesson in ancient history.

'I think I . . . I—' I didn't manage to finish my sentence, as a sudden commotion across the dancefloor grabbed our attention. We stood up to get a better look, and I saw that it was Dan and Greg grappling on the floor. I took the opportunity to slip away from Emma and over to Charlie, who was standing, pint in hand, watching events unfold before him.

'I knew tonight would end in trouble,' said Charlie, motioning to Dan and Greg.

'What's going on?' I asked.

Charlie took a long, slow sip of his beer. 'Greg was snogging that girl he was dancing with, Dan went off on one, and there you have it.' He pointed at our two friends on the floor again. 'Like I said, I knew I should've stayed home.'

The club's door staff, eager to justify their existence, were over in seconds and dragged out Greg and Dan with the minimum of fuss. Charlie and I followed them, and while they were forcibly ejected we pooled cloakroom ticket stubs and handed them to the woman behind the counter. As I turned to leave with Greg's coat in my hand I was stopped in my tracks.

'Were you going to leave without saying goodbye?' said a voice from behind me.

I turned around. It was Emma. In the bright fluorescent light of the lobby she was quite obviously a lot younger than she'd first appeared, but that didn't stop her being pretty. In fact she was just the sort of girl that the seventeen-year-old me would've gladly laid down his life for, and now here I was eleven years later turning her down. At the end of the day it seems everything is a matter of timing.

'I'm sorry,' I apologised. 'As you can see, my mates got themselves into a bit of trouble. I'm going to have to go.'

'I suppose going out next week is off too,' she said quietly.

I nodded. 'Yeah, I think so.'

'It's because I'm sixteen, isn't it?'

I nodded again. 'You could say that.'

Reaching up she straightened the collar of my jacket and kissed me gently on the cheek. 'You'd better be going, then.'

'Yeah,' I said, as the sensation of her kiss slowly faded away. 'I suppose I had.'

By the time I got outside Charlie and Dan were nowhere to be seen and Greg was attempting unsuccessfully to hail a black cab. 'Taxi drivers aren't that keen on customers with blood across their shirts,' I said, handing him his coat.

'Cheers,' he said, and snatched the coat from me. 'If you're looking for your mates, they've gone.'

'What was that about, then?' I asked, studying his bloody nose.

'Hadn't you better ask your mate Dan?' He searched through his pockets. 'I was minding my own business when he came over and started spouting off about how I shouldn't be cheating on Anne, like it's any of his business.' He finally located what he was looking for. He pulled out his lighter and lit a cigarette. 'Then it all kicked off. He's a nutter.'

Dan was totally in the wrong having a go at Greg like that, but he did have a point. I was tired of humouring Greg and his outmoded ways but I wasn't about to lecture him on his stupidity – I just wasn't going to bother seeing him any more. I held out my hand. 'Look, I'm sorry for what's happened, okay? Let's shake on it.'

Ignoring me, Greg threw his cigarette on to the floor and climbed into the back of a red Datsun Cherry – quite obviously not a minicab but some dodgy geezer on the make – and was whisked away into the night.

Alone and a little bit cold, I thought about what to do next. I didn't particularly want to go home, because even though the night air had taken the edge off the alcohol, I was still on a high of sorts. I'd achieved my goal. I was seventeen again – chasing girls and getting into scrapes – and it had felt so good that I didn't want to go back to being Mr Twenty-eight, single and boring.

Desperate to keep the night going a little while longer, I decided to drop into the Comedy Cellar, a small club on Long Acre that Dan and I sometimes played. I knew the guys on the door quite well and there was bound to be someone around to kill time with.

Without hesitating I walked briskly through the crowds in Leicester Square and was about to cross Charing Cross Road when my eyes locked on to a man and woman in the middle of the street holding hands, waiting for a break in the traffic.

I looked at the woman and was horrified.

The woman stared right back at me, also horrified.

The man looked at the woman and then looked at me, equally horrified.

I looked back at the man and the woman and outdid their combined looks of horror to the power of ten.

What were the chances of this happening? A million to one. *If only,* I thought, *this kind of luck could be utilised for the forces of good rather than evil.*

'Duffy,' said an obviously shaken Mel, coming to a halt right in front of me.

'Mel,' I said distractedly.

'Just come from a gig?'

'No,' I replied unsteadily. 'Where have you been?'

'Dinner,' she said.

'Anywhere nice?'

'The Ivy,' she muttered so quietly even a deaf lipreader would've had problems understanding her.

'Oh,' I said. It was the one restaurant she'd always wanted to go to. I'd promised her that the first thing I'd do when the comedy took off would be to take her there.

'Where have you been, then?' she asked, agitatedly fiddling with a button on her coat.

In my head I attempted to create an evening of sophistication and witty repartee but failed miserably. 'A Seventies night,' I admitted. I couldn't help but compare the two experiences. Mel had spent an evening at one of London's top restaurants while I'd plebbed about with my mates in a grotty Seventies club. I'd got my wish: I was seventeen again – immature, impoverished and girlfriendless.

'How was it?' Mel could barely conceal her smile.

'Okay,' I said and shrugged my shoulders.

'Where's Dan?'

'He had to go home early,' I explained weakly.

As if he'd just been switched on, Mel's companion – who I'd been hoping was a garish figment of my imagination – finally decided to speak.

'Hi, I'm Rob,' he said, and offered his hand for me to shake. He was tall and handsome in the clean-cut sort of way that you usually associate with male underwear models in Grattan catalogues, and his voice was deep and authoritative like a newsreader's. I shook his hand.

'I'm sorry, I'm so rude,' said Mel, taking control of the situation. 'I haven't introduced you two, have I? Duffy, this is Rob.' She gestured inadvertently to his chest which seemed to be rippling underneath his dark blue, classically cut suit jacket. 'Rob, this is Duffy.' She gestured (hopefully inadvertently) to my stomach which didn't seem to be doing anything underneath my T-shirt.

'Pleased to meet you, Rob.' I nodded.

'Likewise,' he said, nodding back.

Mel was still looking at my T-shirt. 'You've got blood there.'

I looked down at my stomach and attempted a chuckle. 'It's not mine, it's Greg's,' I explained, and then added hurriedly, 'Too long a story to bore you with now.' I looked at my watch as if I had somewhere to go. 'I'd better be off. Don't want to be late.' I paused, unsure what to do next. 'It's been good to see you again, Mel.' Inexplicably I began shaking her hand enthusiastically. She just looked at me as if I was mad. I nodded in Rob1's direction. 'Nice to have met you, Rob.'

''Bye, then,' said Mel, tacking a sad little smile on to the end of her sentence.

'Yeah, see you again soon,' said Rob, the tone of his voice revealing the sort of intense satisfaction that said, 'Before I met you tonight you had *power* over me but now I see I have *nothing* to fear from you because you are *no one*.'

'I hope so,' I replied, my tone of voice revealing the sort of intense woefulness that said, 'You drive a *big* car, you wear *expensive* clothes and you have a bloody firm handshake – you're right, I am *no one*.'

As in joyful

I opened my eyes and looked around, blinking hard. Only seconds earlier Mel had declared passionately, 'Whoever wins this duel, wins my heart.' Reacting swiftly I'd grabbed the nearest weapon to hand (a small uncooked chicken) and brandished it threateningly in Rob1's direction. *Finally*, I'd thought. *Vengeance!* Unfortunately round one of Duffy *vs* Rob1 was all just a dream.

I was still wearing last night's clothes. I sniffed my T-shirt. Beer. Cigarette smoke. Doner kebab chilli sauce. I looked around again. *Where am I?* I wasn't in bed. I was on a floor – the kitchen floor. *Good*, I thought, pleased with myself. *At least I'm home.* I stood up shakily like a newborn Bambi and surveyed the room while my memory booted up. It was the numerous slices of bread scattered around the room that finally nudged my brain into place. *Toast*. It all came back to me. *I'd gone toast hunting*.

Distraught beyond belief at my encounter with Mel and Rob1, I'd made my way to the comedy club and there continued drinking beyond the point of daft smile and wobbly legs right up to 'Which way is up?' At 4 a.m. I was kicked out of the club and escorted to a taxi. The driver had asked me where I wanted to go and I'd told him Muswell Hill – which was fine for the moment, but things got a bit more complicated when we reached there and I couldn't narrow it down any further. After making him drive around the area for twenty minutes, I finally remembered where I lived. Once home, I'd headed straight to the kitchen to make toast, and somewhere in the three minutes it took for the bread to go brown I'd said to myself, 'I'll just rest my eyes for a moment,' and promptly fell asleep. Why I smelt of doner kebab chilli sauce, however, I have no idea.

It being Sunday I spent most of the day in bed trying not to move. During my third nap of the day Vernie came round, rousing me from a very deep and peaceful sleep, in order to have a huge go at me. Apparently Charle had got a cab home with Dan, and somewhere along the way Dan had been sick over him. This, however, was not why Vernie was mad with me.

'He's more depressed about the baby than ever,' she berated more loudly than was necessary to a man of my weak state. 'Thanks to your clueless big night out he's convinced himself that he's become some sort of pipes and slippers old fart. I could've planned a better boys' night out myself!'

Hours later, when I'd fully recovered from my sister's onslaught, I finally emerged from my nest and bumped into Dan in the hallway. Judging by the state of him, hair flying off at right angles to his head, nine o'clock shadow on his chin, and blood still caked around his nose, he, too, it seemed, was rising for the first time that day.

'All right, mate?' I said as we entered the living room. 'Bagsie the sofa,' I added, speeding up so that I could lie down on it.

'Whatever,' said Dan, grumpily heading for the armchair.

'You've still got blood on your nose.'

He wiped his hand across his face in an attempt to get it off, sniffed his hand and licked it. 'It's not blood. It's doner kebab chilli sauce. Dunno how that got there, though. Haven't had a kebab in a few weeks.' He settled into the armchair and flicked through the channels. Realising there was nothing on, he pressed the mute button. 'What time did you get back?' he asked, scratching the back of his head.

'Must've been about half five, I think. It probably would've been earlier but I forgot where we lived.' I paused, and looked around the room. 'I bumped into Mel last night.'

'Bad news?' he added, reading my face.

'The worst kind.'

'What? She wasn't with her new bloke, was she?'

I nodded.

'Sorry, mate. Life's crap like that.'

'Certainly is.'

'What was he like, then?' asked Dan. 'I kind of imagine him to be a slightly apelike medallion man.

'No such luck,' I said stretching out both my arms to the side of me. 'Imagine this hand is me.' I waved my right hand. 'Now imagine that this hand is him.' I waved my left hand. 'Now imagine all the millions of different types of men in the bloke spectrum in between. That's what he's like. Nothing like me at all.'

'Tidy, affluent, career minded, witty . . . that sort of thing?' said Dan.

'Exactly,' I pronounced sadly. 'My point entirely. I think Mel's finally found what she's been looking for.'

Monday morning!
7.00 AM!
Monday morning!
7.00 AM!
Monday morning!

7.00 AM!

Monday morning!

7.00 AM!

My alarm clock went off, wrenching me from the deepest of deep slumbers into a Nurofen nightmare. When I was seventeen the effects of a big Saturday night used to be over by Sunday lunchtime at the latest. When I was twenty-five I'd be feeling nearly human by *Songs of Praise*. But here and now at twenty-eight, with my brain throbbing like it was going to explode, and coat the inside of my head with grey matter and memories, I began strongly to doubt whether I'd actually ever fully recover again.

Showered, shaved and dressed for work, I checked my watch. I was late. I raced through the flat, trying to find my left shoe, watch breakfast TV and eat cereal all at the same time. Shoe located, TV switched off and bloated Rice Krispies abandoned on sideboard, I shot out of the door, down the stairs to the communal hallway, sorted through the morning's post and was gone.

The collection of motley souls who frequented the bus stop at my regular go-to-work time had disappeared, whisked away five minutes earlier by my regular bus, the 7.33 a.m. 136. In their place was a similar bunch of odd-looking strangers who appeared to be as disturbed by my appearance as I was by theirs. I could see them silently taking me in, thinking to themselves anxiously, 'Who's he? He's not a regular! He's not one of us!'

After ten minutes of their silent stares the bus finally arrived. Breathing a sigh of relief I got on, showed the driver my pass and settled into my usual seat upstairs, left-hand side, right at the back – a compulsive authority-avoiding habit formed during the school trips of my youth. As the bus juddered along Archway Road I riffled through my post: an invitation to receive a Barclays credit card; a 'Greetings From Lanzarote' postcard from an old college friend and an envelope in my mum's handwriting.

Dear Ben,
This letter came for you on Friday. I thought it might be important so I've sent it on. Hope everything's okay with you. Remember, if you need anything at all I'm always here.
　All my love,
　Mum.

I looked inside the large envelope and fished out a smaller one. It was postmarked London and the address was written in a masculine scrawl. I opened it. Read it. Reread it. Looked out of the window. Stared at it again for a bit longer. Screwed it up into a tight ball and got off the bus.

The office where Mel worked was a hive of activity. Telephones rang every thirty seconds and were answered by teams of people sitting at shiny desks on shiny chairs surrounded by shiny potted palms. It was simply the grooviest office I'd ever been in and exactly the sort of place I'd expect to find the advertising sales arm of a TV company. In the two years Mel had been here she'd managed to smash her way through every glass ceiling they had, to become one of their top account managers.

　Standing at the reception I waited patiently for the flame-haired receptionist to finish flicking through her copy of *Hello!* so that I could make my presence known. Just as I'd decided that my being here was an extremely bad idea and that I should go, she looked up from pictures of the Spanish royal family and said serenely, 'It's like a madhouse in here today. How can I help you?'

'I'd like to speak to Ms Benson.'

'Do you have an appointment?'

'No, I'm sorry I haven't.'

'Which company are you from?'

'I'm not from a company.'

She picked up her phone, and looked up at me expectantly. 'Who shall I say is here to see her?'

'Tell her it's the man who used to make milk come out of her nose.'

'You've got exactly one minute.'

I could tell from the second I entered the cool, spacious, aircraft-hangar-sized space that was Mel's office, that she was mad at me for coming to see her at work. I'd never seen her office before. I looked around the room for touches of her personality. There were gerberas on the windowsill (her favourite flower) and a photo of her parents on her desk. There was no picture of me, which saddened me greatly. I knew for a fact that she used to have one because she once told me – it was a picture of the two of us eating ice creams on a beach in Paignton. On the other hand there was no picture of Rob 1 on her desk either, which I reasoned had to be a bonus of some sort.

Hard Mel was back, and as well as looking her usual no-nonsense self, she appeared a little bored too. I wanted her to ask me what was up, but she didn't say anything, and neither did I. She started a countdown: 'Three, two, one.' When she reached zero, she said briskly, 'I'll let you see yourself out,' and started fiddling with the mouse on her computer as if she was going to start working right there in front of me. Without having said a single word, I turned around and walked out.

Standing by the shiny chrome lift waiting to escape from this shiny prison wondering why on earth I'd come here in the first place I heard a door open and turned to see Mel – not Hard Mel but my Mel. It was nice to know that even though we weren't going out any more, she still found it difficult to be mad at me.

'Hold on, Duffy!' she called out. I waited. 'I've got half an hour before my next meeting. Do you want to get a coffee?'

'You know I don't drink coffee,' I replied, and she just smiled.

She took me to a small café around the corner from her office building. I hadn't said very much as we'd walked there, and I could see that for her this was all a bit of an uphill struggle, but to her credit she endeavoured none the less. As it was a warm, bright morning Mel suggested that we sit outside, so while she disappeared into the café for our drinks, I found us a table. A couple of businesswomen were busy in discussion at the table behind me, and at the table to the side of me a young Spanish-looking woman was having a breakfast with a chatty toddler. *No matter what happens*, I thought, concentrating on my reflection in the window of the café, *life carries on as it always has*.

Mel returned with a cappuccino and an orange juice and sat down beside me. 'So what's up?' She lit a cigarette.

She never used to smoke.

'Are we . . . friends?' I asked hesitantly.

'Is that what this is about?'

I nodded. 'Partly.'

She raised her eyebrows and took a sip of her cappuccino. I watched carefully as the froth slowly disappeared from the rim of her cup. 'I don't want to be harsh, Duffy. You must know that I still care about you. But I'm not made of stone. I don't think this friends thing is going to work. I know I said it was what I wanted as well, but I can't see it happening. I can't. Not after all we had.'

I took a deep breath and exhaled slowly. 'I'm not saying it's easy. I'm saying it's what I want. I mean, I think it'll be good for us. I promise I won't interfere in your life. Okay?'

She shrugged noncommittally and took another drag on the cigarette she shouldn't have been smoking. 'We'll have to see how things go, Duff. I can't make any promises.'

We sat in silence while I downed my orange juice in six continuous gulps and Mel sipped her coffee and smoked her cigarette. I watched as the two business women got up and a waitress came out to wipe the table with a cloth. I looked over at Mel again and sensed that she had more to say.

'You're still angry at me, because of the engagement thing.'

'Yes, you're right I am. Why, did you think that I'd just forget that you didn't want to marry me?'

'No,' I said, wincing. 'I don't know how I'm ever going to make this up to you. I don't suppose it's the sort of thing that can be made up for.' I paused. 'Do you think you'll ever stop being angry with me?'

'I don't know,' she replied. She laughed quietly. 'Probably not.'

I attempted to look all doglike, but judging from the reflection of my face in the café's window I didn't have to try too hard. I was getting the hang of this remorse thing. It was coming quite naturally to me now. I sucked on an ice cube, rolled it around my mouth and then dropped it back in the glass. I was trying to find words that said 'I'm sorry' without sounding hollow and empty. I hunted high and low for them but they weren't there.

'That guy,' I said after some moments had passed. 'The one I saw you with on Saturday. New boyfriend?'

She shook her head. 'Not exactly.'

My breathing quickened, I crossed every finger I had and sat bolt upright so quickly that I managed to knock the ashtray off our table. *Please,* I thought, picking it up. *Please let him be just a friend. Or even better, her long-lost brother. Or even better, a stray eunuch she's become maty with. Anything but her boyfriend!*

'Do you remember when I first met you?' began Mel. 'I'd just split up with someone. Well, that someone was . . . Rob.'

I cursed myself inwardly for courting such ridiculously optimistic explanations for her mystery man. *That,* I told myself, *is definitely the last time I look on the bright side of life.*

Rob.

I'd remembered his existence but until now not his name.

Rob.

Though I'm sure she'd told me at the time – I was also quite sure that I jettisoned such information straight away.

Rob.

The names of my girlfriend's previous boyfriends weren't exactly the sort of material I wanted lingering in any of my brain cells.

'You're going back out with *Rob* who you went out with for two years? *Rob* who proposed to you? *Rob* who you said was "crowding" you? *Rob* who you dumped because you didn't want to live with him?' I sighed sarcastically. 'Oh, *that* Rob – yeah, I remember him.'

'Yes, *that* Rob,' said Mel, tolerating my playground wit. 'I bumped into him in Bar Zinc a little while after we'd split up. Anyway, we started talking about old times and exchanged numbers and I thought nothing more of it. He called me at home a few days later and asked me out to dinner. I said no initially, and then I thought, why not? Why should I have to stay in crying myself to sleep every night? Why not just go out and have a good time? And that's what I did. I make no apologies for it, Duffy. None at all.' She paused, calming down her quickened breathing. 'Does that answer all your questions?'

It didn't. Not by a mile. But some things, I reasoned, are best left unknown. I couldn't not ask anything. Her question was a challenge of sorts – defying me to face up to what I'd done. 'Does he make you . . . you know . . . happy?' I found myself asking.

She smiled. 'It's not like you to use euphemisms, Duff.'

Mel thought I was talking about sex, obviously not quite understanding that I would not now, nor would I ever be talking about her and Rob1 having sex. 'No, you've got me all wrong,' I clarified. 'What I meant is exactly what I said: does he make you happy? As in joyful. As in cheery.'

Mel looked puzzled. I don't think she'd been expecting that one. 'Yeah, he does. He makes me happy.'

'That's good,' I said. 'You deserve to be happy.'

Then came another of those long pauses that my life seemed to consist entirely of. It was quite possible that I was becoming addicted to them. 'Just the one pause, okay maybe another one.' How long would it be before I'd be visiting dodgy pubs in pursuit of drug dealers with a side-line in pauses? Pauses – they seemed to be everywhere I went, lurking in the darkness waiting for the right moment to highlight my inadequacies.

'None of this is what you came here to talk about,' said Mel breaking the silence. 'So tell me, what's going on, Duff? What's wrong?'

I looked over to the woman with the toddler; at a half-eaten croissant on a table next to me; at my own reflection in the café window. 'I got a letter this morning,' I began, as I unscrewed the letter I'd received and handed it to Mel. 'It's from my dad.'

'Oh,' said Mel quietly after she'd read it. She pulled her chair closer to me and placed her hands on my hand. 'I'm so sorry, Duff. I really am so sorry.'

This was why I was here. Mel was the only person in the world who would know what I was feeling without my having to explain. In fact she probably knew better than I did. I didn't have a clue what it was I was feeling.

'The letter says he wants to meet up with you.'

'Yeah, I know. Strange, isn't it?'

'Isn't he twenty-eight years too late for that?' Mel's eyes filled with tears as she gently squeezed my hand. Embarrassed by her tears, she wiped them away with the back of her hand. 'I'm sorry I'm getting so upset. It just makes me so angry. Does he really just think he can walk back into your life like this?' She wiped away another tear. 'Are you going to meet him?'

'No.'

'Do you need me to do anything? Do you want me to talk to your mum or Vernie about any of this for you? I want to do something to help, Duff. I really do.'

'I'll be all right,' I said. 'There's nothing more to do really. Like I said, I'm not going. I just needed to talk to someone about it, that's all, and the only person on the planet I could think of was you.'

Mel smiled. 'I'm glad we can still depend on each other.' She paused and looked at her watch.

'Me too.' I replied.

'Will you walk back with me?' she asked.

I nodded.

As we headed towards her shiny office block we chatted avidly, avoiding all the big issues of the day – about hair (she was thinking of having it cut short. I was contemplating growing a goatee); magazine articles (I'd read one that said men would be extinct by the year 2030. She'd read one that said women in America were giving up on men and buying dogs instead); and *EastEnders* (in our separate domains watching the weekend omnibus we'd both been shouting the same advice to the same characters at the same time).

Eventually we reached her office building, glinting in the midday sun, and said our goodbyes.

'Thanks for that stuff you said about . . . well, you know . . . wanting me to be happy.' She reached up and kissed me on the cheek. 'It means a lot to me. I do want us to be friends. I want you to be okay.'

I looked into her eyes and suddenly realised that despite my clumsiness I had a heart crammed full of things that I hadn't said, that I suddenly desperately needed to tell her. I wanted to tell her about my dad and the way my mum had thought he'd love her for ever. I wanted to tell her about Greg and how he'd cheated on his loyal girlfriend. I wanted to tell her about Dan and how he'd taken Meena for granted when they moved in together, and I wanted to tell her about all of the millions of men who'd thought they could do commitment but had ended up walking out on their kids, wives, girlfriends and lovers. I wanted to tell her that I didn't know whether I was like them or like me; whether I really could do commitment or just thought I could, and because of that – the fear that I'd one day do to her what my dad did back then – I could never marry her. And last but not least, I wanted to tell her that despite all this I needed her more than anyone in the world. I didn't say any of this, of course. I just whipped out another one of my interstellar pauses.

'Are you okay?' asked Mel. 'You seem to be somewhere else.'

'Yeah,' I replied ambiguously. 'I think I probably am.'

Cinema, drinking, eating, dancing . . . bowling

A few weeks went by in which I spent a lot of time pretending I wasn't thinking about my dad, before I finally admitted to myself that I was being stupid and that it was time I thought about him in the open. Talking to Vernie about it all helped put things in perspective. Strangely, my dad hadn't been in contact with her, but that didn't bother her in the slightest because if he had, like me, she said she wouldn't have been interested in meeting him at all.

After that, there was nothing more really to say or think, so I did a little rearranging in my mind: I put my dad to the back of it, and the idea that Mel and I might become proper friends to the front. I was just sorting the mess I called my career somewhere into the middle, when something odd came along that completely messed up all my arrangements – I got my audition for *The Hot Pop Show*, and if that wasn't enough, a brief conversation with Alexa just as I was leaving it.

'Is that you, Duffy?' called out Alexa. 'It *is* you!'

I looked up and said hello. I'd actually spotted her in the corridor as soon as I'd come through the double doors of Studio 3, where the auditions had taken place, but I was trying my very best to play it cool. Even though it was five o'clock on a humid Thursday afternoon, when by rights even the most gorgeous of supermodels could be forgiven for looking a bit crumpled, Alexa looked amazing.

'What are you doing here?' she asked, after having done her statutory double-kiss hello.

'I've just had that audition,' I said awkwardly. 'You know, the one for your show.'

'Of course,' she said, a look of recognition illuminating her features. 'I saw your name down on the list, but I completely forgot it was today. How did you get on?'

'I dunno,' I shrugged. I wasn't being modest at all. I really didn't know. I'd felt like I'd been at the audition all day. I'd told them a few jokes from my normal routine, run through a couple of sketch ideas I'd come up with based on the brief they'd given me, and told them my life history. And after all that I was still none the wiser.

'Did it look like they liked you?'

'I suppose so. They didn't appear not to like me. It's hard to say really. They don't exactly give a lot away, do they?'

'No they don't,' she agreed. 'They were exactly the same when I had my audition. I couldn't sleep or eat for days afterwards.' She patted my shoulder in a friendly, reassuring manner. 'I'm sure you'll be fine, Duffy.'

'That's enough about me, anyway' I said. 'How are you? How's the show?'

'It's going really well,' she said enthusiastically. 'I'm just so busy all the time that I feel totally exhausted, but it's a good kind of tired, you know?'

'Yeah,' I lied – the only type of tired I was aware of was the crappy kind.

'And what about you?' She bounced the conversational ball back to me again as if I was a guest on her show. 'Apart from the audition, I mean?'

'Okay,' I said, which was the best answer I could manage in the time allotted.

Fortunately Alexa wasn't fazed for a second by my mono-syllabic answer. She came back immediately with an enthusiastic, 'That's good to hear,' and in return I faked a cough while I thought of something clever to say.

'Have you managed to catch the show at all?' she asked when I'd finished spluttering.

I had indeed, and she'd looked mightily impressive. On the last show I'd seen she'd been surrounded by kids whilst interviewing an up-and-coming boy band dressed in matching purple silky tracksuits and baseball caps. Though barely above school leaving age, they'd attempted to flirt with her by making thinly veiled suggestive comments, all of which failed to impress her in the slightest.

'No,' I lied. The last thing I needed was her thinking I was only talking to her because she was TV's Hottest Totty.

'You don't know what you've been missing,' she said, looking directly into my eyes. She paused. 'I was talking to Mark the other day.'

'Oh, yeah,' I replied. 'How is he?'

'He's fine. We had quite a long chat about you, as it happens. He tells me you're a single man now.'

'Yeah,' I said, as if this thought had only just occurred to me, 'I suppose I am.'

Silence.

'Was it a bad break-up?' she replied eventually.

'Aren't all break-ups bad?' I responded, wondering what was happening to her trademark snappy deliveries.

Silence.

Here was a woman who under normal circumstances didn't know the meaning of the word 'pause', and yet in the last few minutes she'd paused for England. Why was she suddenly acting against type? As far as I could see there were three possible answers:

1. She was bored but was too polite to cut the conversation short.
2. She really was lost for words.
3. She was doing the Hinting Thing.

I studied her face. She didn't look bored or speechless, so she had to be doing the Hinting Thing. *One more silence*, I thought, *and then I'll ask her out.*

'I'd better be going, then,' I said looking at my watch.

'It's been good to see you,' she replied.

Silence.

I needed no further encouragement. 'I was wondering whether . . . if you're . . . free at the weekend?'

'Oh!' She sighed theatrically in a way real people never do. 'I can't. I'm in Los Angeles. There's some big film thingy that's coming out or something and I'm interviewing the star, what's his name . . . (she proceeded to name a Hollywood star of the calibre that gets to do his shopping in Harrods when it's closed to the public).' I reminded myself never to try and tackle the Hinting Thing again in this or any other lifetime.

'But I'm free a week on Saturday if you're not busy,' she added. 'I'm sorry it's so hectic at the minute, but I promise I'll be worth the wait.'

Ignoring what had to be the come-on of the century, for fear of no-saliva dry-mouth choking syndrome, I pretended to check my busy social schedule in my pocket diary. 'Yeah,' I said, brightening up. 'I think I can make it.'

I felt great after that meeting. Strong, independent, even

virile. My life was back on track. I had an audition for a job on TV and was going on my first hot date in over four years, with a kids' TV presenter!!!! Now that I felt this good, I could handle talking to Mel again. I promised myself our friendship was going to work or I'd die in the attempt.

Before I could change my mind I called Mel up and we got on great. In fact for the rest of that week either she called me at work or I called her at work, sometimes even two or three times a day. Out went the pauses and the tension and in came pure unadulterated making each other laugh.

In one conversation on the Wednesday of that week, in an uncharacteristic fit of bonhomie I told her that I was glad she and Rob 1 were getting on so well. I think I said it to hear what it sounded like – a tentative step on to a frozen lake, if you will. The minute it was out there, however, my façade as Duffy The Amiable Ex-boyfriend cracked. I was not glad they were getting on well. If she really needed to be with someone else, I wanted her to be with someone a little less perfect for her. So far I'd learned that Rob had a great eye for colour schemes, could cook without the aid of a microwave and, wait for it, loved shopping for soft furnishings.

Mel thought my confession was the most wonderful thing ever – a sign that we were true friends, a sign that I'd matured. To me, however, it was just a sign that I was losing my mind.

It was a key point in our let's-be-friendsness. From that call forward, the content of our cosy chats changed. Whereas before, her conversation had been ten per cent Rob 1, ninety per cent other stuff, very slowly his percentage began to creep up. 'Oh, Rob did this . . .' or 'Rob did that . . .' she'd say, and I'd grimace silently. Then occasionally she'd let slip some detail that would really cut to the bone. It wasn't the obvious stuff, like her staying over at his house or him staying at hers – although needless to say *that* didn't help matters – it was odd things like them going shopping together or even going to Mark and Julie's for dinner. According to Mel, Julie and Rob1 got on like a house on fire. Even Mark, though he apparently missed my 'funny ways', thought he was wonderful. Everybody loved Rob1 except me. Mel was even trying to persuade me on that score. 'You'd really like him,' she said one day. 'He's on your wavelength.'

What was I supposed to reply to that? Great, bring him round? Fabulous, I must go for a drink with him? Brilliant, because if you were sleeping with a man who wasn't on my wavelength I'd be really upset? So in the way you do when you're talking to your mates on the phone at work and your line manager approaches you, I said, '. . . thanks for calling, Mr Harrison, I'll make sure the message is passed on to the relevant department,' and put the phone down.

The night of my date with Alexa came round quickly. An hour before I was supposed to meet her I found myself in the bathroom mirror staring at my reflection.

I gave myself a pep talk: 'The difference between you and the legendary soul singer Barry White in a spiritual sense is nonexistent.'

I wasn't suggesting that I was a big bloke with a gravelly voice. I was saying that what I saw in the mirror was pure sex. I looked so good, felt so confident, that I had to have been possessed by the soul of Barry White – god of love and gettin' on down. Alexa might have been TV's Hottest Totty, but she didn't stand a chance against my charm offensive.

'Where are *you* going smelling like that?' yelled Dan, as I strode past the open living-room door. The aroma of my

Chanel aftershave – a present from Mel – had obviously managed to cut through the smell of Cantonese-style sweet and sour chicken.

Without even pausing for thought, I yelled back, 'I've got a date with destiny,' before adding an alarmingly hopeful, 'Don't wait up,' and walked out of the door.

'Hi, Duffy.' Alexa kissed me on the cheek. Just as I was pulling away she came round to kiss me on the other cheek and I ended up kissing her ear.

Bloody media types and their two-part kisses.

'Good to see you again,' she said sitting down.

'Cheers.' I replied, taking in her total visual effect. She was wearing a white long-sleeved T-shirt, a black knee-length skirt and trainers. She looked so trendy, so absolutely now, that she sort of reminded me of the shop window dummies in women's clothes shops like Kookaï and Karen Millen – only without the ridiculously pert nipples.

'You look . . . great,' I said. 'I didn't realise you were going to dress up, otherwise I'd have . . .' I gestured pitifully to my clothing, lost for words . . . 'a bit more.'

'You look great, Duffy,' she said, and waved to someone she knew across the bar. 'I live in my jeans normally. I just fancied a change.'

I got the drinks in. I ordered a beer and Alexa had a Martini. I gave the barman a tenner and he gave me back my change on a small saucer. *Yeah right,* I thought to myself as I carefully picked up the coins. *Like I'm going to leave you a tip just because you gave me my change on a piece of crockery!*

'Here you go,' I said, placing her Martini in front of her.

She took a small sip. 'Vodka,' she purred. 'How did you know that's the way I liked them?'

'I just guessed,' I replied, as once more my banal conversation compelled Oscar Wilde to rotate 360 degrees in his grave. I took a sip of my beer to fill in some of what was bound to be a long night of pauses. 'It took me ages to find this place. I walked past it four or five times. What is it with these trendy bars? Why don't they put signs with their name on so you can find them?'

'That would be too easy,' said Alexa, wrinkling her nose in the cutest manner possible. 'If it wasn't difficult to find, it wouldn't be a cool place to drink, would it?'

'It's ridiculous. If they really wanted to be cool, they should make anyone who wants to come here arrive wearing a blindfold. Then no one would know how to get here – not even the bar staff. Now that would be the kind of exclusive bar I'd like to go to on a regular basis.'

Alexa laughed lightly. On a scale of one to ten of sexiness she scored a perfect twelve.

'So?' I said, fearing another pause attack. 'What do you fancy doing?'

'What are the choices?'

'Cinema, drinking, eating, dancing . . . bowling.'

Alexa frowned wrinkling that nose again – it seemed to be getting cuter and cuter by the second. 'Bowling? Isn't that the kind of thing you do on dates when you're fourteen?'

'Probably,' I conceded. 'So this is a date, then?'

'Well, let's see,' she said coquettishly. 'Dating checkpoint number one: are both parties single?' She smiled. 'Well, we know about you.' I nodded coolly. 'And I'm not seeing anyone at the minute. So yes we're both single.' She sipped her Martini. 'Dating checkpoint number two: are both parties keen to get to know each other?' She looked at me and I nodded, cautiously. 'That's a yes from him and I can concur that it's a yes from me too.' She plucked the olive from her glass and dropped it into her mouth. Never before had I so wanted to be an olive. She continued: 'So I'd pretty much say that if we act like we're on a date and look like we're on a date then we probably are on a date.'

'Ah!' I said knowingly. 'But how do we know if we look like we're on a date? We've only got each other's opinions to verify that.'

'Let's find out.' Alexa turned to her left and tapped a stocky man in a long leather jacket on the shoulder. He was in the middle of a conversation with a young blonde dreadlocked woman in a trouser suit. 'Excuse me?' said Alexa. 'My friend and I were wondering if we looked like we were on a date. Do you think we are?'

Bloody TV presenters! While the rest of us were content to tell people what kind of a fun personality we have, people like Alexa always felt a need to prove it. I cringed with embarrassment. Fortunately, the man recognised her and couldn't wait to flatter her ego.

'You look like old college friends,' he said, humouring her. 'You look way too comfortable to be on a first date. What d'you reckon, Olivia?'

'I think you're wrong, Jez,' said his companion thoughtfully. 'They're definitely a couple. Look at the way they're sitting, look at the body language. This is more than companionship: this is about sexual chemistry.' She began laughing. 'I feel quite flushed just looking at the pair of them!'

'Thanks,' said Alexa. She turned to me in order to flash a wide, astonishingly suggestive grin in my direction. 'You don't know how useful your comments have been.'

I see a couple

We left the bar and Alexa put her arm through mine as we walked along leisurely in pursuit of food. She led me to a down-at-heel Indian restaurant off Charing Cross Road called Punjab Paradise, which according to her had become cool with TV and music-business types bored with posh expense-account restaurants and celebrity chefs. Over a distinctly ordinary chicken sagwalla and prawn bhuna we talked avidly about our lives, exchanging stories of our past that presented us in the best light possible. A few times I noticed she tried to steer the conversation on to past relationships, and when I could no longer avoid the issue without appearing rude, I told her simply that Mel and I had broken up because I couldn't marry her. She didn't react, and I think the serious tone of my voice revealed that I was far from over Mel, so she let me change topics.

At about nine thirty we left the restaurant and she suggested we go for a coffee somewhere nice. We reached a coffee bar in Soho, but it was packed full of the type of beautiful people that even she found tedious, so reaching for my hand she suggested that we go for a walk through Leicester Square instead. Convinced this was her being all TV presentery again, I tried to put her off the idea, reminding her that this late at night Leicester Square was turned over to an outlandish collection of tourists, bongo players and

185

pickpockets, but she wouldn't listen. And anyway, a small shallow part of me was flushed with pride at the thought of being out and about in the centre of swinging London holding the hand of one of the most lusted-after women on television.

We walked around for a while, then Alexa said she wanted to sit down for a minute, so we bought two ice creams while we looked for a bench that didn't have someone sleeping on it. A few minutes later and we were sat down watching the crowds pass by. She turned to me fixing me with her deep brown eyes just a moment too long. 'You're quite a laugh really, aren't you?' she said.

'Really?'

'Not like you are on stage though.'

'What am I now?'

'The stand-up you is sharp, funny and slightly irreverent in a good natured kind of way. The real you is more serious, more awkward, like you're in a permanent state of embarrassment.'

'So, you're a TV presenter and an amateur psychologist. An interesting combination.' I smiled knowingly. 'You like to suss out people don't you? You've been doing it ever since I met you.'

'It's true,' she admitted. 'I like to know what makes people tick. It's the key to being a good interviewer.'

'So now that you've got me in a box, are you happy with what you've found?'

'I think so,' she said, and smiled sweetly. 'But I need to do some further investigations.'

Needing no further encouragement I weighed up the pros and cons of attempting to kiss her right there. (Pro: it was a warm night so she might think it was romantic; con: It was a street bench and she might think it was a bit juvenile.)

Before I could come to a conclusion she turned to me and with a mischievous glint in her eye said, 'Let's play Couple Analysis. Like those two people did with us in the bar. Let's make wild, completely unfounded assumptions about couples based on what they look like.' I have to admit I was a little disappointed that she was more excited at showing off her predisposition towards the wacky than having her wicked way with me, but I didn't let it show. In fact I found it amusing because it wasn't the sort of thing I'd ever have suggested doing with someone as gorgeous as her.

Alexa nudged me playfully and pointed to our first victims. They were both about eighteen, and wearing baggy T-shirts, jeans with large turn-ups and brightly coloured trainers. He had on a floppy hat that I suspected he thought made him look like a bit of a hardcase, and was carrying a rucksack that probably had his sandwiches in. She was dressed exactly the same, but had a skateboard tucked underneath her arm.

'They've been going out for six months,' said Alexa between licks of her ice cream. 'It's the longest relationship he's ever had. He thinks she's the best-looking girl in the world. They are in love without a doubt.'

I disagreed. 'Note the way that she's walking just that little bit faster than him. I think they've been going out about a year, but she's been seeing someone else called Darren for the last three weeks. She's just working up the strength to tell him.'

'That's a bit cynical, isn't it?' Alexa pulled a face. 'Give them a chance.'

I shrugged my shoulders. 'I'm just telling it the way I see it.'

She nudged me in the ribs again. 'Okay, your turn.'

I scanned the crowds for a suitable couple. 'Okay, how about those two over there?' I pointed to two Spanish kids who looked like they were fourteen, tops. 'They've been a couple for exactly four weeks. He's fancied her for the last two years. He'll be grateful for this moment for the next ten years. She's the one who's going to establish his pattern. Every girl he goes out with after this will in some way be compared to this one.'

Alexa laughed. 'You're serious, aren't you? Who am I going to be compared to?'

I smiled but didn't answer.

'I think you're wrong,' said Alexa. 'He's too pretty not to have queues of girls chasing him. I think she's been after him for ages, making subtle hints and suggestions, desperately hoping that he'll get the message. But he's too thick or self-absorbed to notice until now. So she makes her move because they're on holiday and he thinks that it's just a spur of the moment thing.'

'Okay,' I said. 'It's your turn. Only one more couple, though, and then we'll find somewhere to have another drink if you like.'

'Sounds good,' nodded Alexa in agreement. 'I see a couple.'

'Where?'

She ignored me. 'She's been very keen for a while. Dropping some serious hints, like that Spanish girl, but he doesn't seem to notice.' I couldn't see the couple anywhere. There was a shady-looking pair standing next to a nightclub entrance who looked like his 'n' hers drug dealers. 'He's not her usual type. He's a bit more down to earth, but she thinks that's good.' I watched a tall dark-haired woman in her late thirties walk past with her young lover. 'She likes him because he makes her laugh and because he's got a look in his eyes that's kind of keen, but then there's something about him that's not quite there.' A young couple with a terrier loitered in front of us as if waiting for friends. 'Like she's not got his full attention. She likes it though. Makes him more of a challenge.'

Well, of course by the time she'd stopped talking I'd stopped searching for this phantom couple and after a token deliberation I commenced what was to become my first public snog on a bench in well over fifteen years.

Like crazed adolescents we kissed in the taxi all the way back to Alexa's flat in Camden. All the time I was thinking, *This is fantastic – I'm snogging an intelligent beautiful woman who not only is not Mel, but has the added benefit of being TV's Hottest Totty.* I was okay with this thought for about ten seconds but then I let my imagination run away with me, wondering what would happen when we reached Alexa's flat. Inevitably, as happens in these situations, she'd invite me up for coffee. And though I hated coffee I'd agree to the idea, and as I sipped my Douwe Egbert's, she'd slip on Miles Davis's *Kind of Blue* and we'd take our clothes off and . . .

'What's up?' said Alexa. The taxi jolted as we pulled up sharply outside a large modern-looking apartment block. She was looking at me intently. I'd been so deep in contemplation that I'd failed to concentrate on the business at hand.

'Nothing,' I said quietly. 'I'll be all right.'

She stepped out of the taxi, paid the driver and held open the door for me to get out. 'Are you coming?'

'Where?'

'Up.' She pointed to her flat in case I didn't believe her. 'Fourth floor, on the right-hand corner, the one with the lights on.' I followed her finger with my eyes, and I couldn't have been more terrified if it had been a moonlit Transylvanian castle, surrounded by dark clouds, thunderbolts and lightning, with the screams of the undead rending the air.

'I don't drink coffee,' I confessed hesitantly. 'Hate the stuff.'

Alexa adopted a suggestive smirk, squinted her eyes and purred, 'Who said anything about coffee?' She lowered her voice to a stage whisper. 'I'm inviting you upstairs to my flat for . . .' she paused, briefly, barely able to control her laughter, and yelled, '. . . hot sex!'

I coughed nervously for the benefit of the cabbie. 'This is all a bit . . . what I mean to say is . . . listen, I've got to get up early in the morning . . . work and all that. I'll call you. Okay?'

'No way,' she said, grabbing my hand. 'You're coming with me.'

Alexa's bathroom was roughly the same size as my flat. It was huge. It had a large circular sunken bath with steps up to it in the middle, and mirrors and chrome just about everywhere. From my position by the wash-basin I could see at least fifteen different views of myself, which was disconcerting, but not as disconcerting as what would happen when I left this safe haven.

Alexa was busy in her kitchen actually making coffee, but I knew she was going to become suspicious if I didn't come out soon. The thing was, I didn't want to come out. I was prepared to stay in the bathroom until she fell asleep, got bored or retired from showbusiness at the age of sixty. I wasn't built to sleep with fabulously beautiful women. I was built to sleep with Mel. Not that Mel wasn't fabulously beautiful, especially when she wore my favourite dress. It's just this was definitely a case of more being less and Alexa was definitely too much.

Ridiculous things were going through my mind like, 'Could I survive the jump from a fourth-floor window?', 'I wonder if there's an air-conditioning tunnel I can escape along like Tom Cruise did in *Mission Impossible*?' and most absurdly, 'How many calories are in a bar of Ulay, because I'm bloody starving?'

Alexa knocked on the door sharply. 'Are you okay, Duffy?'

I scanned the room for something to help me make suitable busy-on-the-toilet noises. 'Yeah,' I shouted as I located a box of purple cubes by the bath, grabbed a handful and dropped them into the loo. 'I'll just be a minute,' I yelled and flushed the toilet. Big mistake. I watched in horror as wave after wave of dewberry-scented bubblebath foam erupted from the bowl like lava from a volcano. When the water finally stopped churning, Alexa's toilet and the surrounding area was covered in a mass of foam. *Surely*, I said to myself, scooping bubbles from the toilet into the bath and mopping the floor with a huge towel, *things can't get any worse*.

Alexa and I were sitting in the lounge. The lights were dimmed and we were gazing out through windows that spanned the room and looked down on to the calming moonlit waters of Camden Lock. She'd laughed until her stomach hurt when I finally confessed the bathroom saga to her, and told me I was the maddest person she'd ever met. She got up and put on some music by a band that I'd never heard of. 'They're playing a gig next week, we should go and see them,' she said as the mellow vibes of the tune washed over us. 'That is, if you fancy it.'

I nodded. 'Sounds great.'

She kicked off her shoes, curled her feet up on the sofa and cuddled up to my chest. 'This is nice, isn't it?' she said, sounding smaller, more vulnerable, more real than Alexa the TV presenter.

I had to agree that she had a point: this was nice. I could smell her hair, and feel the warmth of her body, and in this setting, with this music, things couldn't have been more ideal. We sat perfectly still for some moments, not speaking, barely breathing, just soaking up the atmosphere. And then she kissed me.

Then I kissed her back.

Then I kissed her front.

Then we fumbled about with each other's clothing.

Then we fumbled some more.

And then I noticed something I'd never noticed before.

As a semi-clad Alexa led a semi-clad me to her bedroom, I came to realise that 'something' was wrong, and that the 'something' resided in the department marked 'Boxer Shorts'.

There was nothing going on.

Nothing.

N.o.t.h.i.n.g.

N-o-t-h-i-n-g.

As barren and lifeless as the surface of Mars.

I wasn't just being pessimistic. I'd had this body twenty-eight years. No one knew it better than me. And I knew that no amount of coaxing, jostling or shouting was going to make a jot of difference to the situation.

'What's wrong?' said Alexa as we reached her bedroom door.

Everything, I wanted to say. *Everything*.

'Look,' I said, panic now having worked its way fully into my voice. 'I can't do this.'

'Yes, you can,' she said, smirking. 'It's really quite straight-forward.'

'No it isn't,' I remonstrated sadly.

She tugged my arm. 'Of course it is!'

I'm going to have to tell her.

'Alexa?'

'What's wrong?'

'It,' I said, looking down at my groin.

'What?'

I pointed silently.

'Oh!' she exclaimed, casting a pity-filled glance at my boxer shorts.

'Oh, indeed.'

'These things happen, don't they?'

'Not to me they don't,' I said despondently.

'I mean . . . I've read in magazines . . .' Lost for words, she tapped her finger on her lips as if thinking of a solution. She had none. 'Are you sure?'

'Of course I'm sure,' I snapped. I apologised immediately. 'Look, I'm sorry, this is just too embarrassing for words. Why don't I just go, eh? We'll put this down to experience.'

'Is it my fault?' asked Alexa. 'Have I done something wrong?'

I really did want to go home now. Go home, get into bed and never get up again. Ever. I did not want to stand here, in this flat, with very few clothes on, talking to a virtual stranger about something so intimate that the very thought of it had me reeling in anguish. 'Look, Alexa. In case you've forgotten, you're TV's Hottest Totty. It's not likely to be your fault, now, is it?'

She looked crestfallen. 'Well, I'm sorry anyway.'

'Not as sorry as me,' I replied, searching around for my trousers. 'Believe me, no one is as sorry as me.'

Not a sausage?

'Are you okay, Duffy? You seem a bit odd.'

It was the day after the sleepless night before and I was round at my sister's, lying across one of her armchairs pouting like a toddler who'd just broken his favourite toy. Charlie was in the garden mowing the lawn, while a now visibly pregnant Vernie was sitting with me, eating a bowl of ice cream and staring at me like I was slightly touched. Not many men would've gone to their sister's to talk over this sort of problem, but I had to talk to someone and there was no way on earth I was going to mention anything this sensitive to Charlie or Dan.

I needed a woman's perspective on this, because women, I reasoned, were more at ease with their bodies. Vernie certainly was. From the day she hit puberty she was forever discussing periods, swollen breasts and the benefits of evening primrose oil. I tried to tell her that as a young boy not even into his teens, I wasn't even vaguely interested. I used to cover my ears and sing loudly, but somehow the information seeped into my consciousness. Over the following years I eventually became so well informed about the technicalities of so-called 'women's problems' that girlfriends had in the past asked *me* for advice. It therefore required only a short leap in the imagination to conclude that although Vernie wasn't in possession of the same equipment as me, she might have a handy miracle cure or words of advice that would make everything all right.

'No, I am *not* okay,' I said, answering her question grouchily. 'I am *not* in the *least* bit okay. In fact right now I believe this is the *abso-bloody-lutely* least okay I've ever been.'

'What's wrong?' Vernie asked.

'Everything,' I said dejectedly, and proceeded to tell her about my evening with Alexa in all its gory detail.

Perched on the edge of the sofa my sister listened to my tale of woe carefully, and occasionally, in between huge spoonfuls of ice cream, let out gasps of 'Oh!', 'How awful!' and 'Poor you!' When I concluded my narrative she put down her empty bowl on the carpet and stared at my groin in disbelief. 'Are you sure?'

'You know in *Some Like it Hot* when Marilyn Monroe kisses Tony Curtis in that incredible dress and you think to yourself you'd have to be dead not to get excited about that? Well, this was a little bit like that, only about fifty billion times worse because it was happening in *my* pants.'

'Yeah, but are you sure? Maybe you're, you know, nervous because she's on telly.'

'Believe me,' I sighed, casting my mind back to the night before, 'I was totally relaxed.'

'Maybe you'd drunk too much?'

'I'd hardly touched a drop.'

Vernie got up, taking her bowl with her, and left the room. When she came back she was carrying an entire tub of Wall's Chocolate Swirl virtually fat free dessert with a spoon jutting out of it. She really was milking this pregnancy craving thing for all it was worth. She settled herself down and recommenced eating.

'Do you know what I think?' she said after two mouthfuls.

'What?' I said sulkily.

'You know how men always think with the contents of their boxer shorts?'

'Yeah?'

'Well, I think the contents of your boxer shorts are still in love with Mel.'

'You're joking, aren't you?'

'Think about it. It used to work, right?'

I opened my mouth as if to say something but Vernie put her hand up to silence me.

'Spare me the details, oh brother of mine. A simple yes or no will do.' I nodded. 'And it doesn't work now.' I nodded again. 'That's it, then. It's psychosomatic. Your . . . you know . . . is still in love with Mel!'

'That's absolute rubbish,' I said, quashing Vernie's eureka moment dismissively. 'And you know it.'

'Okay! Okay!' she said defensively. 'It was only a suggestion, Duff. There's no need to be so bloody touchy.'

'Well, if you've got any more suggestions like that, I suggest you keep them to yourself,' I said irritably and stood up to leave. 'I came round here for your advice, Vern, but if you think that I'm going to go and ask my GP for previous partner aversion therapy or pop down to Holland and Barrett's for some organic anti-Mel rescue remedy or ask at Boot's chemist counter for the ex-girlfriend equivalent of a nicotine patch, you've another think coming! This has got nothing whatsoever to do with Mel. Nothing.' I calmed down, having finally become aware how ridiculous my indignation sounded. 'I'm going to go now and do what I should've done in the beginning instead of coming round here. I'm going to sort out this whole sorry episode myself and when you see me next I will be a whole man once more. Goodbye.'

*   *   *

Over the following seven days, in an attempt to right the wrong that had happened to me, I saw Alexa twice. Both times we got on incredibly well. We'd laugh, flirt and have a great time, but the minute things started to get even vaguely heated, well . . . nothing. Bizarrely, she seemed keener on me than ever before. It was as if her reputation as TV's Hottest Totty was at stake and she was determined not to lose her crown. Time and time again she asked me up for 'coffee' and time and time again I said no, not wanting a repeat of that deflated Saturday night. The more I said no, the more she wanted me to say yes. This was a unique position for me to be in and one that would've been of great benefit in my youth. Had I managed to convince girls at sixth form that it was *me* refusing *them* sexual congress, rather than the other way round, my 'A' level life would've been considerably more bearable. None of this mattered, however: despite everything I'd done to try and alleviate the problem – purchasing baggier pants, eating Bran Flakes and browsing the female underwear sections of clothing catalogues – the problem remained.

'Are you okay, Duff?'

It was a week later and I was round at Dr Vernie's sexual ailment surgery once again. This time I was prepared to take her advice for a miracle cure, whether it involved leeches, losing a limb, or even my ex-girlfriend.

'No,' I said sulkily.

'Is it still . . . ? She pointed to my lap and raised her eyebrows questioningly.

'Yes.'

'Nothing at all?'

'Nothing.'

'Not a sausage?' Vernie doubled up with uncontrollable

laughter, barely stopping herself from falling off the sofa. She wiped the tears of mirth from her eyes and sniffed. 'I'm sorry, Duff, I couldn't help myself.'

'Yeah, I'm sure you couldn't.' I held my head in my hands in despair. This really was becoming a nightmare from which it was possible I would never wake up. 'Do you really think that it's got something to do with Mel?'

'Don't you?'

'I'm not sure. Your theory fits. It's just—'

The sound of the front door opening interrupted our conversation. It was Charlie coming in from work. He came into the lounge carrying two large plastic Threshers bags that were making excessive clinking noises. 'Bumped into Dan on the Tube,' he said to Vernie, explaining not only why he was an hour late but why he smelt of Guinness too. 'He's just nipped to the newsagent. He'll be up in a minute.'

'Is that right?' said Vernie, now unquestionably annoyed. 'Why didn't you phone to say you were going to be this late?'

A man after my own heart, Charlie pretended he hadn't heard her question and instead opted to create a diversion. 'What's so funny?'

'Nothing,' I said abruptly. There was no way I was going to let him use my current infirmity to get him out of trouble with Vernie.

Charlie refused to give up, though. His only hope was to harangue me into submission. 'I could hear you laughing from outside. Come on. What's going on?'

Vernie opened her mouth as if about to begin a sentence.

'No, Vernie!' I yelled and leaped over to cover her mouth.

Charlie looked at me and then at Vernie, clearly bewildered, but aware that with a little more pushing he'd be off the hook for good. 'I'll find out sooner or later, you know.'

'It's private,' I said with my hand still over Vernie's mouth as she giggled wildly.

She bit my hand forcing me to let her go. 'I can't keep secrets from Charlie, he's my husband,' she said, trying to suppress her laughter. 'We tell each other everything, don't we, Charlie?'

'Of course we do, darling,' said Charlie, adopting an angelic tone of voice in order to mock me. 'What is it that your dear, dear, brother doesn't want you to tell me about?'

'You are *not* telling him anything!' I barked at Vernie threateningly.

'Oh, Duffy,' pleaded Vernie. 'Charlie only wants to help. Anyway, I think it might help for you to talk it over with another man. He might have some advice on what to do in this type of situation.'

'What kind of example are you showing your unborn?' I pointed to her moderately pregnant stomach. 'He can hear you, you know. He's probably thinking to himself, 'Why's Mummy tormenting uncle Duffy like this? She can't be a very nice lady. I'm going to show my disapproval of her shocking behaviour by taking fifty-two hours to come out.'

'Any more than twelve hours and I'll drag you out myself!' yelled Vernie at her bump. 'Anyway, if the baby is a *he*,' she said patting the sides of her stomach fondly, 'he's learning a valuable lesson – not to be anything like his uncle Duffy. Baby Jacobs, when you grow up, don't keep things inside. Talk. You can talk to me. You can talk to your dad – though I wouldn't recommend it – and you can even talk to your uncle Duffy. One day the whole of the world's male population will spontaneously combust because they've kept too much stuff in for too long, and I don't want it happening to you.' She paused. 'If you're a girl, Baby Jacobs, let me tell you how very lucky you are. Life is so much easier being a woman. We're so much more . . . I don't know . . . unburdened.' Vernie then looked up at me smirking. 'Try it, Duff. Try a little unburdening. Share your problem with Charlie, he might actually be able to help you.'

Charlie looked at me eagerly while I grimaced at Vernie's attempt to be earnest. 'Has it happened to Charlie then?'

'Never,' said Vernie barely able to suppress a snigger. 'Not my stud muffin.'

A look of horror crept across Charlie's features as the unmentionable of all unmentionables reared its ugly head inside his consciousness. 'You mean your . . . y'know . . . oh mate, I'm so sorry. I had no idea.'

I bowed my head in shame.

'I've heard it's quite common,' said Charlie, clearly trying to bolster my spirits. 'I shouldn't worry about it, mate. Leave it alone for a while and it'll be all right.'

'Leave what alone?' said Dan, who had just entered the room carrying a family-sized packet of Quavers.

'Duffy's you-know-what,' said Vernie matter-of-factly. 'He thinks he's impotent.'

Dan shivered visibly. 'Oh, mate,' was all he initially managed to say by way of comfort, then he added shakily, 'I agree with Charlie. Leave it alone for a while. It's probably resting or hibernating or something.'

'You lot are hopeless!' chided Vernie. 'You and your "It's only a flesh wound" mentality. Go on, listen to Charlie and "leave it alone for a while" – just make sure when it drops off you bring it to him to fix for you, and not to me. Get yourself down to a doctor, Duffy. Doctors see people with things that are wrong with them all the time! That's what they're there for.'

'Nah,' said Dan warily. 'Bunch of quacks, mate. You do not

want to be lowering your trousers in a doctor's surgery. You don't know what might happen. One minute you're following orders, slipping on to the examining table with the paper towels on it and the next he's telling you all sorts of things have got to come off. Ignorance, my son, is bliss.'

'Oh, stop, it you two,' said Vernie finally taking pity on me. 'You can take a thing too far, you know. Duffy's worried enough as it is thinking that it's all got something to do with Mel.'

'What's it got to do with Mel?' asked Dan quizzically.

'Everything,' said Vernie.

'You know what you've got to do, don't you?' said Dan after Vernie had expounded her theory.

'What?' I said, expecting this to be yet another joke at my expense.

'Exorcise it.'

'Exorcise it?'

'Well not "it" exactly,' said Dan laughing. 'I don't think there's a priest in the world that would want that job. But I think you've got to confront your demons. Vernie reckons that you're like this because you still find Mel attractive, right? So if you stop finding her attractive you'll be okay, won't you?'

I nodded.

'You've been talking for ages about wanting the two of you to be friends, so all you've got to do is stop talking and start doing. Once you see Mel as a close friend rather than your ex-girlfriend your troubles will be over.'

'Makes sense,' said Charlie, his tone of voice revealing that he was somewhat shocked to discover Dan could make sense. 'It's the only thing you can do, mate.'

'He could have a point,' said Vernie, looking at Dan,

barely able to comprehend that she too was agreeing with him.

'Friends it is, then,' I said, looking at all three of them. 'I just hope it works.'

We should do this more often

'So how are you, Duffy?'

'Okay. And you?'

'Not bad. Not bad at all.'

It was mid-afternoon, that post-lunch pre-hometime period of the day when it's impossible to do anything at work but sleep, stare into space or phone your mates. I chose to phone Mel. During the call I updated her on Vernie's recent pregnancy scan ('It looks just like a wizened Winston Churchill only smaller and without the cigar'), and Charlie's continuing battle to get to grips with fatherhood ('He did the introductory quiz in *Pregnancy For Fathers* and scored three out of twenty') and Dan's latest attempt to reinvigorate his comedy act with a character called Trip Master Monkey ('He pretends he's a monkey that keeps falling over. You have to see it to believe it'.) Then for no reason at all Mel said, 'This is good. This being friends lark.'

'Yeah,' I replied. 'It shows that we're growing up. Maturing like cheese and fine wine.'

Mel laughed. 'I'm the fine wine. You're the cheese.' She paused. 'I'm glad we're talking like this, because I want to tell you something and you may not like it, but I think if we are friends I should tell you anyway.'

'Okay,' I said, my stomach muscles tightening, waiting for the blow. 'Go for it.'

'Rob and I . . . we're going to go on holiday to Tuscany next week with Mark and Julie.'

'Oh,' was all I managed as I imagined the two of them frolicking next to a sunkissed lake, laughing gaily, and later sitting down on their sunloungers to write a postcard that said, 'You wish you were here.' It was too much. 'I didn't realise you were at the holidaying abroad stage. We didn't reach that stage until year two.'

'That was only because up until then five days in the Lake District with me was about as much of a commitment as you'd make.'

'There's no need for that.'

'I'm sorry,' said Mel. 'You're right.'

'I've got some news of my own.' I'd been meaning to tell Mel about Alexa for a while and as we were being truthful, now seemed as good a time as any. 'Remember that woman who knew Mark who came to see my act . . . the one who's a presenter on *The Hot Pop Show* . . . well, we're kind of . . .'

'Oh,' said Mel and fell silent for a few moments. 'So how long have you and TV's Hottest Totty been . . . ?'

'A while,' I confessed. I didn't want to hurt her any more than she'd wanted to hurt me with her holidaying arrangements. We both knew life had to move on but that didn't make it any less painful.

'It had to happen some time,' she said impassively. 'I'm pleased for you. I really am. Does she make you happy?'

We were back to that old one. 'I wouldn't go that far,' I said reassuringly. 'We're getting on okay though.'

Silence.

'So now we've both moved on,' I said finally.

'Looks like it,' she replied.

'So this means we can be proper friends.'

'Yeah,' she said. 'I suppose it does.'

I paused. 'Will I get to see you before you go off on holiday?'

'I don't know,' she said. 'I've got loads on at work. I'll just check my diary.' Her voice disappeared for a while, leaving me alone with my thoughts. 'Thursday's the only night I can do.'

'Okay, Thursday.'

Mel tutted loudly. 'Oh, hang on, I've got a presentation Friday morning, so I'll have to work late.'

I really was disappointed. I hadn't seen her since the day I'd visited her at work, and I desperately wanted to see her. To see with my own eyes that we were friends. This wasn't about exorcising her memory from my pants, this was about consolidating what we had. I felt that unless we did, she'd return from her holiday closer to Rob1 and further away from me than ever.

'What about just a quick drink, then?' I suggested hope-fully.

'I'll be too tired to be out in public,' she said dolefully. 'I'll tell you what, though, I can do better than just a drink. How about coming round to mine? You bring a bottle of wine and I'll bag something tasty from Marks & Spencer's chill cabinet.'

'Sounds great,' I said, brightening immediately. 'See you Thursday.'

It took me fifty minutes longer than my usual five to get ready to go to Mel's. My bed was covered in clothes that I'd been trying on and taking off for most of the evening. In the end I wore my jeans, trainers, a white T-shirt and my corduroy jacket. I looked a bit scruffy, but I didn't care because that was the point entirely. I had to make it known to Mel that I hadn't made an effort. She was an expert on the semiotics

Mike Gayle

of my wardrobe. The slightest bit of an effort on my part would be immediately construed as a covert attempt to get into her pants.

I arrived ten minutes late (I was working my 'No Effort Theory' to the max), and rang the doorbell.

After some moments Mel opened the door. 'Hi,' she said and kissed me on the cheek. 'Come in.'

I followed her upstairs to her flat. She was wearing dark blue jeans, a shiny black top and a green cardigan. The look was understated, homely and comfortable. She obviously had a 'No Effort Theory' of her own. I handed her a bottle of wine, my contribution to the evening's meal. I'd bought it from Safeway. I didn't have the faintest clue whether it was any good or not. All I cared was that it had passed my three basic criteria of wine purchasing:

1) Does it have a nice label?
2) Do I know anyone who has holidayed in the country of origin?
3) Is it under a fiver?

The label on the bottle had a picture of a cedar tree on it, and it was made in Italy (a country Dan had visited on a school trip many years ago), but the thing that had really swung it for me was that it was £4.99 – not quite cheap and yet not exactly reassuringly expensive.

'I'll get the glasses.' Mel headed off into the kitchen, leaving me alone in the lounge. I looked around the room for any changes. There were some new curtains and she'd moved the large uplighter that used to stand next to the sofa over into a far corner. There were a couple of new videos in her collection – *The Big Blue* and *La Grande Illusion* (undoubtedly presents from Rob1) – but apart from that nothing had changed. This pleased me immensely and immediately set me at ease.

We sat down to eat at the kitchen table. There was a huge pile of bills, a Next catalogue and a copy of *Elle* at one end and us and a candlestick at the other. Mel really was a big fan of the 'No Effort Theory'.

I bet she's never this relaxed with Rob1.

I poured more wine into our now half drunk glasses and we began our meal which was undoubtedly the best thing I'd eaten since we'd split up. As I chewed a mouthful of fondant potatoes Mel apologised for not cooking something proper and I told her not to worry. Why? Because this was yet another thing she . . .

. . . would never do with Rob1!

The meal over, two empty wine bottles on the table and a third already open, we tucked into dessert, a summer fruits pudding for her and a cherry cheesecake (my favourite) for me. Everything felt relaxed. Everything felt . . . okay.

'This is nice,' said Mel, moving her chair next to mine so that she could sample my pudding as well as her own without stretching. 'We were always friends as well as boyfriend and girlfriend, don't you think?'

'Yeah,' I nudged her gently with my shoulder, 'buddy.'

She nudged me back, slightly harder. 'Yeah . . . mate.'

I nudged her in return harder still. 'Yeah . . . chum.'

She then proceeded to nudge me so hard that I fell off my chair. Laughing hysterically from my position on the floor I managed a 'Yeah . . . pal!' as Mel tried to help me up. Holding on to my hand, she lost her balance and ended up on top of me in a fit of giggles. Having determined that the wine was making it too difficult for either of us to stand up, I grabbed the remaining bottle from the table and on all fours we crawled our way to the living room to relax.

'So, you're okay?' I asked, slouching back on the sofa sipping another glass of wine. 'I mean, everything's good in your life?'

Mel didn't answer. I nudged her again. 'Yeah.' She shook her head as if waking herself up. 'Sorry, you must excuse me. I was just thinking . . . Sitting here, drinking too much wine, talking, laughing. This kind of comfortable doesn't happen overnight.'

'No.' I kicked off my trainers. 'You're right it doesn't.'

'People always go on about how fantastic relationships are in the beginning, and of course everyone hates relationships when they end, but what about the middles? The middles where you know everything there is to know. Where you can look at the person you love and know what they're thinking; see something on the telly and know how they'd react; when you know exactly what they'd wear to come round and see you.'

I smiled fondly. 'Did you know what I'd be wearing tonight?'

'Look under Fat Buddha's bum,' she said.

I slid off the sofa, crawled over to the mantelpiece and picked up the small ceramic Buddha Julie and Mark had brought back from a trip to Thailand several years ago. Fat Buddha used to be the butt of all our politically incorrect jokes about fat men when we were together. I picked him up by his neck and underneath was a torn out page from a pocket diary. It read, 'White T-shirt. Jeans. Trainers. Corduroy Jacket.'

'Are you trying to tell me that you knew exactly what I was going to wear?' I said, crawling back to the sofa.

'I'm not *trying* to tell you anything,' she laughed. 'I bet you've even got your marl grey underpants on.'

This was typical Mel. I remember her once telling me that as a teenager she'd been a massive fan of the pop band Wham! So much so that she knew every personal detail about George Michael and Andrew Ridgeley, right down to their shoe sizes. I'm sure back then she didn't question why she collected all this information – she did it simply because it made her happy, not realising that she was actually learning skills that she'd one day need in the future. Seventeen years or so down the line, she was still an avid collector of personal details, only this time round they were mine. In the four years we'd been together Mel had learned off by heart every detail about me – chest size, name of first girlfriend, favourite episode of *Dad's Army* – everything. I'd often wondered why she'd done this, but it was only now, as I sat on the sofa that I realised that there was indeed a method to her madness. To her, to know truly, was to be intimate. To be intimate was to know the person you love as well as you know your own self. She'd built up the information inside her head to the point where she had created a virtual me, a model which she could use to predict my behaviour down to the last detail – even to the choice of colour of underwear. I was impressed.

'Congratulations,' I mocked. 'When's your membership to the Magic Circle arriving?'

'Ahhhh,' she joked. 'Have I hurt your feelings?'

'No,' I said, faking a sulk.

Mel leaned towards me. 'Come here,' she said rubbing my cheeks. 'Let me make it all better.'

Then she kissed me.

Then I kissed her.

Then we fumbled about with each other's clothing.

Then we fumbled some more.

And life came back to where there had been none.

And so we did it.

Twice.

Okay, once and a half.

Rays of sunshine broke through the curtains, rousing me from my slumber. Consciousness came immediately, but I didn't move in case I woke Mel. Instead I slowly opened my eyes and carefully manoeuvred my body to face her. I quickly realised I needn't have bothered being so quiet. She was already up and making shower noises. I lay back on the pillow, arms behind my head, and savoured the sweet smell of victory.

I always knew we'd get back together. I knew it would just be a matter of time. We meant too much to each other to give up so easily. I think we'll take things slowly to begin with. See each other twice a week until we're safe. And then everything will carry on as it was before. Except this time I'll make sure that I never lose her again.

Mel entered the bedroom wearing her hooded white towelling dressing gown, brandishing her hairdrier sternly. Her hair was still wet. She didn't look happy.

'My hair drier's dead, Duffy,' she said. 'This is a sign.'

'Of what?'

'A sign to punish me for what we did . . . there . . .' she pointed to her bedroom rug . . . 'and there . . .' she pointed at a small peach armchair her gran had given her . . . and there,' she pointed to the bed. 'My hair, Duffy. What am I going to do? I can't go to an important meeting with wet hair.'

I sat up in bed and tried to do that sexy, ruffled look that characters in big Hollywood films always have the day after. I caught a glimpse of myself in the full-length mirror on the wall. I looked about as sexy as an alcoholic tramp. 'It's probably the fuse,' I said helpfully.

'You don't know that,' she snapped exasperatedly. 'You

know bugger all about DIY. Remember, you were the one who fitted a handle on my bathroom door upside down, and three years later it's still the same way.'

This was not the mood I'd expected. I was hoping for a little joy. Maybe even euphoria. Irritability at my presence expressed through a knackered electrical appliance wasn't really what I had in mind.

'I take it you regret last night.'

Mel flopped down heavily into her peach armchair. 'Regret? Duffy, this is beyond regret. I cheated on Rob! I can't believe I did that.'

I instantly felt relieved. She didn't regret last night at all, she was merely torturing herself because she felt bad that she was going to have to hurt Rob1 when she dumped him. She needed help. She needed Bloke Logic.

'There you are wrong, Mel,' I said pointedly. 'What you did . . . what we did, well, it's not cheating. Not really. It's just a question of timing. You were going to dump Rob1 anyway, so the fact that we did what we did before you'd told him, is at the very worst a grey area.'

Mel's face transformed from neutral to thunderous instantly. 'Point one!' she yelled. 'Will you stop referring to Rob as Rob1? It's really annoying! Point two: it's not a grey area, Duffy! It's very black and white. Point three: I'm not going to dump Rob. You and I should not have done what we did. It was very wrong.'

I felt my body deflate in humiliation. 'But I thought . . .'

'Well, you thought wrong. Has your position on together-ness changed?'

I didn't answer.

'Yes, well, mine hasn't either!' She stood up and came over to sit on the bed next to me with her head in her hands. Her anger disappeared as quickly as it had arrived. 'Now look what we've done,' she said. 'What about this friends thing we had going?'

'It's still there,' I said dejectedly. 'Just as long as we stay away from £4.99 bottles of red wine.' I searched around for my underwear. It felt ridiculous being the only one naked in the room. 'Can you pass my clothes, please?'

Mel picked up my jeans off the floor and threw them at me playfully. 'You did this on purpose, didn't you?'

'What?'

'You came around to seduce me. Looking all cute and worn out.'

'I did no such thing!' I protested.

She laughed. 'Why not? Aren't I good enough to seduce, eh?'

'What about you?' I said accusingly. 'You only invited me round here because you were jealous that I was together with Alexa. All this time I've had to listen to you go on about Rob1, but it was okay, because *you* had someone else. The minute I found someone else, though, you didn't like it, did you?'

I knew I shouldn't have said it. Yes, it was true. Yes, it scored a few points on the self-righteous scoreboard. But was it worth it? Not at all. Yet another 'LEAVE WELL ALONE' option that I'd failed to exercise. *Why do I always say the wrong thing at the wrong time?*

Mel didn't say another word to me. Instead she got dressed, put on her jacket and shoes, grabbed her briefcase and hermetically sealed the door with a slam so forceful something fell and crashed on the floor next door. I got up and looked into the living room. Fat Buddha was lying smashed on the floor with his head rolling towards the sofa. I picked up the pieces sadly and placed them on the coffee table.

I walked back to the bedroom and looked out of the

window. I watched as Mel got into her car, slamming the door shut behind her. It was a bizarre scene to watch, because all the time I kept thinking, *Her hair is still wet.*

. . . and your plan is?

'Duffy, it's Mel.'

'Hi,' I said cagily. It had been two weeks since I'd last heard from her. 'When did you get back from Tuscany?'

'Half an hour ago.'

'How was it . . . your holiday, I mean?'

'It was all right,' she said dismissively. 'I don't think the food agreed with me. I kept being sick all the time.'

Was it too much to ask for Rob1 to be ill too? A touch of gastroenteritis. A smidgen of dysentery. A tinge of beri-beri. 'Did Rob suffer too?'

'He couldn't go in the end. Something came up at work.'

Excellent! Better than disease – penalised by hard work.

'I'm sorry to hear that,' I said airily.

'I'm sure you are,' she said sardonically. 'But none of this has anything to do with why I've called. I've been thinking a lot about what you said last time we were together. You were right: I think I *was* jealous about you and Alexa. It was wrong of me to invite you round and to let what happened happen. I suppose I just wanted to see if you still wanted me, and if you're truthful you wanted to know exactly the same thing. You have to admit it, Duff.'

'No, I don't.'

'Of course you do,' she persisted, her voice revealing a complete lack of doubt. 'Don't forget how well I know you.'

217

'Okay, you're right,' I admitted finally. 'But where does that leave us? You still have feelings for me. I still have feelings for you. You want one thing, I want something else, and to top it all we're both seeing other people.'

'The way I see it,' said Mel authoritatively, making it clear that she'd given the matter a great deal of thought, 'we've got to face up to the fact that, irrational as it may seem, we still mean a lot to each other but want different things from life. We were together for a long time, and that kind of intense feeling isn't just going to disappear. We undoubtedly still feel the need to be part of each other's lives—'

I interrupted. I could feel that Mel was going into over-analysing mode – finding fifteen different ways of saying exactly the same thing. I'd had enough. I just wanted her to get to the point. '. . . and your plan is?'

'If only you knew how annoying that is, Duffy!' she snapped exasperatedly. 'My *plan* is that as we can't live with each other and we appear to be unable to live without each other, we have to do the mature thing. The adult thing.' She still wasn't getting to the point.

'And that is?'

'Well, the way I see it, one of us has a well-developed conscience while the other likes to pretend that he hasn't, even though I know he bloody well has. And so in the same manner that criminals are sometimes forced by courts to face up to their wrongdoings by meeting the victims of their crime, we should meet each other's new partners.'

I coughed nervously. 'You're joking, right?'

'It totally makes sense, Duff.'

'On Planet Psychotic perhaps, but here on earth I think you'll find that what you've suggested is deranged.'

Mel continued, unruffled. 'Once we meet each other's new partners they'll both become real. This way I can convert the image of Alexa as "that bitch off the TV who's sleeping with my ex-boyfriend" to "Alexa the human being who finds herself in the middle of this terribly entangled situation". She becomes real.'

'But aren't you forgetting one small thing?'

'What?'

'I've already met Rob1 "that tosspot who's going out with my ex-girlfriend", so I can be excused from this nightmare. He didn't become "Rob1 the unfortunate individual caught up between two people who . . ."' I chose my words carefully . . . '"have strong feelings for each other". I loathed him before I met him and totally despised him after the event. It's just the way it goes.'

'Let me explain this to you, Duffy,' said Mel, adopting a businesslike tone I suspected she used at work with difficult clients, 'in terms you can understand. We can't carry on being friends if we don't try to do something to rectify this situation. That's no phone calls. No meeting up together. No Letters. E-mails. No communication whatsoever. I know it'll be difficult but it's the only way if you won't do this.'

'You're serious, aren't you?'

'Yes, I am,' she said. 'Anyway,' her voice was much lighter in tone now she'd got my attention, 'you haven't met Rob properly at all. He's a really nice guy. He likes you. He told me so.'

It was all I could to do stop myself from tutting contemptuously. 'I bet he's told you he's not jealous that you phone me either; that he's happy we're still in each other's lives; that it doesn't bother him when you mention my name . . .'

'Yes,' snapped Mel.

'Mel, these are guy lies! Can't you see that? It's not in

our natures to like He-Who-Was-There-Before-Us. It's natural selection. The selfish gene.'

'Look, I'm serious. We have to do something. And we have to do it now.' She played her trump card. 'Have you got a better solution?'

'No,' I said.

'Then it looks like we're going with mine, then, doesn't it? Next Saturday night. You and Alexa come round to mine. I'll make something nice and we'll sort out this whole thing.'

'But won't they think it's suspicious that we're suddenly having this meeting? I mean, you're not going to tell Rob1 about what happened, are you?'

'You know what a terrible liar I am. I feel like I'm going to be struck down by a bolt of lightning every time I tell my mum that I didn't skip breakfast, but this would hurt Rob too much.' She paused. 'How would Alexa react?'

'She'd be really mad,' I lied. I hadn't the faintest clue what Alexa would think. 'Absolutely furious.'

It was the day of the dinner invitation and I'd just arrived at Alexa's. I was wearing a dark burgundy suit without a tie in a bid to look both smart and casual. Alexa, however, had insisted on dressing up. She was wearing a purple top that had all the seams on the outside by a Dutch designer whose name I couldn't pronounce, and black wide-legged trousers from Joseph. I knew all this information about the labels because she'd insisted that I accompany her on a shopping spree in New Bond Street for the whole afternoon. It was a truly frightening experience. Not only did she not bother looking at a single price tag the whole time we were out, but she deliberated over a pair of shoes for three hours and still didn't buy them. Shopping for soft furnishings with Mel was a doddle compared to this.

'Come in,' said Alexa, holding open her front door. I followed her into the lounge. 'Do you want a drink? I'm having a glass of wine.'

'Yeah, go on, then,' I said, sitting down on the sofa. I looked down at Alexa's feet as she handed me the glass of wine. 'Are those what I think they are?'

'Yes,' she laughed. 'The second I got home I knew I wanted them after all. I called a cab and went straight back to the shop and bought them. And even if I do say so myself, they look fantastic.'

'They do,' I said. I took a moment to take in her whole outfit. 'In fact all of you looks fantastic.'

'You don't look too bad yourself.'

She sat down next to me and took a sip of her wine. 'I've got to tell you something that I know you're not going to like,' she said.

'What is it?' I asked, hoping she was going to deliver the 'this isn't working out' speech. It had been obvious for quite a while that Alexa and I were never really meant to be. She was beautiful, fun to be with, and for all her pretensions actually quite down to earth, but she wasn't right for me. Though cured, I was still feigning impotence – a sign, if any were needed, that things weren't quite right – and when I'd explained Mel's suggestion to her earlier in the week she'd said yes without even blinking an eyelid. No one normal should want to meet their current partner's ex-partner that much. If it had been the other way round and Alexa had wanted me to meet any of her ex-boyfriends, there would've been no way I'd have done it. We just weren't suited. I didn't mind, though, because I really did think we could be friends – especially as, technically speaking, we hadn't seen each other totally naked.

'It's about the audition,' she said.

I stopped breathing.

'The executive producer called me about an hour ago to let me know she'd made her decision. I'm sorry, but you didn't get the job. I tried really hard to swing it for you. I really did, but they kept going on that you weren't what they were looking for, whatever that means. But they don't know anything. Don't worry about it, Duff. Something else will come up soon, I'm sure.'

I drained my glass of wine and didn't say anything. I purposely hadn't been thinking about the audition, because I knew that if I gave it any thought at all, by the time I'd finished churning out vast numbers of hope-filled 'what ifs', it would become the biggest thing in my life. Unfortunately, it was only now as I sat on this sofa, not saying anything and feeling like the whole world was collapsing around my ears, that I realised how misguided I'd been. Despite my efforts, the audition had been the biggest thing in my life this past few months. It had been the one thing keeping me afloat. It had been the best thing that had happened to me in the eight years of being heckled, ripped off and lied to. It hurt not to have it happen. It hurt more than I could bear. I looked at Alexa and then at the room that I was sitting in. None of this felt right. This was all wrong.

'You win some, you lose some,' I said eventually. 'Who got it in the end?'

She picked up a scrap of paper by the telephone. 'Some guy called Greg Bennet. I think I even met him at one of the auditions.'

'Grim-looking, balding man with a massive Napoleon complex, talks a lot about football?'

'Yeah,' she said, puzzled. 'Come to think of it, when I spoke to him he did say that he knew you too.'

I've had enough, I told myself. *This is the end.* 'I'm quitting comedy,' I said, letting my thoughts roam free. It felt odd saying those words at long last, and yet at the same time I was relieved.

'Not because of this stupid audition, surely?'

'Exactly because of this stupid audition. I've given this comedy lark my best shot for over eight years, and this audition was the biggest thing that's happened to me in all that time. Maybe it's a sign. I don't know, maybe it's time I realised I'm going to be one of the ones who doesn't make it. I'm not bitter.' I paused. I wasn't fooling anybody, least of all me. 'No, I *am* bitter. I'm as bitter as it's possible to be. I've given up everything chasing stupid dreams. Too much. Now it's time to bail out before it's too late.'

'This is a bad idea. You're really talented, Duffy. You've just had a knockback. We all get those once in a while. You wait. Take a few weeks off, forget all about the audition and then everything will look different.'

'Did you know,' I said, wondering how I was ever going to tell Alexa that I didn't want to see her any more, 'that Margaret Thatcher once said, "If a man finds himself a passenger on a bus, having attained the age of twenty-six, he can account himself a failure in life"?'

'No.'

'Yeah, she did. I read it in an article in the *Guardian* last year. I pinned it on the cork noticeboard in the kitchen'. I sighed heavily. 'Do you know how I get to work every day?'

'By bus?'

'For the last three years,' I said. 'I'm two years past Maggie's sell by-date and I'm still catching the bus. That's why I'm giving up comedy. I need to get real. I need to stop travelling on buses.'

'Come on, Duff. What would you do? Get a permanent office job? You'd be banging your head against the walls within a week.'

I shrugged. 'I could go back to college maybe. I don't know. Do something constructive.'

'You're just feeling depressed about not getting the job. Everyone knows what it feels like to be disappointed. There'll be other auditions, other opportunities.'

'Maybe.' I sighed again. 'And maybe not.'

'But that's not all, is it?' she said, her eyes searching my face.

'What do you mean?'

'Us.'

'Us?'

'Yes, us.'

Alexa had obviously developed the same mindreading technique that Mel possessed.

'Yeah, well, I was going to get round to "us". The thing is—'

'You're still in love with your ex.'

'That's not what I was going to say.'

'I know, but it's true. You were going to string me some old line about things not working out between us, because you're too scared to admit what's really going on. I'm no expert on love, but I am a woman. It's totally obvious you're still in love with Mel. There are only three reasons why any man would agree to go to dinner with his ex and her new boyfriend. One: he's mad. Two: he's stupid. Three: he's still in love with her. You're not mad or stupid, so what's left? You talk about commitment like it's an alien concept. This thing that you just can't do. But all this time hasn't it dawned on you that "commitment" is what you're doing right now? I read this brilliant thing once in a book: 'What's the difference between involvement and commitment? Think of eggs and bacon. The chicken was involved. The pig was committed." You, Mr Duffy, are, probably always were, and definitely always will be, a pig.'

Alexa's words slowly began to sink in. 'So what you're saying is I've been acting like a fool because I'm already committed to Mel . . .'

She nodded.

'So if I'm already committed to her, then it's ridiculous being afraid of commitment. So there's nothing stopping me from . . .' I stood up. 'I've got to go.'

'I know,' said Alexa.

'Aren't you mad at me or anything? I've led you a right dance: I've helped you spend hideous amounts of money on clothes you needn't have bought, and if that's not enough, I wouldn't sleep with you even though you practically begged me.'

'Well, now you put it like that . . .' Alexa started to laugh. She leaned forward and kissed me. 'Look, firstly I love buying clothes. Secondly, you're kidding yourself if you think me and my brand-new shoes are staying in tonight pining for you while you're proposing to your ex-girlfriend. And thirdly, rejection is good for the soul. Even if you are TV's Hottest Totty. Duffy, you're a nice guy, you really are, and I hope we can be friends, but the real reason I'm not bothered is because at the end of the day I'm just a sucker for a happy ending.'

In the back of a cab with a wet late-evening London whizzing past in a continuous blur I could hear nothing other than the sound of my heart beating. With the benefit of my new enlightenment, the key mistakes I'd made in all my time with Mel were suddenly clear to me in a way they'd never been.

For starters I'd entered our relationship determined to stay exactly the same – which I'll admit is pretty stupid, but at the beginning had made perfect sense to me. Changing meant that I wasn't the man I used to be, and I quite liked the man

I used to be. Mel, however, had taken me on a journey out of the wilderness I inhabited with Dan and led me part of the way to the land of the living, where there were three different types of shampoo in the bathroom, duvet covers that matched pillows and food that didn't come out of a tin or make its appearance accompanied by toast. Admittedly, sometimes I'd felt like I was slapbang in the middle of no-man's land – not quite my old self and not revised enough to be a new self – and yes, there were occasions when I found myself wanting to run back to what I knew. But I'd tried being a super stud of seduction and it hadn't worked, precisely because I was a changed man. In the past my deepest thoughts used to be about stand-up, music and women. Thanks to Mel's influence I'd expanded my repertoire of subjects to include life, the universe and everything.

Mel was the best girlfriend I could've asked for. She was funny, gentle and most of all, loyal. She was one of a kind and I'd nearly blown it for good because I had a problem with all the stuff that seemed to come with the relationship. Like IKEA. Like dinner parties. Like . . . marriage. The one thing she most wanted but the only thing I couldn't deliver.

Well, I could now.

Blue

The taxi pulled up outside Mel's and I sat motionless in my seat as my head occupied itself with the following problem: how on earth was I going to announce to her that I didn't just want to have dinner with her, I wanted to spend the rest of my life with her too? I looked out of the cab window for inspiration. Mel's 2CV was glistening brightly in the rain but I couldn't see Rob1's coolmobile anywhere. *He's probably got a taxi so he can have a drink*, I reasoned. A thought which led me to consider the bottle of wine in my hand. During my afternoon shopping trip with Alexa, in a bid to be wild and unpredictable like her, I'd abandoned my normal strategy for wine purchasing and picked a bottle at random in Selfridges and bought it. It had cost me £17.99, which to my mind meant that it had better be up there with the best the sensual world had to offer or I was asking for my money back.

Enough of the procrastinating, Mr Duffy, I reproached. *It's now or never.* I stood and watched the cab pull away. My legs felt incredibly unsteady, like I'd just run a marathon. It was amazing. They just wouldn't work properly. In addition to this, my saliva had turned tinny and watery. With each swallow the scales of digestion were tipping further and further towards projectile vomiting. I was comforted by this fact because it meant that both my conscious and unconscious selves were in agreement that this situation I was about to get myself into was a momentous one.

I rang the doorbell and waited, practising my proposal, so that when the moment came, at the very least I'd be word perfect.

Mel, I love you. Will you marry me?

Nice.

Mel, I've been a fool. Will you be my bride?

Okay, but a touch melodramatic.

Baby, I'm thinking me in a suit, you in a white dress and the vicar in whatever he wants.

Who am I, John Travolta?

I closed my eyes, breathing deeply, and tried to calm myself down. Eventually I heard the lock on the front door turning and I opened my eyes to see Mel standing there. She'd been crying.

'What's wrong?' I exclaimed, observing the traces of smudged mascara across her face. 'Are you all right?'

She wiped away a stray tear with the palm of her hand and said, 'You'd better come in.'

I followed her upstairs into the living room, wondering what could've happened. I thought that perhaps she'd had a row with Rob1, but it seemed to be more than that. Then it occurred to me that something might have happened to her parents. Mel's mum had suffered a slight stroke a couple of years ago and had been in and out of hospital ever since.

'Are you all right?' I asked when we reached the lounge. 'It's not your parents, is it?'

'No,' she said. 'They're fine.'

I put my bottle of wine on the table and scanned the room for evidence of Rob1's presence. 'Where's Rob?'

'He's been . . .' she said, sitting down on the sofa . . . 'and he's gone.'

I sat down next to her, and all I wanted to do was put my arms around her. 'Have you had some sort of row?'

'You could say that.'

'I'm sorry to hear it,' I said quietly. In a strange sort of way I actually meant it.

'There's no need to lie, Duff.' She smiled weakly. 'At least not for my sake. Me and Rob were never going to go anywhere. I've known that from the beginning. It's funny: I think I was only with him because he was so much the opposite of you.' She paused. 'Anyway, he's not the reason why I've been crying.'

'I don't understand,' I said, moving closer to her. 'What's upset you so much?'

'I'm pregnant,' she said, not looking at me.

I tried to grasp the meaning of what she'd said, but it just seemed to escape me. It was like my brain was stuck. I had no reactions at all. I was totally calm. I didn't say anything. I couldn't say anything. I couldn't feel anything and could barely hear anything apart from the sound of my own heart.

'Before you ask,' she said, 'it's not Rob's. Practical impossibility. Call me old fashioned, but I couldn't sleep with someone I didn't love, and I didn't love Rob.'

'When did you find out?'

She looked at her watch. 'Three hours and twenty-seven minutes ago. Not that I'm counting or anything. I was over a week late. I've been late before, but like they always say, this time I knew. I bought three tests, three different brands. Any less than three opinions isn't enough for a woman like me.' She laughed softly, stood up and walked over to the mantelpiece and picked something up. 'I thought I'd keep them as a memento.' She unwrapped a tissue and laid the three test sticks on the table one by one. 'Blue. Blue. And Blue. It's a baby all right.'

She looked at me expectantly. It was my turn to say something. The best I could muster was, 'I thought we . . .'

'That's life,' she said sharply. 'Accidents happen.' She began pacing the room nervously. 'If this is a shock for you, Duff, I'm sorry, but it's a whole lot bigger shock for me. It's turned my whole world upside down.'

'Listen, Mel,' I interrupted. I had to say something. I had to let her know that I loved her. That I wanted to be with her. That whatever happened *we* were going to be all right. 'I've got something I need to tell you.'

'Will you not do that!' she yelled, tears now streaming down her face. 'I'm speaking, Duffy! I'm fed up of you talking over me all the time. For once just shut up and listen!' She closed her eyes and breathed deeply. When she spoke again her voice was calmer and more controlled. 'I want you to know that I've made up my mind that I'm going to have this baby, Duffy. But I have to make it clear to you here and now that we won't be getting back together. That's what you were going to say, wasn't it? Let's get back together?'

'It's not like that, Mel. It's not like that at all. I want you back. That's what I came here to say. That's why Alexa's not here. Because I want to be with you.'

'Oh stop it, Duffy! Just stop it. Why won't you listen to me? I don't want you to do the right thing. I don't want us to be together because I'm pregnant. I wanted us to be together out of love, but it's too late. It's funny. In all the time we've been apart I've not once told you that I love you. We used to tell each other "I love you" every day. When we split up that stopped and I missed it more than anything. Instead we've been going on about how we "care" for each other and "need" each other, afraid to admit that we still love each other. Well, I love you, Duffy. I love you so much it scares me, but I can't do this any more. I just can't.'

'So what are you saying?'

'I'm saying that even though I love you it's over between us. I'm saying that right now I can't even handle having you near me. I'm saying that things have changed now beyond our control. I've always tried to do what's best for you but now I've got to think about me.'

I looked into her eyes, overflowing with tears, and could see that she meant every word, and as the tears filled my own eyes, I knew that she was right. If I'd thought that there was even the slightest chance I could change her mind I would've gladly spent every second from then on trying to convince her. But she was never going to believe me. It wasn't the situation that was impossible, it was her. I could see already from the way she spoke and looked at me that she'd created a barrier between us to protect herself, and she was never going to take it down.

Standing in front of her, my head swimming with thoughts and my heart overloaded with love, I pleaded with her. 'Please, Mel, I'm begging you. Is there anything I can do, anything at all that will change your mind?'

'No,' she said. 'Some things just aren't meant to be.'

Rituals are important. Nowadays it's hip not to be married. I'm not interested in being hip.

—John Lennon

The Italian Job

Friday. 11.30 p.m. The flight from Paris arrived three hours late into Heathrow's Terminal Four, which was just about typical of the entire torturous fourteen days I'd spent there. On my very first night in Paris I came up with the great idea of sleeping rough in the Gard du Nord, thus saving me the many francs I would've squandered on a room with such frivolities as a bed, toilet and running water. It was only when I saw the state of the premier Paris train station that I realised what a mistake I'd made. The air was thick with fumes from the trains, and even the pigeons cooing quietly in the rafters were a dirty, sootish grey. At three o'clock in the morning, which is when I arrived, the only place with a higher concentration of criminals would've been a prison. Within half an hour I'd been solicited by four prostitutes, offered hard drugs by a man wearing a dressing gown, and received threatening glances from a group of young men who had nothing better to do than hang around a train station at 3 a.m. After a sleepless night in which I did nothing but wish I was back in Muswell Hill, I booked into a hotel.

Over the next two weeks I saw all the sights that Paris had to offer: the Louvre, the Eiffel Tower, the flea market, the Left Bank, but without anyone to share them with, it all seemed kind of pointless. Everywhere I went there were couples smooching; gazing into each other's eyes; feeding each other food across restaurant tables. I knew Paris was supposed to be the city of love, but this was ridiculous – it was like going to IKEA on a bank holiday, only worse because there was no escaping it, and it all served to remind me just how alone I was.

Even checking in for the flight home was a nightmare. The woman on the desk had asked me if I wanted a window or an aisle seat and I told her that I wasn't bothered. The clerk tapped away at her computer keyboard and told me that all the window seats had gone for my type of ticket. Now that I couldn't have one, of course I wanted a window seat, I needed a window seat, I would've torn off my right arm for a window seat. Where did she put me? A middle-row seat right at the back of the plane. When she asked me if I'd packed my own bags I briefly contemplated telling her that my mum, the renowned diamond smuggler, terrorist and drug overlord, had done it for me, but I chickened out because I didn't know what other punishments she could inflict on me with her mighty seating computer.

All in all, I had a crap time from start to finish, but I suppose it didn't really matter where on earth I'd disappeared to, my mood would've been just the same.

Mel had absolutely refused to listen to reason. The night that she told me she was pregnant, I'd stayed round at her flat until four the next morning just holding her and crying. Nothing changed, though. She still believed that it would be best for both of us to go our separate ways. During my time away I'd tried really hard to put myself in her shoes. To understand what it was she was feeling. Here she was, twenty-nine, single and pregnant, with a ex-boyfriend whose track record for reliability wasn't exactly perfect. Of course she'd be scared to rely on me; to let me back into her life when she wasn't sure whether I had what it took to go the distance. Given my past performance, I'd failed her. Why would she believe in me?

That was only one side of the story though. My side was equally complicated. I hadn't set out to be unsure of my ability to love one person for the rest of my life – it had just happened. Unlike Mel, who seemed to have been handed a map and compass of her emotional landscape at birth, I didn't know what I was capable of, and it felt like I was being punished for my deficiency.

Mel and I were a badly dubbed, out of-sync kung fu movie, with Mel as the action and me lagging behind as the dialogue. I thought I'd never catch her up. But which was more important: us reaching the same conclusions, or us reaching the same conclusions at the same time? Mel had arrived at the idea of marriage before me, but now I'd reached the same point that she'd been at, she'd raced ahead again. Once again, it seemed, everything came down to timing.

Mel told me that she needed time alone, and I agreed that space was probably what I needed too. So I went home and told Dan everything that had happened – the splitting up with Alexa, abandoning comedy, my road to Damascus conversion to commitment, and of course my impending fatherhood. He asked me if there was anything he could do to help and I replied, rather melodramatically, 'I don't think there's anything anyone can do to help me now.' That's when I decided I needed to go away. Why Paris? Why not?

Initially I'd intended not to tell anyone when I was coming back home, but Charlie and Vernie wouldn't take no for an answer. They'd harangued me vigorously when they dropped me at the airport to catch my flight, so I gave in and promised to contact them from France. I wasn't trying to be enigmatic. I just didn't want to come back to England until I'd vaguely sorted my head out. This level of intense emotional trauma was all new to me and I hadn't the faintest idea how long a decent headsort would take, but given that I'd only packed twelve pairs of pants and loathed handwashing with a vengeance, my time away was always going to be limited.

In the end, the thing that made me come back (other than hating the food, boredom or running out of clean underwear) was Dan. Before I'd left he told me that he was thinking about going to Meena's wedding after all. He didn't ask me to go with him. He would never do that. But if at the age of twenty-eight I was allowed to have anything approximating the playground title 'best mate', then Dan was it, and I wasn't going to let him go through something like that alone.

As soon as I came into the arrivals lounge I found a phone booth and dialled Mel's number. I'd felt like calling her a million times a day when I was in Paris, but had always resisted for fear of making her feel like I was crowding her. The phone rang out and eventually her answerphone picked up. I put the receiver down without leaving a message and made my way to meet Charlie and Vernie outside the Sock Shop.

'How are you?' said Vernie. Her stomach was now so round with her pregnancy that I had to hug her from the side when she greeted me.

'I'm fine,' I replied unconvincingly. 'I'm still standing, as they say.'

'It's good to have you back,' she said, holding on to my arm. 'I wouldn't say this under normal circumstances, but because I'm about to pop a sprog any time in the next fortnight I think I can get away with it – blame it on hormone imbalances or something.' She paused and smiled. 'Baby brother Ben, I have missed you.'

'Me too,' said Charlie, giving me a blokey hug. 'It's been

weird coming home every day to find there's still food in the fridge, beers in the cupboard and no one hogging the remote control. It's unnatural, just didn't seem right.'

'Are you excited?' I said, looking at Vernie's stomach.

'Of course I am. I'm going to be a brilliant mother.' She paused. 'Talking of brilliant mothers, Mum's coming down to stay with us in a couple of weeks. Charlie can't get that much time off work, and when the baby arrives I'll be rushed off my feet, so she's volunteered her services for a while.'

'Great. With Mum only up the road there'll be no hiding how messy my flat is!' I protested jokingly. 'Mother's intuition doesn't stretch from Leeds to London, but Crouch End to Muswell Hill will be a doddle for her. She'll have psychic visions of the state of the kitchen and she won't be able to rest until she's nagged me to death to clean it up or done it herself. How much do you want to bet that when you pick her up from the train station she'll arrive with a mop, a duster and twenty quid's worth of cleaning products?'

Vernie laughed. 'Pregnancy might mean my brain is shrinking, but not even in this condition would I bet against a dead cert like that!'

Charlie wandered off, trying to remember which of the NCP car parks he'd left the car in. Vernie and I, meanwhile, sat down on a bench outside and waited. I could tell that she wanted to ask more about how I was feeling but was holding back for fear of her concern being interpreted as nagging.

'It's okay,' I told her. 'I can see that you've got something to say, so you might as well say it.'

'I just want to know that you're okay. You're the only baby brother I've got.'

'I'm fine,' I said. 'Admittedly I'm not brilliant but I am okay.'

'You don't look fine, Duffy. You look terrible.'

Mike Gayle

'Cheers,' I said sarcastically.

'I know you told me not to say anything to Mum, but with her coming to stay you know that you're going to have to tell her about Mel being pregnant, don't you?'

'Yeah.' Even the idea of telling my mum all about this made me feel ill. 'But not yet, eh?'

'If you don't tell her, she'll find out somehow. That what's mothers do best. If she does find about it by accident, it'll really hurt her that she didn't hear it from you.'

'I know,' I said. I glanced up at Vernie to see if she'd finished. 'I'll sort it out.'

'All right, mate!' yelled Dan triumphantly as I walked into the living room and dropped my rucksack on the floor.

'You look like a stick insect,' grinned Dan. 'I'll get you a lard drip feed to fatten you up while you're asleep. You look way too healthy.' He sat up and rubbed his head. 'How was it, then?'

'Not too bad,' I replied as he handed me a tin of Red Stripe. 'Six out of ten at a push.'

'I've got three pieces of news for you, all of which will make you believe that there is a force working for the greater good against all the evil in the world.'

'Give me the news that will make me most happy first.' I sloped into the armchair. It felt good to be back.

'Well, Alexa called while you were away. She said she had some news that she just couldn't wait to tell you. It turns out that the telly job Greg got wasn't as good as it sounded after all. Apparently the producers decided against using him to write gags and sketches, and instead preferred to utilise his skills as . . . wait for it . . . the voice of one of the programme's studio puppets! I taped it last week, and honestly, Duff, I nearly

240

had a heart attack I was laughing so much. You can tell it's Greg from a mile off. Who says there's no justice?'

'What's the other news?' I said, laughing. 'It can't be anywhere near as good as that, surely?'

'Greg update number two. I bumped into The Lovely Anne last week in the Haversham, and guess what? She's dumped him!'

'Result! So she came to her senses after all?'

'Not exactly. It was more a case of her having no other choice. Get this.' Dan leaned towards me as if too shocked to impart the news in the normal way. 'Apparently Anne had thrown a party at their flat to celebrate Greg's new job and invited all their mates. Half cut on Jim Beam, who should try it on with Bethan Morgan – Anne's best mate – but Greg! Anne hit the roof and chucked him out!' Dan paused. 'I wish I'd been there.'

'So what's the third piece of good news?' I asked. 'Don't tell me you've got your own sitcom?'

'Better than that. Guess what's on in half an hour on BBC2?' he said, pointing at the TV with the remote.

'Dunno.'

'*The Italian Job.*'

'Nice one,' I said. It was mine and Dan's all-time favourite film. 'Any other phone messages?'

'Nah,' said Dan.

I was still hoping Mel would've called by now. I looked at my watch. *It's late – if she's gone out she'll be back by now. How many places can a pregnant woman be at this time of night?* Getting up off the floor I went to the phone and dialled her number. Her answerphone was still on. I left a message telling her I was back and that I'd try to call her again when I knew whether Dan and I were going to

Meena's wedding. Dan must have overheard the last bit of the message because when I turned round he was looking at me pensively.

'You don't have to come with me tomorrow, you know,' he said solemnly. 'I still haven't made up my mind about the wedding, but if I do go I'll be all right on my own.'

'I know you will,' I replied, 'so you won't mind if I tag along, will you?'

Realising that it was futile to argue, he laughed and said, 'Cheers. At least I'll have someone to talk to.' He sat up straight and turned off the TV. I looked at him questioningly, and he said, 'There's something else.'

'What is it?'

'We need to talk.'

'What about?'

'Us,' he said.

'Us?'

'Yeah, let's talk about us.'

'I don't know what conclusions you came to out in Paris about you and Mel or about what you're going to do with the rest of your life, but I've been thinking seriously about my own future while you've been away. I've also been thinking about you leaving comedy, and it's a really bad idea. The worst you've ever had. I know we've both got a lot of other stuff going on in our lives, but the comedy has always been a laugh. We're not too old to stop having a laugh, so what I'm trying to say is . . . I think we ought to try working together.'

'What do you mean?' I said. 'Be partners? Form a double act?'

'Like Abbott and Costello.'

'Morecambe and Wise.'

'Hope and Crosby.'

'George and Mildred.'

We ran out of double acts.

The only conclusion I'd come to in Paris was that Alexa was right. The minute I took any permanent job with no hope of escape I would be banging my head against the walls, constantly calling in sick or being escorted off the premises by security guards within a week. Some people can do the nine-to-five thing and not worry, but I knew I couldn't.

Dan took my hand and laughed. 'Do you, Benjamin Dominic Duffy, take Daniel Aaron Carter to be your lawful wedded partner in comedy?'

'I do,' I said, grinning like an idiot. 'Do you, Daniel Aaron Carter, take Benjamin Dominic Duffy to be your lawful wedded partner in comedy?'

'I do,' said Dan, adding, 'Then by the considerable power invested in me I now pronounce us officially a double act. Carter and Duffy. Has a nice ring about it, don't you think?'

'Not as nice as Duffy and Carter,' I replied, 'but it'll do for now.'

The groom's handsome too

I woke up with a start and studied the alarm clock carefully. My stomach tightened and I put my hands behind my head and stared at the ceiling, lost in thought. Today was the day. Today was D-day for Dan. Before we had gone to bed (after falling asleep halfway through *The Italian Job*) he had told me that he'd definitely decided to go to the wedding. I knew there was no point in trying to talk him round, so I reminded him I was going with him no matter what, and went to bed hoping that the intervening hours would bring him to his senses.

Pulling on a T-shirt that had been lying on the floor, I got out of bed, knocked on his door, yelled, 'Morning!' and walked in. Though the curtains were closed, chinks of light coming through the gap between them illuminated the room enough for me to make out the shape of Dan sitting up in bed. The sound of Marvin Gaye's album *What's Going On* was coming from his CD player. He turned on his bed-side light.

'Morning,' I said again.

'Yeah,' he replied unenthusiastically. He looked at his watch but remained silent.

'I suggest that we stay in London, laugh at Greg on kids' TV, meet up with Charlie for a drink and count our bless-ings – and if you're really good we can go to that café on

Archway Road that does those fried breakfasts. I'll even pay.'

My transparent attempt to take Dan's mind off things failed abysmally. 'Not today,' he said, rubbing his eyes and stretching. 'I've a wedding to go to.'

'So you're still going?'

'What do you think?' he said.

I didn't reply.

'I didn't mean that sarcastically, Duff. I actually want to know what you think I should do. Do you reckon I should go to my ex-girlfriend's wedding?'

Even though I already knew what my answer was, I weighed up the situation as truthfully as I could and I still thought it was a bad idea. 'No,' I said finally. 'It's not going to do you any good whatsoever if you stay here and mope, and it's certainly not going to do you any good if you go there and watch someone you still . . .' I searched around for the right terminology . . . 'someone you still obviously have *strong feelings* for, marry someone else.'

'I knew you were going to say that, Duff,' said Dan, turning off Marvin Gaye. 'I knew it because that's exactly the kind of advice I'd give you. Thing is, we're both so crap at giving and receiving advice that I wonder why we bother. The easy thing would be not to go, which is exactly why I have to go. Sometimes it's not always about the easy life. I can see that now. All I've ever wanted was the easy life. Not too much stress, not too much boredom, a bit of a laugh here, some mucking about there. Nothing too strenuous. Now look where that's got me. It's got me losing Meena. It's got me living here with you for the last eighteen months and maybe for ever. It's got me living exactly the same life that I've always led. I've lost her, Duff. She's going to marry someone else and there's nothing I can do. So I'm going to act like I'm twenty-eight instead of eighteen. I'm going to go to the wedding and I'm going to wish her well, because it's the only way I'll ever learn.'

Dan put on a suit and tie, which made him look kind of odd. The last time I'd seen him in it was during a momentary lapse in his faith in comedy two years ago. He'd bought it from Burton's for a job interview with an IT company. Twenty minutes after he got the letter telling him he had a second interview, the suit was back in the wardrobe and he was back in the world of laughs, late nights and hecklers.

We caught the train to Nottingham and were silent for most of the journey. Dan was obviously wrapped up in thoughts of Meena. Meanwhile I was wondering how Mel was. I constantly worried about her and the baby, whether she was sleeping okay or how she was getting on at work. She was always on my mind, but it never felt like a burden.

At the station we caught a taxi to the registry office and twenty minutes later we were there. Large groups of people milled about with that wedding vibe about them: the smart clothes, the anxiety about what time it was, and the facial expressions that managed to combine 'This is so exciting' with 'These shoes are killing me'.

Dan and I sat on the wall of the registry office car park and loosened our ties. Although it was September and not exactly hot, I could feel the sweat running down my armpits, and I considered starting a discussion with Dan about the differences between antiperspirant and deodorant, but just at that moment Meena's brother, Chris, tapped us both on the shoulder. It was a matter of public record that Chris had wanted to give Dan 'the kicking of a lifetime' for the way Dan had treated Meena, and if there was anyone that you wouldn't want to receive the kicking of a lifetime from, it was Chris.

The only thing that had prevented him from killing Dan was Meena's protests that Dan wasn't worth it.

'Carter and Duffy,' he said flatly, making us sound like the veritable comedy double act we now were. 'There's a surprise.'

'All right?' said Dan. 'How's things?'

'I'm going to say this once and once only,' spat Chris. 'This is my sister's wedding day and you're not going to spoil it. If you do anything at all to screw this up I will spoil you beyond all recognition.' He jabbed a muscular finger into Dan's chest. 'Do you understand?'

'I'm not here to spoil anything!' protested Dan, consciously avoiding looking Chris in the eye, as you would any wild animal that was looking for an excuse to tear you limb from limb. 'I'm here to see a close friend get married. Okay?'

Chris glared at Dan and then glared at me and then combined his glares for the benefit of the both of us before walking off.

I turned to Dan, about to remark upon Chris's ability to walk upright without the aid of his knuckles, when we were interrupted again. Standing next to us was a balding man in his late fifties, with a full beard who was so large he reminded me of an off duty version of the wrestlers that my mum loved watching on a Saturday afternoon when I was a kid. The austere-looking woman next to him, in a matching cream suit and hat, I assumed was his wife. They just had to be Meena's parents.

'I would've thought you'd have had the decency not to turn up,' said Mr Amos to Dan. He raised his eyebrows when he said the word 'you' for emphasis.

'Your daughter invited me, Mr Amos,' said Dan. 'She's a friend. It would've been wrong not to have come. The coward's way out.'

'Well, you still shouldn't have come,' muttered Mr Amos, lost for words at his daughter's stupidity.

'Why?' asked Dan.

A look of confusion spread across Mr Amos's features. His huge eyebrows suddenly met in the middle, the furrows in his forehead deepened and his lips tightened.

Mrs Amos, obviously unfazed by the unexpected, stepped into the fray on behalf of her husband. 'Because you don't deserve to be here,' she said, and then added a loud, dismissive tut to back her husband's disapproval.

'Don't think you're going to mess things up for our daughter,' Mr Amos said threateningly. 'I promise you this: you will not spoil this day.' He looked at Dan with such scorn that I thought he was going to throw a punch.

'Look,' I said, and stood up, pushing him back gently, 'you've said what you wanted to say. Now leave it, eh?'

'You'd better take your hands off me, son, if you know what's good for you.'

The last thing on earth I needed was to get into a fight with anyone. Least of all a man with a son as preposterously homicidal as Chris was. However, he was threatening my friend, so I stood my ground regardless, despite possessing all the pugilistic presence of an eight-year-old girl.

'Just leave him alone, okay?' I said, trying my best to sound hard.

Throwing a look of disgust in my direction, he and his wife turned and walked away, leaving me to bask in the glow of winning such a potentially lethal face-off. I sat back down on the wall, my legs were shaking slightly.

'Maybe it wouldn't have been such a bad thing if he had hit me,' Dan said quietly.

'Nah,' I said. 'He would've knocked his wig off in the process.'

'You reckon he was wearing a wig?' Dan looked over his shoulder at the departing Mr Amos. 'Who'd have thought it, eh? I always knew there was something about the old git that didn't add up. Meena always told me he just didn't like having his hair cut.'

For a moment he almost seemed like his old self, but within a few minutes he slipped back into his New Dan depression.

I was just wondering what to do to cheer him up when a voice from behind us said, 'Feeling sorry for yourself?'

I looked round, semi-startled, at a tall dark-haired man whose distinctive attire singled him out as the groom. Next to him were two other men, who by their dress could only have been ushers. Without a doubt we were once again going to be threatened with violence. I handed Dan a cigarette, and took one out for myself.

'Don't,' said Dan, taking control of the situation by refusing to turn around. 'Just don't. There's no need to, Paul. You've won.' He inhaled deeply on his cigarette. 'You've got Meena, and watching the odd episode of *Casualty* and *The Bill* I can see that your acting career has indeed gone from strength to strength since we left college. Meanwhile, I've got no Meena, and as for my career . . . well, let's just say it's nowhere near as illustrious as yours. So, please, there's no need to prove your manliness with fisticuffs – I believe you. Let's just leave it at that, eh?'

One of Paul's ushers, eager to prove his solidarity with the groom, shoved Dan in the back, and would've followed it up with some other act of violence had I not stood up, dropped my cigarette and pushed him back forcefully. He lost his balance and fell into the other ushers. He was about to launch himself at me and tear me limb from limb when Paul held him back.

'Leave it, James,' he said. 'If we start anything here Meena will go mad.'

James calmed down, but not before spitting in my direction. 'You're a dead man,' he said, pointing at me threateningly. I nodded, smiled and gave him a silent but effective internationally renowned gesture of disdain. Where all this bravado was coming from I had no idea, but I was going to enjoy it while I had it.

'I'll leave you alone,' said Paul while Dan observed him coolly. 'I don't know what Meena ever saw in you. I really don't. You were a waster at college and you're a waster now.' He paused. 'It was Meena who invited you here and I've respected her wishes in having you here. But this I will say: do anything to spoil this day and you will regret it.'

'Why does everyone think I've come here to spoil Meena's day?' said Dan to me rather than the assembled besuited apes behind him. 'I loved Meena. Why would I want to spoil her day?'

'Paul, we'd better go, mate,' said the groom's only pacifist usher. And with that they walked off without saying another word.

The registry office was set on the edge of a park five minutes away, so for the remaining twenty minutes we wandered about looking at flowerbeds, sitting on benches and smoking too many cigarettes. By the time we made our way back to the registry office a large group of people from the last wedding party had just exited and were milling around with the guests for Meena's wedding. At five minutes past two everyone's attention turned towards the driveway as a white Rolls-Royce carrying Meena and her maid of honour came to a halt. Watching her get out of the car was a totally surreal experience. I was no expert on wedding dresses, but even I could appreciate that she looked absolutely stunning. Meena's father helped her out of the car and she held on to his arm proudly.

'I can't believe it,' said Dan, his voice faltering slightly. 'I'm jealous of Mr Amos. Meena's relying on his support to get through this. I want to be Mr Amos. I want Meena to rely on me, even if she is marrying someone whose finest hour was as bank robber number two on *The Bill*.'

The interior of the registry office was decorated in a soulless cream that made the room feel cold and impersonal. Dan and I thought it best to take seats at the back, well away from the groom, ushers and Meena's family. We sat down on cushioned plastic chairs that had seen better days, and smiled at an old lady dressed in orange taffeta who had moved along for us. The organist began playing Mendelssohn's Wedding March, and everyone stood up.

'She looks wonderful,' said the old orange lady to Dan as Meena and her father made their way up the aisle. 'The groom's handsome too.'

Dan nodded.

'I'm so happy for her,' said the old orange lady. 'Of course it nearly didn't happen. Her mother was saying that she had cold feet this morning. Wasn't going to go through with it.'

'Really?' said Dan. 'Why was that?'

'I haven't the faintest clue, but I'd love to know,' she said ominously. 'Apparently she's only been courting Paul for a year. Maybe that was the problem. Although, the way I hear it she's not had a very good track record with men altogether. According to her mother, Meena's previous young man was a bit of an undesirable.'

'I heard he was just a bit stupid,' said Dan. 'Didn't know a good thing when he had it.'

'He's meant to be here somewhere,' said Orange Lady

scanning the room, presumably in search of someone with hooves and a pointed tail. 'Apparently he had an invitation! Can you imagine the audacity of such a man? Turning up to Meena's wedding like this?'

Dan shook his head.

'Well, he doesn't matter any more,' said Orange Lady dismissively. 'The important thing is that she's here today. Whatever worries she had, she must have resolved them.'

I looked across at Dan, but his eyes were fixed to the front of the room.

Now, I'd seen *The Graduate* and countless Hollywood imitations. I knew that when the registrar got to the part where he says, 'If there's anybody here who knows of any reason why these two should not be married, let them speak now or forever hold their peace,' Dan was supposed to say something, anything that would mean that he wouldn't lose Meena, but he didn't. He just kept his mouth tightly closed and tried to hold back the tears.

Everyone clapped when Meena and Paul were pronounced husband and wife. I didn't at first, as a show of support for Dan, but then Dan started clapping and I felt a bit stupid being the odd one out.

Orange Lady looked at Dan sadly while the happy couple signed the register. 'It was quite emotional, wasn't it?' she said, handing him a tissue from her handbag. 'I hope you don't mind me saying, but it's very rare that men cry at weddings. You must have been very close to her.'

'Yes,' he said. 'I was.'

Like that bloke in *Groundhog Day*

Dan and I were offered a lift to the reception by two of Meena's old college friends, Jenny and Lisa. In the car they asked me how we knew her and I lied and told them we used to live in the flat above Meena when she lived in Muswell Hill. Dan wasn't really saying much about anything, and although I tried to make up for his reticence by talking all kinds of complete and utter rubbish, it quickly became obvious to them that he was acting a bit strange.

Eventually Lisa got annoyed enough to make a comment when an innocent question to Dan about what he did for a living was met with complete silence. 'I don't know what your problem is,' she said to Dan as the car pulled up at a set of traffic lights, 'but there's no need to be so obnoxious. Last time I looked, manners didn't cost anything.'

Without pausing for thought Dan opened the car door and got out, slamming it behind him.

'Er, d'you want me to pull over?' said Jenny, addressing me agitatedly, about to indicate. There was now a long queue of traffic either side of us.

'I didn't mean to upset him,' added Lisa apologetically. 'He was just being so strange. Don't you think you should go after him?'

'No,' I said quietly as I watched Dan dodging through the lines of cars to the other side of the road. 'No, I don't think

I should go after him, and no, I don't think you should pull over.'

They both looked at me as if they were witnessing the worst betrayal of friendship ever committed. Right now, however, Dan didn't need my opinion, sympathy or comfort, which is what these two strangers wanted me to offer him. What he needed was to be alone.

'He'll be all right,' I explained. 'He's just had a bit of a weird day, that's all.'

The white Rolls-Royce that had taken the bride and groom from the registry office to the reception at the Piermont Hotel, was surrounded by a gang of children. They were pointing and yelling, 'Chitty Chitty Bang Bang!' in unison at the car's chauffeur. They'd been at it for some five minutes now and I could tell from the look on the driver's face that he'd got to the stage where he was weighing up whether it was worth losing his job to enjoy the simple satisfaction of telling the lot of them to bugger off. The rest of the wedding guests milled around aimlessly on the hotel's front lawn sipping glasses of bucks fizz, chatting with friends and relatives they hadn't seen in years and generally wondering what would happen next. Meanwhile Meena and Paul and their immediate families were being herded around the hotel grounds by a team of wedding photographers keen to give the couple's day of happiness a varied selection of softly focused backdrops.

Jenny and Lisa had abandoned me in order to 'mingle' almost the very second we'd arrived, leaving me to loiter alone at the front of the hotel lobby examining the ornamental ivy growing up the windowframes like a dedicated amateur botanist. Quite obviously appearing bored out of my mind, I was approached by a number of people who all endeavoured to draw me into conversation. I chatted to Mrs

Kapur (Meena's great auntie) about the latest trends in men's ties, Samantha (the groom's second cousin's ex-girlfriend) about how much she hated the groom's second cousin, and Lucy (a six-year-old who hadn't the faintest clue what her connection to the bride and groom was) about what she was getting for her birthday in two weeks' time. Thankfully after half an hour of this an announcement was made for the guests to take their seats at the banqueting hall. There was no way I was going to sit down at a table of strangers, eating melon and swapping wedding anecdotes, and I had made my mind up to call a taxi and get the train back to London when I spotted Dan walking up the hotel drive, looking pensive.

'All right, mate?' I said as he reached me.

He nodded, hands dejectedly lodged in his trouser pockets. 'Yeah. I'm all right.'

'Let's sit down for a second.' I gestured to a wooden bench overlooking a large pond. 'These shoes are killing me.' Dan nodded and together we walked across the lawn, crunching sun-dried duck poo underfoot.

'Did you walk here?' I asked as we sat down.

'Got a taxi,' said Dan. He scratched the back of his neck animatedly. 'Sorry about . . . you know.'

'No, problem,' I replied, and there we sat, not moving or talking, just sharing a silence – a big, fat empty pause filled with nothingness. I'd forgotten how much of a strain it was constantly to have to translate the world and how I saw it into words for the benefit of those who didn't understand. It was nice to enjoy a moment when I could just sit back, relax and think about nothing.

'Duff?' said Dan, after having shared over half an hour's worth of noncommunication.

'Yeah?'

'Do you love Mel?'

I paused and lit a cigarette before answering. It was a big question to begin with, but the fact that it was Dan who had asked it, only seemed to make it even bigger. 'That's a bit deep, isn't it?' I stalled. 'Where did that come from?'

He shrugged indifferently, acknowledging both my attempt to sidestep the question and my right to do so. 'I was just wondering whether if I had the power to time-travel, I'd have done things differently . . .' His attention was distracted by the roar of an RAF jet passing overhead. He stopped and stared up at the sky momentarily. 'Do you know, I'm not sure I would. That's the thing about hindsight: over time you gradually forget how stupid you've acted in the past. Time and time again I've made the same mistakes. Like that bloke in *Groundhog Day*. Only I never learn. Knowing you've got to do the right thing doesn't amount to much if you never actually do it. I mean—'

'I thought I'd find you both out here,' interrupted a female voice from behind us. It seemed like everyone was coming up behind us these days.

Dan and I turned round simultaneously to see which new member of Meena's family and friends had come over to warn us off spoiling the wedding. My money had been on Meena's chief bridesmaid, because I'd noted somewhat warily that she was built like a professional arm wrestler, but it was the bride herself. She was standing there quite innocently, her wedding dress appearing much whiter than it had done before. Every now and again a shallow gust of wind caught the loose fabric of the skirt, giving it an almost liquid appearance.

'Hello, Dan, hello, Duffy. How are you both?'

'All right, Meena?' I said nervously. I stood up, preparing for evasive action. This was bound to turn into a Situation, and I really didn't want to be here when it did. 'I think I ought to leave you two alone. You've probably got stuff you want to talk about and you don't really need me hanging about, do you?'

'No,' said Dan firmly. 'I think you ought to stay, Duff. You need to hear this more than anyone else.' He stepped over to Meena and kissed her lightly. 'Congratulations,' he said warmly. 'It was a good wedding as weddings go.'

'Thanks,' said Meena. 'I'm . . . glad you could come.'

'Wouldn't have missed it for the world.'

'You two weren't at the lunch, were you?'

'No,' said Dan apologetically. 'It was all my fault. I had a bit of a wander around Nottingham and lost track of time.'

'There's more food if you want it,' she said, gesturing towards the hotel. 'There's loads of it knocking about. If you don't fancy it now you can always wait until the evening reception.'

'Are you having a disco later?' asked Dan, grinning.

'No,' laughed Meena. 'Paul's parents paid for the hire of a band. They're called the No Tops. They play all sorts, but they specialise in covers of cheesy Sixties Motown hits.'

'No disco,' said Dan with a hint of gentle sarcasm in his voice. 'No "Come on, Eileen"? No "Three Times a Lady"? Not even a "Birdie Song"?'

Meena laughed and held his gaze a few seconds longer than necessary or indeed appropriate for a recently married woman.

'So what's it like being married?' asked Dan. 'Do you feel any different?'

'I don't know,' she said thoughtfully. 'No, no different. At least not yet.'

'D'you remember that wedding we went to?' said Dan. 'It was one of your mates from the first theatre you worked at, what was her name . . . Lynne Hodges that was it . . . and there was that huge fight between the best man and her father-in-law.' He paused, slightly confused, as if he'd lost his train of thought. 'Do you think our wedding would've been like this? I can't help thinking it wouldn't have been. I think at least it might have been a bit smaller. My family's nowhere near as big as yours. My mum—'

'Don't, Dan,' interrupted Meena. 'Don't make out like we're old mates. Don't pretend that you're just another wellwisher. If there's one thing you can do for me, please just be honest.'

'I'm sorry, you know,' said Dan quietly.

'What for?'

'For everything. I know I've done everything wrong. I can't believe I let you go. I loved you when I lived with you, and I think I still love you now. I wish I'd had the guts to tell you all this yesterday. Or even this afternoon. When the registrar said, 'Does anyone know why these two people shouldn't be married?' I wanted to say what I felt.' Staring right into her eyes, he asked her a question that up until this point in my life I would never have imagined him saying. 'If I had spoken up,' he said, 'would you still have married him?'

She paused before answering. 'We'll never know, will we?' Then she looked away as tear after tear fell from her eyes and ran down her face. She wiped them away with her hand, smearing a dark line of mascara across the bridge of her nose in the process. 'After today I never want to see you again, Dan.'

'I know,' he said. 'That's why you invited me and that's why I'm here: to say goodbye.'

Meena looked at me for the first time since her hello. I felt embarrassed to still be here; I felt embarrassed to have witnessed this most private of moments; I felt embarrassed for being me.

'Have you got a spare cigarette?' she asked. I handed her the lit one that was in my hand. She puffed on it frantically for a few seconds as if she were more in need of nicotine than oxygen, threw it on the floor and walked away without saying another word.

Dan didn't move. He just stood and watched her walk off silently.

'C'mon, Dan, let's just call a cab and go home, mate,' I said, checking my pockets for change for the phone. 'You've done what you came here to do. I think it's best that we just go. Even you must have had enough by now.'

'We can't go yet,' said Dan, subdued.

'Why not?'

'Because Mel's here.' He pointed across to the hotel lobby where Mel was indeed getting out of a taxi with Julie.

'I can't believe this,' I sighed.

'What's she doing here?' asked Dan.

'Meena invited Mel and me ages ago – just when we'd split up. I told Mel that I wasn't going, so she obviously assumed that it was safe for her to come up here and wish Meena well.'

'Are you going to talk to her?'

That was a good question. After all that had happened today, I wasn't in the right mood to make small talk. Julie's presence was bound to wind me up, and the last thing on earth I needed was to start a row. Mel and I certainly needed to talk, but not here, not now, and certainly not in front of a million wedding guests. *No*, I decided, *this is going to be the one time that I actually choose the 'LEAVE WELL ALONE' option*.

'Let's just go,' I said quickly, 'before today gets any crappier. It will, you know, I can just feel it.'

'Earlier,' said Dan, staring at me with the same searching

look that he'd given to Meena, 'when I asked you if you still loved Mel, you didn't answer me.'

'I know,' I admitted reluctantly. 'What about it?'

'Well, do you?'

I nodded.

'So why don't you do anything about it?'

'Look, Dan, just let it go!' I said, losing my temper with him in a way I never had before. 'I've told you, Vernie and Charlie – all of you a million times – the reason why. Mel thinks I only want to be with her because she's pregnant. She doesn't want me.'

'Calm down!' said Dan. 'I'm not attacking you, Duff.'

'Look, I'm sorry, mate,' I apologised. 'I know you're only trying to help me out, but this isn't just about me any more. I've got to think about Mel and the baby too. I've messed her around too much in the past. There's no way I'm going to be able to convince her. It's just my tough luck.'

'No,' said Dan firmly. 'It isn't . . . well, at least it doesn't have to be. Look, you've seen what's happened to me today. I can't stand by and watch the same thing happen to you. She loves you, Duff. You know that as well as I do. You two, weird as it might seem, are made for each other. You've got to make her see that.'

'How? I've tried everything. I can't get through to her.'

'Look,' said Dan, 'there was no guarantee that if I'd spoken up in the church today that Meena would've changed her mind. In fact I'm pretty certain that she wouldn't have. But at least I'd have known that I tried. That's what really galls me, Duffy – that I didn't *try*. It's just like the day that she walked out. I knew I could've talked her round, I knew that I could have convinced her to stay, but it was easier to let it go. If you believe in something, Duff, you can't let it go without a fight. You just can't.'

*   *   *

'The Piermont Hotel welcomes you to the Halcyon Suite, for the wedding reception of Paul and Meena Amos-Midford,' read the sign outside the main banqueting hall. I opened the doors and scanned the room for Mel, but I couldn't see her anywhere at first. Eventually I spotted her sitting at a table in the far corner of the room. It was weird, but at that exact same moment she looked up, saw me and smiled.

I was halfway across the room, less than thirty feet away from her – less than thirty feet from asking her to marry me – when the best man began tapping his dessert spoon against a wine glass to get everyone's attention and announced that it was time for the speeches. I didn't want to stop, but I knew if I continued walking, the whole room would be watching me, so with my heart racing, barely able to concentrate at all, I sat down in an empty seat and waited.

'Hello again, young man,' said a voice next to me. It was Orange Lady from the registry office, holding a large glass of wine. 'Where's your friend?' she whispered loudly.

'Outside,' I explained. 'Doesn't like speeches.'

'Me neither,' said Orange Lady, then added, 'Do you know, this is my fourth glass of wine?' She leaned unsteadily towards me until we were almost touching noses, and whispered loud enough for everyone at the surrounding tables to hear, 'Very good stuff it is too. But I do believe it's gone straight to my head!'

The best man's speech was loaded with jokes about the groom's ex-girlfriends, acting skills and personal habits. Meena's dad thought this bloke was hilarious and kept patting Paul on the back heartily. The groom's speech was even worse: he just harped on about how wonderful his new family was. There was no love in evidence at all, only gratuitous backslapping. He finished by proposing a toast to the newest Mrs Amos-Midford in the world, and everyone in the room raised their glasses. There was a huge round of applause, and waiters appeared, filling everyone's glasses with champagne. The band started to play an uptempo version of 'I've Got You Under My Skin'. Paul and Meena made their way to the centre of the room for the first dance and began twirling around as if they'd been beamed straight from some 1930s cocktail party. During the whole time it took for all this to happen, Mel didn't take her eyes off me.

Edging around the wedding photographer and a man armed with a video camera, who were recording Meena and Paul's every move, I made my way to Mel's table.

'Hi,' I said, smiling. She looked beautiful. More beautiful than ever. Her hairstyle had changed yet again, and now it was short and messy in the kind of sexy way Meg Ryan could only dream of.

'Hi, Duff,' she said, standing up to hug me. 'How are you? How was Paris?'

'Fine,' I lied. 'And you? How's everything with you?' I'd wanted to ask about the baby too, but didn't want to bring it up in so public an arena.

'Okay,' she replied. She could obviously still read minds when she wanted to, because she then looked down at her stomach and added, 'Everything's fine there too. No need to worry.'

'Good.'

Silence.

'Didn't I see you here with Julie? Where is she?'

'She's just nipped to the toilet,' said Mel hurriedly. I could tell that she was lying, because she was fiddling nervously with her hair. She always did that when she lied. I took this as a good sign, however: Julie had obviously disappeared on purpose so that Mel and I could talk.

'Gone to look for more victims to turn into the undead, has she?'

'Don't start, Duffy,' reprimanded Mel sternly. 'Julie's having . . . well, she's having a tough time at the minute.'

What could possibly have fazed the mighty Julie? I wondered. Had they run out of polenta at her local Sainsbury? Had her Dyson vacuum cleaner spontaneously combusted? Or worse still, had she discovered that she and Mark would never be able to afford to live in their beloved Notting Hill Gate? I didn't ask any of these questions of course, because it didn't feel right baiting Julie without her being there.

'What's wrong with her?' I asked. 'Nothing too painful I hope.'

'I can't tell you, Duffy. At least not yet.' She paused. 'I've got some news of my own, but you might not like it. I was going to call, but since you're here I might as well tell you now. I told my bosses at work that I was pregnant and that I wanted to leave and they offered me a deal to make me stay.'

'That's good,' I said. 'If it's what you want.'

She smiled. 'It is . . . well, at least I think it is. The company has just taken over a group of radio stations in the North and I'll be overseeing the restructuring of their sales divisions. It's only a temporary project – around three months – but it's a step up into higher management and if I do well it could mean big things in the future.'

'Sounds like you've come up trumps. So what's the problem?'

'It's away from London. I'll have to spend Monday to Friday up there and then I'll fly back to London at the weekends.'

'Mel,' I said nervously, 'you're being vague on purpose. Whereabouts up North is it?'

'Glasgow.'

I didn't say anything. I couldn't say anything. I could feel a massive pause coming, until suddenly, from an unknown source, words came to rescue me. 'Don't go,' I said so quietly that I could barely hear myself.

'What?'

'I said, don't go. I don't want you to go, Mel. Stay here in London and marry me. I miss you. Whatever it is that makes you different from any woman I have ever met or could ever hope to meet – the very Melness of you – I miss that more than anything. It's just over four months since we first split up and since then a lot has happened that I need to explain to you . . .' I stumbled as I searched for the right words to express what I wanted to say.

'The reason why I didn't want to get married when you asked me was because I lacked faith in myself. I thought the minute we got married I'd feel trapped. I just couldn't get it into my head that marriage wasn't a conspiracy to hijack my independence. You knew that, and that's why you broke off the engagement, because you didn't want to make me do anything I'd regret. Well, I regret more than anything not marrying you. I regret that I'll never be able to have the time back that I've missed with you. I promise you it's not the baby that's changed my mind. I changed my own mind. I want to marry you because I can see now that the benefits outweigh the disadvantages. No, I don't mean that, what I mean is that . . . that . . .'

'I think what you're trying to say is that you're not scared any more,' said Mel softly.

'That's right, I'm not scared – okay, maybe I'm a little nervous, but I'll be all right. I'm not scared about sleeping with one person for the rest of my life, in fact I'm looking forward to it. I'll admit I still feel a bit shaky about going to IKEA, but that's something we can work out. The big thing is that I'm no longer scared I'll ever fall out of love with you . . .

or that you'll ever fall out of love with me. I have to commit to . . . I *am* committed to you because without you nothing makes sense. Without you I'm not even myself. Without you I'm nothing.'

That was it. That was my big speech. I'd given my all and now it really was up to her. I studied her face for clues to her state of mind, to see if I'd finally managed to convince her to believe. There was a look about her that I couldn't explain, but it made me feel that I'd managed to breach the barrier that had come between us. We were now standing barely inches apart.

Without speaking she reached for my hands, held them tightly and gazed deeply into my eyes, searching for the answers to everything she wanted to know. Then she started to cry.

'I want to believe you, Duffy,' she sobbed. 'I want to believe you more than anything in the world. I look at your face and I hear your beautiful words and I'm nearly there, Duff. But nearly just isn't good enough any more. How do I know that you really mean what you say? How can I be sure that those old feelings won't come back again?'

'I don't understand. You've always gone on about how well you know me. How you know me better than I know myself. And it's true. I've never met anyone who knows me like you do. So why can't you see that I'm telling you the truth when I say that I want to marry you? Why can't you read my mind?'

Her tears were in full flow and we had become the main attraction in this corner of the room. I didn't care. I couldn't see anyone but her.

'That's just it,' she sobbed. 'I don't trust myself any more. I don't trust myself to make a decision that will affect not just your life, or my life, but the life of our baby too. I can't tell what it is you're thinking because I don't know what I'm thinking and it scares me. I love you, Duffy, but I'm too scared to gamble everything when I can't be sure.'

I couldn't believe it. This was supposed to be our happy ending, the last reel of a romantic comedy, the point where the guy gets the girl, but somehow it had turned into *A Nightmare on Elm Street*.

'I know I have to make a decision one way or the other for both our sakes,' she continued. 'We just can't carry on like this any more. I know this is selfish of me, but I can't make this decision right now, so I'm asking you for more time – time to think things through and get my head round all of this.' She leaned forward and kissed me. 'My new job starts on Monday. I'll be up in Glasgow all week but I'll be back in London late Friday night and I promise you that by then I'll have an answer for you.'

Bet you're happy now

On the train back from Nottingham, frustrated at being unable to do any more than wait for Mel to make her decision, I formulated a plan. The perfect plan. A plan that would without a doubt convince her once and for all that she had nothing to be scared of, that I did love her and would always do so. The only drawback, however, was that it required the assistance of Julie. As in Mark and Julie. As in Nosferatu. As in the person who last time I checked ranked me lower on the evolutionary scale than pond scum. But that's great plans for you – they always carry with them an element of danger. By the time Dan and I got home from the wedding it was quite late so I decided to sleep on my plan in case I was being rash. When I woke up early on Sunday morning and still thought it was the best idea I'd ever had (totally eclipsing past highlights such as baked beans on cream cracker sandwiches and taping *EastEnders* while I watched it in case I thought of something clever to yell at the characters after it's over), I knew I had to do it.

Coming up the escalator at Shepherd's Bush Tube I worked out my strategy for dealing with what was bound to be an impossible situation:

1) Go round to Mark and Julie's.

2) Beg for her mercy.
3) If needs be, cry.

I didn't give myself the option of steps one to three not working. There was no plan B, and without Julie there'd be no plan A. Julie was essential. It was then, as I stood on her doorstep, my heart racing wildly and my index finger hovering over the doorbell, that it occurred to me that this was about karma. I was being punished for the sins of my previous life, the telling of ex-girlfriends that I was dead, the half-truths to Mel and the skeletons in my cupboards. It was as if life had decided that if I really wanted true happiness I was going to have to pay for my indiscretions.

I rang the doorbell and waited.

When Julie finally came to the front door she was wearing nothing but her dressing gown. What are *you* doing here?' she exclaimed.

I decided in the light of what Mel had said about Julie having some sort of crisis, that a delicate touch would be required. 'Hello, Julie,' I replied as chirpily as possible. 'I'm sorry I didn't get to talk to you yesterday at the wedding, but by the time you came back from the loo my taxi had arrived.'

Julie fixed me with a menacing stare as if I was some horrible practical joke writ large. 'Duffy,' she growled, 'it's eight o'clock on Sunday morning. It's freezing cold out here and I haven't got the patience or indeed the inclination to humour you. So I'll say this: I don't care that you didn't speak to me yesterday because I don't like you. I don't care if I never see you again because I don't like you. In fact I don't care about you full stop because I've never liked you. So now we've got that sorted, what do you want?'

'Is Mark about?' I asked innocently. I was hoping that his presence might soften Julie up a bit.

She bristled instantly. I knew that bristle. It was the bristle Mel used to use on me when I was in her bad books, just as, it would appear, Mark was in Julie's. 'He's in Los Angeles on a shoot,' she said sharply. *They've probably had a row about him going off around the world again,* I reasoned. *This is bound to be Julie's big 'crisis'. I'll give them two simpering twenty-minute transatlantic phone calls and they'll be back to their usual smug selves.*

'He won't be back in England for a few days,' she said and then added, 'Was it him you wanted to see?'

'No, Julie,' I said. 'It's you I came to see. I need your help.'

She was visibly shocked. All her facial expressions went into free fall. She looked very odd indeed. Then as quickly as the panic came it disappeared. 'You don't really expect me to persuade Mel to get back with you, do you?' she sighed dismissively. 'Not even you can be that stupid, surely?'

I coughed uncomfortably. 'I know we've not always seen eye to eye about everything, Julie, and I'm sorry about that. I'm also sorry about the time I was sick over your bathroom floor, I'm sorry that I've always been so rude about your dinner parties and I'm really sorry that I used to call you Nosferatu behind your back.'

'You called me Nosferatu?'

'Damn. I thought you knew. Well, now I'm really really sorry I called you Nosferatu. I'm sorry for just about everything, but please, I'm begging you for just ten minutes of your time while I explain what I need from you. Please.'

I studied Julie's face to see how many points I'd scored in my favour. Judging by her posture (defensive) and her facial expression (overflowing with disdain) I reasoned it was a figure somewhere near, as they say in Eurovision circles, to *nul points*.

'No way, Duffy,' said Julie firmly. 'Mel told me everything that you said to her at the wedding. And do you want to know what I advised her? I told her that she was mad to think that you were capable of growing up, let alone changing.'

I took a long deep breath and held it. I wasn't going to breathe again until the impulse to commit manslaughter had passed, which it did surprisingly quickly as it finally dawned on me what this was all about. Julie was protecting Mel in the same way that I would've tried to protect Dan had someone like Julie wormed their way into his affections. I had to convince her that I was good for Mel. That I'd do anything to make her happy. I took another long deep breath.

'Okay, Julie,' I said, pulling up my trousers at the thighs. There was only one person on earth for whom I'd normally do what I was about to do, and that was Mel. 'You want me to beg, well, I'll beg.' I got down on my knees, put my hands together as if in prayer and wailed at the top of my voice, 'Pleeeeaaase!'

Julie's first reaction was to check if the neighbours had started looking out yet (they hadn't), her second was to look at me as if I'd lost the plot (which to all intents and purposes I had), and her third was to take great pleasure in exclaiming loudly, 'No!'

'Please!'

'No!'

'Please!'

By now the twitching-curtain brigade were out in full. Julie knew this. I knew this. It was just a matter of whose nerve would break first. She stepped back inside and slammed the door shut. Determined not to give up, I stood my ground and continued to yell at the top of my voice on Julie's front doorstep.

'Julie! I know you're still there and I'll stay right here on your doorstep keeping your neighbours awake for as long as it takes for you to let me in and listen to me. I don't care if you call the police. I really don't care. Not any more. So you see you've got two choices: let me in for five minutes and listen to what I've got to say, or have me carted away by the Old Bill and really give the neighbours something to talk about. Which is it to be?'

There followed a long silence in which I contemplated what a night in gaol would be like. It didn't seem that bad in theory. The main thing that bothered me was that they'd take the laces out of my trainers. It always took me ages to lace up my trainers. Julie opened the door just as I'd decided that if I did get arrested I'd give my trainers to the desk sergeant for safe keeping rather than unlace them.

'Okay, okay,' she said wearily. 'Come in. But you've got exactly five minutes and no more.'

She let me in and I followed her through to the lounge. The room seemed emptier somehow, less furniture. *Metropolitan minimalist chic agogo*, I commented to myself silently. Julie sat down on the sofa and rubbed her eyes. It was strange seeing her just-got-out-of-bed hair and and Clinique-free features, because although on the one hand she now really did remind me of one of the undead, on the other, for the first time ever she almost looked human. I decided to soften her up with flattery. 'You look fantastic, Julie.'

'No I don't,' she snapped. 'I look hideous. It's how people who have been woken up on a Sunday morning look. Don't flatter me. Don't make small talk. Tell me what it is you want and then disappear.'

'Okay, I'll be straight with you. I'm trying to butter you up because I've got a huge favour to ask. There's no reason in the world for you to do it other than that you're the only person who can help me. Please. I don't want to cry in your living room but I will if I have to.'

'What do you want?'

I outlined her role in the Plan, although not the plan in its entirety. She listened, didn't say anything one way or the other, and as soon as I'd finished looked just as unmoved as she had done before.

'Firstly,' said Julie, 'it's a ridiculous idea. Secondly, I don't think anything can convince Mel to spend the rest of her life with you, and thirdly . . . no. A plain and simple no. In fact, let me put it this way. Not now. Not ever. Let me tell you, Mr Duffy, you have put my best friend though hell. You weren't the one who had to console her when she was falling apart when you first split up. You weren't the one who had to watch your best friend get back together with the man you loathe most on earth. You weren't the one who had to mop up the tears when she found out she was pregnant. Why? Because you're never the one who has to clean up after the devastation you cause.'

'I know what you think of me,' I said, 'but there's another side of me, Julie. You've got to know that. I admit I've been selfish in the past, but I've changed.'

'You say that now,' said Julie passionately, 'but what about in six months' time? Men leave. That's what they do. They get tired of what they've got and they get up and go.'

I was confused. This was more than a general 'all men are crap, get a dog instead' speech. She sounded if she was talking about something specific.

'I don't get this, Julie. What are you trying to say?'

She shook her head. 'Nothing.'

'Mel told me that you're having a hard time at the minute.

She wouldn't tell me why. Is it something to do with Mark being in Los Angeles?'

'No.'

'Then what's wrong? I know it's not like me to show concern but if it's serious—'

'Mark and I have split up, okay?' she said without looking at me. 'He's gone.'

I was stunned. It was worse than when I discovered at the age of eight that Father Christmas didn't exist. At least then I still knew that I'd be getting presents from my mum, Father Christmas or no Father Christmas. But if the king and queen of togetherness couldn't make their love work, what hope was there for mere mortals? No wonder Mel was unsure about getting together with me: not only had I provided her with enough doubt, she was also having to deal with the fact that everything she'd idealised about Julie and Mark had been broken in two. 'I'm sorry, Julie. I really I am. I had no idea.'

'Well, now you know. He moved out about a month ago. I told Mel not to tell you because I knew what you'd say. I know you used to think that Mark and I were smug. What was the phrase you used? Oh, I remember now. "Keeping up with the Mark and Julies." Bet you're happy now.'

'No, I'm not, Julie. It's crap when things fall apart. I wouldn't wish it on anyone. I am sorry about you and Mark. Is there anything I can do?'

She shook her head.

I sat and watched her for a moment. A shadow of her usual venomous self, I found myself actually feeling sorry for her. As much as I'd derided Mark and Julie, I'd always thought that they were right for each other. I suddenly felt guilty sitting here asking her to help out my relationship when she was so obviously on the verge of falling apart.

'Listen,' I said, standing up, 'I'd better go.'

She pointed at the door. 'I think you'll find that's the way out.'

I wasn't going to say anything, I was just going to get up and leave, but then I thought about Mel and what was at stake and I suddenly got angry. 'There's nothing I can do to get you and Mark back together. If there was I'd do it. But can't you see that you've got the chance to help me and Mel? I know that I can't change her mind if she's doesn't want me, but I can show her that I meant every word I said when I told her that I loved her.'

'I don't believe in love.' Julie stood up in a bid to hasten my exit.

'Because Mark left you?'

'*Because* no one means anything they say any more. Because everything is temporary. Because nothing lasts. Because that's the way it is.' She looked over at me expectantly.

'It doesn't have to be,' I said, meeting her gaze.

'I think you've had your five minutes.'

'Yeah,' I said, wondering what I was going to do now. 'I suppose I have.'

This is little Elvis

'Are you cold?'

'No, Mum.'

'You must be cold.'

'I'm not, Mum.'

'These hospital waiting rooms are incredibly draughty and you're only wearing a shirt.'

'But I'm not cold.'

'You're bound to catch a cold. Why don't you go home and put on a cardigan?'

'I'm fine, Mum,' I said, making contact with my inner Dalai Lama. 'Honestly I'm fine.'

Three days had passed since Julie had ruined the Plan. Three event filled days that had begun on Tuesday with a telephone call and ended with me lodged on a hard plastic chair in a waiting-room in Whittington Hospital.

It all began at the beginning of the week with a long and confusing answerphone message left by Pete Berry, a comedy promoter at the Chuckle Club in Hackney. In it he informed Dan and me that he wanted to book us for a gig in a fortnight because he'd been hearing good things about our new act. He then went on to reveal that if the gig went well he would consider us as a support slot for the previous year's Perrier Comedy Award Winner on a six date national tour he was organising. All of this was news to me because to the best of my knowledge Dan and I hadn't written a single joke together, and the only people who knew about Carter and Duffy the double act were Carter and Duffy the double act.

I had to wait two hours for Dan to get back from his weekly shopping trip to Muswell Hill Sainsbury's before I discovered that all this was his doing. 'If you're going to make a splash,' he said, 'you've got to make a few waves.' By 'waves', I think that he meant the following complete and utter fabrications:

a) that we'd been approached by Channel Four to develop a new sitcom called *Dexter's Plectrum* about a bunch of geeky no-hoper sixth-formers who turn out to be the next U2.
b) that we'd accepted a 'substantial five-figure sum' to do voiceovers for a series of adverts selling a well-known brand of cooking oil.
c) that a talent scout from a US talent agency had spotted our act and signed us up and we'd already been flown to Los Angeles for casting auditions in two Hollywood pictures as 'Limey bad guys'.

Dan had pitched his lies perfectly. In the world of comedy, where one day you could be bottom of the bill in the Dog and Duck and the next taking meetings in Hollywood, anything was possible, and our fictionalised success was just wild enough for anyone who heard it to believe every single word.

'Honestly,' said Dan, nearly doubled over in laughter, 'I told two of the regulars on last Sunday's bill at the Laughter Lounge in Hammersmith, and by Monday night the whole of the London comedy circuit knew about it. We are hot!'

The second event to occur was the arrival of my mum

at Euston station on Tuesday afternoon. One of the first things she'd said to me when Charlie and I picked her up from the station was that she was coming round to see where I lived first thing Wednesday morning. As the flat was in the worst state I'd ever seen it, I made Dan stay up with me until three o'clock in the morning so we could have it tidy for her inspection. In the process we discovered £7.86 in change down the back of the sofa, fungus the size of a small yukka plant at the side of the washing machine, and Dan's car-boot-sale copy of *ET* lodged behind the sideboard.

By the time we'd finished it looked like a completely different flat. My mum would've been well impressed by our efforts had she ever got to see them, which she never did because of the next big event: Vernie going into labour.

Mum called me from the hospital on Charlie's mobile to tell me. This was just about the funniest thing ever: my mum and 'newfangled technology' just did not go together, so for the first few minutes all she said was 'Can you hear me?', 'Am I speaking into the right end?' and 'Am I doing it right?' As it was 3.20 a.m. and I was on my way to bed after my cleaning fit, I told her that I'd be there before lunchtime on Wednesday. She promised to call me if there was any other news and I went to sleep.

As soon as I woke up I made my way to the hospital and I sat in the waiting room, listening to Mum's constant questions.

'Do you want a cup of tea or coffee from the machine?' she asked, her purse open to display a vast collection of coins of the realm. My mum liked to be ready for every sort of occasion and collected change like some people collect stamps.

'No thanks, Mum,' I said, refusing for my usual reasons.

'I was going to have a cup of tea,' she said, closing her purse, 'but I think I'll wait just a little bit longer as well.'

She dropped her purse into her handbag, rooted around a bit and pulled out a packet of sweets. 'Trebor Mint?'

'No thanks, Mum.' I smiled. 'You're nervous, aren't you?'

'Of course I am,' she said. 'Aren't you?'

That thought hadn't occurred to me. Was I nervous? I think I was. I was excited. I was going to be somebody's uncle. There was going to be a child who would have an uncle Duffy; someone to whom I'd be able to pass on the skills of making the perfect slice of toast, and read books Mum used to read to me as a kid. Someone to be around for when they wanted to talk about how much their parents drove them up the wall. This felt good.

It didn't require a huge leap in my thought processes to make the connection between what was happening here and what was happening in my own life. I was going to be somebody's dad too quite soon. I hadn't thought about it in France, or since I'd got back, or even when Mel had told me. It was easy not to think about it because it hadn't happened yet. But sitting here in this admittedly now chilly waiting room, it struck me: I'm going to be a dad.

Suddenly I felt sad. Sadder than I'd ever felt before. Not about the baby, but about Mel and me. Our having a baby was bound to be one of the best things that would ever happen in my life, and yet here I was not making the most of it. Whatever decision Mel made, nothing would change the fact that I was going to be responsible for a life other than my own. A greater privilege than that, I couldn't think of.

'Mum,' I said, 'I've got something to tell you.'

'I know,' said my mum.

'How do you know?'

'I don't know exactly what it is, but I can tell when you're troubled, Ben.' She handed me a mint, took another one from the packet and put it in her mouth. 'I've got something to tell you too. Two secrets, in fact. One big, one not so big. I'll tell you my secrets first – that way it'll make it easier to tell me yours.'

I was kind of perturbed by the whole situation. I couldn't imagine what kind of secrets my mum would have that she'd think I needed to know about.

She put her hand on mine and began. 'The small secret first: I may be moving down here to London permanently. Vernie's been asking me to come and live with her and Charlie since they knew about the baby. I told them I didn't want to, but she said that she didn't want the baby just to see her gran on special occasions. I told her I'd visit as often as I could, but then Charlie insisted too. I finally gave in, but I told them I'd give it a go for a few months first to see how it went. I'm keeping the house in Leeds until I'm sure.'

'That's great,' I said. 'Vernie will love having you around. Me too.' I couldn't think of anything more to say, so focused was my mind on secret number two. 'So what's the big thing you've got to tell me?'

'Confess rather than tell,' she said quietly. 'I don't know how to say this so I'll come straight out with it: when you broke up with Mel I was really worried about you. I know that you're a grown man and I should've kept my nose out, but I couldn't help thinking it was wrong: you loved each other – anyone could tell that. When you told me you'd split up because you weren't sure you could commit, I blamed myself. I hated the idea that you weren't getting married because of what happened with me and you dad. Which is why I wrote to him and asked him to get in touch with you.'

'*You* wrote to *him*?' I could hardly believe what I was hearing. 'You've been in contact with my dad?'

'I got his address from his sister in Tamworth and I told him that he had to get in contact with you and arrange a meeting to explain to you that you're nothing like him.'

It was odd being subjected to this much love. To think that my mum would open all sorts of painful memories just to try and make me happy. I gave her the biggest hug I could manage and she started crying.

'I was only trying to help, Ben,' she sobbed quietly. 'He wrote and told me that you never got back to him. I didn't want to upset you. I just wanted you to see that you were nothing like him. You're your own person. You always were and you always will be.'

When she'd finished crying I fetched a cup of tea for her from the machine and a coffee for myself so that she didn't feel like I was being left out. While it went cold I told her the story of Mel and me, right from the beginning, from when I first saw her four years ago through to the last time, less than a week ago at Meena's wedding.

Mum didn't say anything for a moment: I think the shock that in a few months she'd be a grandmother for a second time had left her speechless. She drank her tea silently. 'So Mel's going to make her decision in two days' time?'

'The arrangement is she comes back from Glasgow on Friday,' I explained. 'She'll call me as soon as she gets home. I'll go round to her flat and one way or the other we'll sort this whole thing out. We both want what's best for the baby, and for what it's worth, if she decides that she doesn't want to be with me, then at least I think we've learned enough from the past to make it work as friends.'

Mum looked at me and said in the manner that only mothers can use convincingly, 'Don't worry. Everything's going to be all right.'

'I know, Mum,' I said. 'I believe you.'

*   *   *

'Look,' said Charlie, holding up his daughter for mum and me to see as we walked into the delivery room. 'I'm a dad!'

It had taken ten and a half hours for Vernie to give birth, which according to the doctors was an 'easy labour'. Judging by the state of Vernie, who to be frank looked like she'd just ran a marathon, the phrase 'easy labour' was something of a misnomer.

Still holding the baby, Charlie pointed to me. 'This is your uncle Duffy! He's the one who'll be giving you your pocket money.' He pointed to my mum. 'This is your gran and anything you want she'll get it for you!' As he passed the wriggling bundle into Vernie's outstretched arms he introduced the baby. 'And finally everyone, the star of the show . . . this is little Elvis.'

'Don't start, Charlie,' sighed Vernie in a good humoured sort of way. 'No matter how much I love you, we're not calling our baby Little Elvis.'

'But she looks like Elvis,' said Charlie.

'She's bald, her head's a funny shape, and in case it has escaped your attention she is a little girl. Her name's Phoebe. You know her name's Phoebe because you helped choose it. If this child grows up thinking that her name is Little Elvis I promise you there will be trouble.'

Charlie smiled. 'Beautiful baby Phoebe.'

The next half hour was spent playing pass the baby. After Vernie it went to Mum, who then passed her back to Charlie, who then passed her back to Vernie when she started crying, who then quieted her down and then offered her to me.

'I think I'll pass this time,' I said, declining as politely as I possibly could. Babies always made me nervous – they were so fragile that I felt they'd fall apart in my hands if I so much as looked at them in the wrong way. Plus, I wasn't entirely convinced by the Theory of Universal Baby Cuteness that so many people subscribed to. I mean, she looked fairly okay, but not exactly what I'd call attractive. My main problem, however, with babies was that I couldn't reason with them. It was why I've never been all that keen on cats either. It's the ability to reason that separates us from the animals, and until Phoebe could talk, an animal she would remain. *She may well be my niece*, I thought, *but I'll wait until I can chat to her like a regular human being before I really bond with her*.

In the end Vernie passed Phoebe to Charlie who clearly couldn't get enough of her.

After five minutes she began crying again. 'She's crying again,' said Charlie needlessly to Vernie. 'What shall I do?'

Vernie smiled at him all sweetness and light and said, 'You're her dad. *You* do something.'

Ten minutes and two circuits of the ward corridor later and Charlie handed her back to Vernie in triumph. 'Somehow she's managed to scream herself into a sort of blissful state of peace,' explained Charlie.

As she lay in Vernie's arms, her eyes firmly shut and her tiny fingers flinching sporadically as she dreamed of whatever it is that babies dream of, I peered at her closely.

'She looks like you,' I said to Vernie.

'I think she looks like aunt Margaret sucking a sherbet lemon,' said Vernie. 'The likeness is uncanny.'

By the time I got home it was late afternoon. I felt totally drained and was just contemplating a long spell in bed when I heard the electronic beep of the answerphone. I listened to the messages: a sycophantic Greg congratulating me and Dan on our sitcom deal; Dan calling to see if the baby had been born yet; my old temping agency to see if

I was interested in a six-week block at an accountancy firm; and one other. I listened to the one other twice. Searched out my address book. Picked up the phone and dialled.

'Julie, it's Duffy here. I just got your message. You said you had something to tell me.'

I heard her taking a deep momentous breath. 'You know that thing that you asked me to do?'

'Yeah?'

'Well, I'll do it.'

I was stunned. Miracles could happen. The plan was back on. 'Excellent!' I cried a little too enthusiastically, and then added calmly but sheepishly, 'I couldn't ask you for another favour, could I?'

'What is it, Duffy?' sighed Julie impatiently.

'You couldn't meet me tomorrow after you've been to work, could you? I sort of need a lift.'

'Where to?'

'IKEA. A new addition to the plan.'

She paused. 'You want me to ask, don't you? Well, I'm not going to, because I don't want to know how that mind of yours works. Some things should remain a mystery.'

'So you'll do it?'

'I'll see you round at mine at six thirty sharp.' She paused again. 'Duffy?' she said, a hint of warmth entering into her voice. 'I really do hope that everything works out for you.'

'Thanks,' I said. 'I hope so too. Because to tell you the truth, I really don't know what else I can do.' It was my turn to feel uncomfortable. 'Julie?'

'What now?' she said with mock impatience. 'Do you want me to drive you to Marks and Spencer as well?'

'Not this week,' I returned quickly. 'I just wanted to ask: what made you change your mind?'

'I'm going to hate myself for saying this, but *you* did – *you* changed my mind. I thought about everything you've said and done recently, and I don't know why, but I really do believe that you love Mel and that you want to make her happy. All I've ever wanted is for her to be happy, and if that's what you do, then I'm all for it.'

'Cheers.' I sensed an awkward moment coming over the horizon. 'I'd better go, but I'll see you tomorrow at half six.'

'For what it's worth,' she said hesitantly, 'I just want you to know that what I said yesterday was wrong. Well, at least I've changed my mind. For better or worse I'm back believing in good old-fashioned love.'

Finally, everything was coming together. There was just one more thing that I had to do. I picked up the phone and made a call.

Monkeys

Here's how my first ever conversation with my dad went:

Me: Hello, is that George?
Him: Yes.
Me: It's Ben Duffy here.
Him: (Pause.) Hello. (Hideously long pause.) How are you?
Me: I got your letter a while ago. Do you still want to meet up?
Him: Yes, of course.
Me: How about tomorrow?
Him: Sounds good to me.
Me: Where shall we meet?
Him: Wherever you like.
Me: (Painfully long pause.) I dunno.
Him: (Excruciatingly long pause.) I don't know either.
Me: (Quite obviously siezing on the first thing that enters my head.) London Zoo!
Him: The zoo? Aren't you a bit old for that?
Me: (Brusquely.) Okay, you choose.
Him: No . . . London Zoo sounds fine. Eleven o'clock suit you?
Me: Fine. (Pause.) Okay, then, 'bye.
Him: 'Bye.

The zoo. The sodding zoo! I couldn't believe that I'd just arranged to meet the man who was half responsible for my conception, in a zoo. It had just flashed in my head like a beacon. Later I wondered if deep in my subconscious what I'd wanted more than anything while growing up was to be taken to the zoo by my dad. Well, here I was some two decades later and finally my dream was coming true.

I had made the decision to call him as I'd sat in the hospital waiting room with Mum and she'd told me how she'd contacted him for my sake. I didn't like the thought of her feeling responsible for something that had nothing to do with her. I already knew that I wasn't my dad. I already knew that unlike him I could do the commitment thing. But I felt that for Mum's sake, for my sake and for the sake of everyone whose dad just waltzed off and left them when they were kids, I had to do this one thing. And anyway, the parallels between my own life and that of Luke Skywalker in *Return of The Jedi* were so uncanny that I couldn't resist. Was I, like Luke, going to discover that my dad was someone powerful like Darth Vadar, or was he just going to be some old rent-a-dad, with regulation paunch, bald patch and extended nasal hair? When I was a kid I used to tell people that my dad was in the SAS and that was why he was never around. But then Mike Bailey got a book out from the local library on the SAS that said that they weren't even allowed to tell close family members they were in the crack army battalion, which pretty much blew my cover.

The next day I got up early and put on the suit that I'd worn to Meena's wedding. It was a bit crumpled but I wore it anyway. While I didn't really give a toss one way or another what my dad thought of me, I couldn't help but feel a little insecure. Something in me didn't want him to be disappointed when he saw me. I even put on a tie. The funny thing was, as I approached the entrance to the zoo dead on eleven o'clock I spotted him a mile off because he was wearing a suit and tie too. So there we were. Two grown men in suits and ties going to the zoo.

'Hello,' I said, giving him a short and very awkward wave. 'Are you George?'

'Ben,' he replied, offering me his hand. 'Good to meet you.'

I thought about correcting the 'Ben' thing but left it. He squeezed my hand very firmly in a handshake that seemed to last for ever. He was shorter than I expected. Both Vernie and I were quite tall, and as my mum wasn't, I'd always assumed that we'd got it from my dad. It felt odd discovering that we'd inherited our height from one of our less immediate ancestors. He had a full head of grey hair (so I couldn't blame my receding hairline on him either) and a kind of long, drawn-out face that along with his thick eyebrows and moustache gave him the appearance of an ageing TV private detective. The only thing we had in common was our eyes. Almond shaped, and dark brown. 'Shall we go in?'

'Yeah,' I said. 'Let's do that.'

He paid for the two of us at the kiosk near the entrance and we pushed through the turnstile into the zoo. As it was a damp Thursday in October and school half terms had not yet started, the zoo wasn't exactly crawling with activity. There were a few preschool kids with their mums dotted about the place, and that was it. Leading the way, George decided that we ought to go and visit the lions first. Which is exactly what we did.

It was the strangest thing, because we didn't talk about the missing years, his life or mine; instead animals dominated the conversation. Never have two people who so obviously know bugger all about the animal kingdom found so much to say about it. We read plaque after plaque, informed each other of nature documentaries we had seen in the past and dredged up all manner of ridiculous animal facts. ('No, I didn't know that whales give birth to live young. But did you know that the kangaroo has a forked penis?') After the lions, we visited the reptile house, the penguins in the pool, watched the llamas, the elephants, in fact everything there was to see.

We spent a particularly long time in the ape house, for my benefit. I was running out of stuff to say and the orangutans were so entertaining that we used them as a talking point for at least half an hour. The zookeepers had given the orangutans clothes to play with. One particular orangutan, who had to have the saddest, most mournful face in the primate world, was sitting on the ground next to a tree, with a lady's long raincoat over his head. His body was huddled up and his long hairy arms were wrapped around his back as if he were giving himself a hug. We watched him for ages as he began doing forward and backward rolls for no reason at all. If Mel had been here she would've wanted to cry.

After three hours of wandering around, we decided to take a break for lunch. Queuing up in the restaurant, George told me that he'd treat me to lunch, which struck me as very funny – I'd worked out on my way to the zoo that at the very least he probably owed me a few thousand pounds in backdated birthday presents alone. He chose a ham baguette wrapped in cellophane and I had a plate of French fries with three sachets of tomato sauce.

'Do you want a coffee?' he asked as we reached the drinks dispensers.

'I don't really do hot drinks,' I told him.

'Me neither,' he said, pulling a face. 'I hate things that are too hot to sip.'

As the sun had come out briefly, we sat at the tables outside the zoo's restaurant to eat, even though the plastic chairs were damp. As we chewed in silence, I could see how difficult this was for him, but it was hard for me too. There was this massive thing between us – a conversation that we both knew we had to have, but that neither of us particularly wanted to begin.

I was just about to offer up another animal fact ('Did you know that bulls see in black and white?') when George suddenly put down his half-eaten baguette. 'I was just wondering what made you change your mind?'

This is it. This is The Talk.

'About seeing you?' I asked, playing for time. He nodded. I thought deeply about his question and avoided eye contact while I spoke. 'I've just sorted out my life in a way I never thought possible. I've spent a long time avoiding stuff that I used to be scared of, and if there's one thing I've learned it's this: nothing is ever as scary as you think it will be.'

George laughed, a kind of big baritone laugh that made me envious, given that my voice was nowhere near as deep. 'I think it was Mark Twain who said, 'I am an old man and have known many fears. Most of which have never happened.''

'I think I prefer my version,' I said. 'It has a sort of awkward charm about it.'

'I prefer yours too,' he replied.

There was a big silence. 'I used to hate you. In fact I spent most of my life hating you. You made my life difficult for no good reason as far as I can see.'

'I deserve that,' he said. 'There's no good excuses for what I did. You're right I made your mother's life a mess and made things hard for you and your sister.' He paused. 'You said "used to hate". Does that mean that you don't hate me now?'

I swallowed hard. 'I think I've just come round to the idea that it's pointless hating you. When I was at school, most of my mates had absentee dads of some description. It was weird. Like a whole generation of men had held some sort of secret ballot and decided universally to bugger off pronto. They were all at it. Like the monkeys.'

'Monkeys?'

'Yeah,' I said and then proceeded to tell him Dan's dead monkey joke. 'You were just doing the dead monkey like everybody else, which is no surprise given that the difference between monkey DNA and human DNA is as little as one per cent.' This startling statistic forced me to take a moment of self reflection: *Where are all these animal facts coming from?* 'You weren't necessarily a bad person,' I continued. 'Just weak willed.' I looked up at George for the first time. He was watching me intently.

'You know I'm sorry, don't you?' he said. 'It's useless apologising – it's only words after all – but I mean it. I've missed your growing up and Vernie's growing up and it's stuff that I'll never get back. I tried not to think about you at all when I first left, which was difficult, but I knew your mum would give you everything you needed. Eventually it got easier and easier to forget that you existed. It was almost like you were a dream, or you were somebody else's life.'

Over the next half an hour we tried to cram in as much as we could about the last twenty-eight years. I told him about Vernie and the baby, my stand-up career so far, and even a bit about me and Mel and the baby (although I didn't go into too much detail).

In return George told me about his life. He'd remarried and divorced, never had any more kids and had spent his life in shoe sales. Now he was retired he spent most of his time in the garden of his house in Enfield. He seemed moderately happy with his lot, which annoyed me slightly, so I made up a stack of lies about my mum having won a modest sum on the National Lottery and her having a retired suitor who was forever taking her on exotic holidays to the Caribbean. Although I no longer hated George, there was no way that I didn't love my mum a billion times more than anything I'd ever feel for him.

'Well, I'm glad she's happy,' was all he managed to say.

'She is,' I replied. 'Very.'

We decided to call it a day when it started to rain. As we headed for the exit George talked about how this hadn't been as scary as he thought it would be and so we should do it again. However, I think he knew as well as I did that we were never really going to. We'd both done the thing that we'd been waiting a lifetime to do, and now we'd crossed it off our lists there wasn't a lot more to say other than goodbye.

'Goodbye, then.' I offered George my hand.

'It's been good to see you,' he said, shaking it firmly. 'For what it's worth, I think you're a fine young man.'

'Cheers,' I replied. I don't think he expected me to reciprocate his compliment, but if he did he was sadly mistaken. His statement did, however, call for something more substantial than 'Cheers', so I found myself saying, 'I've got your eyes.'

'I know,' he said, taken aback.

'Mel thinks my eyes are the reason she fell in love with me,' I said quietly as it began to rain. 'I'll let her know that they're just like yours.'

He smiled gently. 'Meet up soon, then?'

'Yeah,' I said. 'I'll see you around.'

Every man has a poem in his heart

'Are you sure it goes in there?'

I looked at Julie exasperatedly.

'Maybe you've got it upside down or something? Have you tried wobbling that funny-looking thing?'

I gritted my teeth and wobbled irately.

'This isn't going to work, is it?'

Julie, I thought carefully, *may well have a point.*

Up until now everything in the Plan had gone like clockwork. As arranged I'd met up with Julie and we'd driven to IKEA. Half an hour and several hot and bothered assistants later and part one of the Plan was complete. In my pockets were parts two and three but on the way to Clapham I had a flash of inspiration and a potential fourth part of the Plan occurred to me. A quick detour via the freezer section of a nearby Safeway and my job was nearly complete. By eight o'clock we'd arrived at Mel's flat where Julie's role in the Plan came to the fore – she handed me the spare keys she kept to the flat. I'd told her I'd be in and out in under an hour. That was then.

'What time is it?' I asked, rubbing my temples gently whilst surveying the havoc I'd wreaked in Mel's living room. *It's going to take ages to tidy this lot away.* 'It feels like midnight.'

Julie looked at her watch and did the sort of comedy

double take that usually only ever happens in films. A look. Another look of disbelief and then another look just to check that the first two weren't part of some sort of hideous hallucination. 'It's one o'clock in the morning,' she said.

'You're joking?'

'I'm not. I'm deadly serious. Look, Duffy, we're going to have to go. I've got work in the morning. I can't stay up all night while you make a mess. I'm sorry, but I think we ought to tidy up and leave.'

'We can't go yet,' I protested. 'I haven't finished doing what I'm doing. Mel's going to be back tomorrow night. I wanted everything to be perfect . . .' I ran out of steam as the futility of my big plan finally hit me. 'This really isn't going to work, is it?'

'Look, it's just one part that's not going to work. The rest will be fine. Let's just tidy up and make the most of what you've done.'

'Will you put in a good word for me? Explain to her what I was trying to do?'

'Of course I will,' said Julie. 'The more I think about it, the better this idea of yours gets. It won't matter that you didn't get it all done. All that matters is you tried. Mel's not stupid, she'll know how hard you've worked. It's the trying that matters. She'll know how much you love her.'

Julie then did something she'd never done before. Something I never expected her to do in this lifetime or any other – she hugged me. At first, still somewhat shocked, my body went rigid with fear as if I'd come face to face with a black widow spider. Slowly, however, I overcame my initial reaction as I recalled the qualities of New Julie – the one who had gone out of her way to help me – and I found myself returning the hug. And there we stood, wrapped in each other's arms, sharing a moment that up until yesterday had been right at the top of the least-likely-event-to-occur-in-the-next-twenty-four-hours Top 40.

Just as I was wondering what the second least likely event might be, Julie whispered in my ear, 'I think someone's in the room.'

We immediately let go of each other as if we'd just been connected to the national grid, turned and stared wide eyed at the doorway to the living room. Standing there, holding a small suitcase and wearing a look of sheer bewilderment, was Mel.

'What are you doing here?' asked Julie, trying for all the world not to sound guilty. 'You're not meant to be back until tomorrow evening.'

'What am *I* doing here?' said Mel, switching on the main light. 'What are *you* doing here, more like? It's one o'clock in the morning, I'm knackered and I've just walked into my own flat to discover my best friend in an embrace with the father of my child. I don't think I'm the one who needs to be bloody explaining anything.'

'It's not how it looks,' I said sheepishly. 'Honest, Mel, this is all just a hugely hideous mistake.'

'Of course it's not how it looks,' Mel sniggered. 'Just look at the two of you! Terrified rigid that I'm going to accuse you of having an affair. Do you honestly imagine for one minute I'd think that?' She stepped into the room, and for the first time noticed the sheer havoc I'd wreaked in her living room. 'Okay,' she said, hand on hip. 'What's going on? And why have you decided to turn my flat into a bombsite?'

'Mel,' I began, 'It's not Julie's fault, it's all mine. I had a plan, something that was supposed to convince you how serious I was about you, but it's all gone horribly wrong . . .'

'It hasn't, Duffy,' prompted Julie sternly. 'Just do what you've got to do.' She walked over to Mel, gave her a hug and said warmly, 'Go easy on him. He's not half as bad as he seems.' Mel looked at Julie in silent amazement. 'My work here is done,' continued Julie, 'so I think I'm going to leave you two to sort this out by yourselves.' She went out, closing the door softly behind her. Now Mel and I were alone I knew this was it – my big moment.

'I've got some things to give you,' I began, as I felt my breathing quicken. My head started to feel slightly fuzzy as the blood rushed to my brain. 'The original plan was that you were supposed to come home tomorrow and just find them here in the flat. *I* wasn't supposed to be here at all. But since I am, I might as well give them to you myself. They're not gifts exactly – sort of non-gifts to be accurate – but they do all have something in common that I want you to think about.'

'This is all really weird Duffy, even for you,' said Mel. 'The fact that you've managed to rope Julie into your schemes worries me greatly.'

'Close your eyes,' I said, 'while I give you your first non-gift.' Mel closed her eyes. 'Put out your hands.' She did as I requested and I placed my first non-gift in her hand.

'Yeurgh!' exclaimed Mel. 'It's all soggy.'

'I know. I forgot to put it back in the freezer and put it in the fridge by accident. You can open your eyes now.'

'It's a bag of broccoli,' she said blankly, looking at me for explanation.

'I know, you left some in my freezer ages ago before we broke up. I threw it away but I've bought you some more.'

'Thanks. It's just what I wanted,' said Mel pulling a face. 'What's next?'

'You know the procedure.'

She closed her eyes and I handed her the second non-gift. 'It's the remote control for *my* television!' exclaimed Mel.

'Er . . . thanks very much! This is like some sort of twisted version of Christmas.'

'This bit's a little more complicated,' I said, ignoring her asides. 'You close your eyes again, but this time I'm going to have to guide you over to the other side of the room.' Holding on to her hand tightly, I navigated her carefully across the room. 'You can open your eyes now.'

'Great!' Mel looked around her. 'Bits of wood and metal. Now I know for a fact that unless you've been dismantling my furniture none of this is mine.'

'Ah you see bits of wood and metal,' I corrected. 'But I see *very* important bits of wood and metal. This mess here,' I pointed to a pile of short metal rods, two large door panels, a massive instruction sheet, and a pile of brackets and side panels, 'in my hands all amounts to a bunch of bits of wood and metal but in the hands of someone with more common sense than your average house brick they all fit together to make an IKEA wardrobe.'

Mel's faced changed as she began to get an inkling of what I was doing. She opened her mouth, about to speak, but I put my finger to her lips to silence her.

'Not now. You can speak when I've given the last of my non-gifts.' I searched around in my jacket pocket and knelt down in front of her. 'This is for you.' I handed her a small gift-wrapped package.

She tore open the wrapping paper revealing the box inside, and opened it hurriedly. She was quiet for some moments and then she looked at me with tears in her eyes and knelt down beside me. 'It's my engagement ring.'

'I know you're probably wondering what this is all about. You probably think this is just me having a laugh, and in a way it is. I love making you laugh, Mel, I want to be the one who makes you happy all the time, but there's a serious side to this too. You see, the broccoli *was* yours and I give it back to you. The remote control *is* yours but I used to use it most and so now I give it back to you. The wardrobe *should've been* yours on that day we argued in IKEA, so I give it to you now. And finally this ring, in your hand, which represents my heart, is, was, and will always be yours. Even if you turn me down, I can't ever take it back because it's yours for ever.'

I sat down on the hardwood floor, exhausted. 'Charlie once said to me that when it came to winning over the one you love, "every man has a poem in his heart". Well, this, Mel, was my sonnet. The only thing I regret about tonight,' I said, wiping a tear away from her cheek as she moved herself closer to me, 'is that I was defeated by that stupid wardrobe.' With that I closed my eyes like a blindfolded deserter about to be shot and waited for her answer.

There was a brief moment of silence, and then I felt Mel's arms around me, squeezing me tightly as she whispered the words, 'I love you,' into my ear.

'Will you marry me?' I asked tentatively.

'Of course,' said Mel as I opened my eyes. 'That's why I've told my bosses today that I couldn't carry on the job in Scotland and asked for my old job instead. That's why I came back a day early. I couldn't wait any longer. I didn't need frozen broccoli, a remote control, a ring or even a wardrobe to know that you love me. I just know.'

'You're sure?'

'Of course,' she said wiping her nose on the sleeve of her jacket. 'If it's really what you want.'

'Even though I can't build flat-pack wardrobes?'

'Especially because you can't build flatpack wardrobes.'

'Even though I still hate shopping in IKEA?'

'Especially because you hate shopping in IKEA.'

'Even though I don't always understand you, I wind you up with the stupid things I do and occasionally try to shush you when the TV's on?'

'Don't push it,' she said as she moved in closer to kiss me. 'Quit while you're ahead, Mr Duffy.' She kissed me again. 'All you need to know is that I love everything about you. I love you exactly the way you are. I don't want you to be like me and I certainly don't want to be like you. I want us to be the way we are.'

It'll reduce puffiness around the eyes

We set a wedding date for as soon as was possible, which turned out to be some four months away, and in the meantime I went back to temping, gigged like a demon with Dan up and down the country and fell more deeply in love with Mel than I thought possible.

Like these things do, the big day came up faster than either Mel or I had expected, but it was none the less welcome, and my last twenty-four hours as a single man went something a little like this:

12.30 p.m.
Took the afternoon off work and met up for a drink because Mel said I wasn't allowed to go out the night before the wedding, as the previous Thursday's stag do resulted in a ten-week ban from the Haversham. Dan, Charlie, myself and various other mates headed to the Haversham wearing joke-shop false moustaches.

3.10 p.m.
Landlord of Haversham saw through disguises instantly, and we were escorted off the premises. We headed for the Newton Arms, in Tufnell Park, the definitive old man's pub – Woodbines behind the bar, no carpet on the floor and grumpy-looking old men just about everywhere. We spent

the afternoon drinking bitter, laughing ourselves silly and smoking Woodbines with aforementioned grumpy old men.

6.00 p.m.
Mel's official cut-off point. As responsible best man, Dan let me know it was time to go. We all agreed that it was indeed time to go home.

6.10 p.m.
Okay, just the one.

7.10 p.m.
After this next one we're off. I mean it.

7.30 p.m.
No, really.

8.10 p.m.
Just as we were finishing what we promised ourselves would be our last drink, Charlie's mobile began an annoying electronic rendition of the 'William Tell Overture'. He answered it, expecting it to be work, but it was Vernie trying to find out where we were. Thinking on his feet, he told her that we were just on our way home, but his cover was blown by Dan and two of his new octogenarian best buddies, Albert and Reg, singing 'Can't Smile Without You' at the top of their hoary voices. Needless to say, Vernie pulled a strop, yelled loud enough for us all to hear and slammed the phone down. Now it really was time to go.

8.15 p.m.
Vernie called back and threatened Charlie with all manner of torture should anything untoward happen to me before my wedding.

8.32 p.m.

Dan, Charlie and I said our goodbyes to Albert and Reg and all our mates and and then grabbed a taxi home. Despite our protests, the driver insisted on keeping his car radio tuned to an easy-listening station which happened to be playing back-to-back Phil Collins. Though he clearly did not know the words, the driver insisted on singing along to 'Easy Lover', twice forcing me to correct his completely inaccurate rendition of the chorus.

8.51 p.m.

Thanked the very nice waiter at the Star of the Punjab in Kentish Town for taking our orders (onion bahjees, chicken vindaloo, prawn korma and chicken sagwalla). It was all Dan's idea. Honest.

9.01 p.m.

Vernie called Charlie on his mobile again and issued the severe reprimand: 'If anything happens to make Duffy late, ill or unpresentable tomorrow, you will never ever see me naked again in this or any other lifetime.' For the sake of Charlie's sub-duvet activities we asked the waiters to hurry up.

10.15 p.m.

Taxi arrived at the Star of Punjab and we bid fond farewells to Harpreet, Hassan and Steve, the Star of Punjab waiters. As they waved their goodbyes, they promised faithfully that they'd come to the wedding as I'd requested. We got the taxi to drop Charlie off in Crouch End first. Vernie came out the minute we pulled up, gave Charlie her best Death Ray look and peered into my eyes. 'I don't want my brother looking haggard on his wedding photos!' she berated loudly and then handed me a Clarins bottle. 'It'll reduce puffiness around the eyes,' she added sagely.

10.25 p.m.
Dan and I arrived back at the flat. Our good moods in full swing, we decided to invite Will and Alice, the couple who lived in the flat beneath us, to the wedding in a gesture of niceness. At first they looked at us strangely, but when I eventually managed to persuade them that although I was drunk I was telling the truth, they said they'd love to come. We also considered inviting the couple who lived in the flat above us, Matt and Monica, but Dan still held a grudge against them because he was convinced it was they who had called the police round to pull the plug on our New Year's Eve party last year. I, however, was still overflowing with the milk of human kindness so I invited them anyway.

11.30 p.m.
Mammoth toast-making session. Dan and I toasted a whole loaf of Hovis just for the hell of it. Whilst opening a can of Red Stripe I had a brief tender moment with Dan. 'You know, you're all right for a Northern toast-muncher,' he said, buttering a slice of toast. 'And you're not too bad yourself for a soft southern git,' I replied. Touchy-feely moment over, we slipped into the living room to consume the fruits of our labours.

12.03 a.m.
Asked Dan who the mystery guest was he was bringing to the wedding, and he refused to tell me yet again. He'd asked me a month ago if he could bring someone. I'd said yes of course, but when I asked who it was he went all furtive, so I didn't bother asking again. Mel reckoned it was Fiona,

the new girl who had just started working behind the bar in the Haversham. Charlie and Vernie were of the opinion he was bringing one of my ex-girlfriends as a surprise guest, but my money was on it being someone nobody knew – that was much more Dan's style.

1.12 a.m.
Tiredness came over me in a massive wave so I retired to bed. Before I did so, I wrote down on a notepad, 'Getting married tomorrow,' in case it escaped my memory, and then read and followed set of instructions pinned to my pillow by Vernie:

1) Set bedside alarm clock for 7.30 a.m.
2) Set Dan's radio alarm clock on the floor next to the bed for 7.30 a.m.
3) Set Mickey Mouse alarm clock at the bottom of the bed for 7.30 a.m.
4) Call BT and ask for 7.30 a.m. wake-up call.

1.22 a.m.
Attempted to sleep.

1.55 a.m.
Still not sleeping. Counted sheep.

2.28 a.m.
Ran out of sheep and began counting other farmyard animals.

3.30 a.m.
Called Mel and told her how much I love her. Her only reply was a very sleepy, 'That's nice.'

3.32 a.m.
I called Mel again in case she thought I was a crank caller. 'Of course I knew it was you,' she said patiently. 'Only you would do this to me!'

3.40 a.m.
Still unable to sleep, so I got up and flicked through Dan's videos in the front room. Selected Dan's car-boot-sale copy of *ET* to while away the early hours as I'd never seen it.

4.20 a.m.
Due to heightened emotional state caused by impending wedlock, *ET* had me in floods of tears. 'Why are people so horrible? He only wanted to go home.'

4.30 a.m.
Fast forwarded film to the end to make sure he wasn't really dead.

5.21 a.m.
Satisfied with happy ending, I suddenly felt tired and went to bed.

7.30 a.m.
Multiple alarms woke me and probably everyone in North London apart from Dan. I felt awful and wondered if I was in fact dead. Went back to sleep.

7.45 a.m.
Woken by doorbell. Eyes barely open I made my way downstairs to discover Mum, Charlie, Vernie and baby Phoebe on the doorstep dressed up in full wedding gear. They all came

upstairs and made themselves at home while I showered. When I emerged from the bathroom half an hour later, Mum was washing the dishes, Vernie was grilling sausages and Charlie had Phoebe on his lap and was watching *ET*. Dan, meanwhile, was still asleep.

9.00 a.m.
Cars arrived to take us to St Faith's in Barnet. Estimated Time of Arrival: 9.30 a.m.

9.30 a.m.
Stuck in traffic. ETA now 9.45 a.m.

9.45 a.m.
Still stuck in traffic jam. ETA now 9.55 a.m. I managed to convince myself that Mel wouldn't marry me if I was late, and that I'd be condemned to live with Dan until the day I died.

9.54 a.m.
Arrived at the church. Thankfully Mel hadn't arrived yet. Mum kept checking my suit for fluff and dusted me over every thirty seconds like one of her prized Capo Di Monte figurines. Remembered to ask Dan if he'd got the ring. Few panicky moments when after checking every conceivable pocket and orifice he still couldn't find it. Fortunately he discovered it on a piece of string around his neck just as I was about to kill him with my bare hands. Good man!

10.00 a.m.
Said hello to waiters from the Star of Punjab, Will and Alice and Alexa. No sign of the New Year's No Noise Neighbours,

or for that matter my fiancée. Spotted Dan behind a Vauxhall Astra in mid-snog with his mystery guest . . . none other than The Lovely Anne, Crap Greg's ex-girlfriend. Hurrah for Dan indeed!

10.05 a.m.
Still no sign of Mel. Mum helpfully reminded me that it's a woman's prerogative to be late. Didn't reply for fear of being unable to locate my inner Dalai Lama. Julie came over and introduced me to her new man and former pottery teacher, Leon, who lives in Notting Hill Gate. Leon handed me a large gift-wrapped box on behalf of Julie. I tried and failed to resist taking a crafty peak. Typical! Dinner set from Habitat.

10.15 a.m.
Managed to convince myself that Mel had got cold feet and had done a runner. My mum just shook her head and told me me to 'stop being so ridiculous'.

10.21 a.m.
Mel's car is spotted by Dan coming up the road. She loves me!

10.25 a.m.
Following a brief moment for explanation from Mel's mum and dad (the car was stuck in the same traffic as us) we're nearly ready to begin.

10.45 a.m.
Standing at the front of the church, I turned to see Mel on her father's arm, striding up the aisle. It was like seeing her for the first time in my life all over again – that walk, that living

breathing version of Chrissie Hynde singing 'Brass In Pocket' – even in a wedding dress and six months pregnant! When she reached me I whispered in her ear, 'You look amazing,' and she beamed and whispered back, 'Don't say things like that, because I'll only cry and I'm desperate to look calm and serene on the wedding video!'

10.55 a.m.
She said, 'I do.'

10.57 a.m.
I said, 'I do.'

10.59 a.m.
'I now pronounce you husband and wife,' said the man in charge. 'You may now kiss the bride.'

11.00 a.m.
We kissed.

The Best Man

Ladies and gentlemen, on behalf of the bride and groom I'd like to welcome you to the wedding of Melanie Lara Benson, and of course, the one and only Benjamin Dominic Duffy! As best man it falls to me to come out with a lot of stuff about how wonderful the bride is and then crack a few jokes about the groom . . . and who am I to truck with tradition? No, seriously, although this is a happy day, in some way it's a sad day, too, because I'm going to miss Duff. Over the last couple of years he has been the best flatmate ever. He is easy going, reasonably house trained and never ceased to amaze me with his ability to make lost fridge food edible simply by scraping the fur off it and shoving it into the microwave. Someone said to me this afternoon that I shouldn't think of today as losing a flatmate, I should see it as gaining somewhere nice and clean to be invited for Sunday lunch – they may well have a point. Decent food apart, though, I hope I'll also be gaining another friend as good as Duffy. Mel really is the best thing that has ever happened to him and I couldn't think of a better person to hand over responsibility to for his supervision. And so, I ask you to join me in a toast to these two brave people – brave because no matter how much in love someone is, it is still a leap of faith to make the sort of promise they've made today and mean it. So I ask you to join me in raising a toast: to Duffy and Mel – Mr and Mrs Commitment.

The Bride

Hello, everyone. Due to thousands of years of patriarchal oppression women have been denied the right to make speeches at weddings and make jokes at the groom's expense. As a fully-fledged flexible feminist I'm not about to have my wedding day dictated to me by anyone – especially as I paid for half of it. Anyway, I've prepared a few words that I'd like to say. When Duffy and I first planned to get married, I'd had my heart set on a huge wedding. Now it's me who is huge and not the wedding. But to be serious for a second, I'm glad we've done it small – just the people we love and care for most. I couldn't have wished for a better day. Anyway, I'd like to thank everyone for coming: you really have made today a day to remember. I'd especially like to thank my mum and dad for all the hard work they've put in to making this day a success, and Julie for being there for me, and Charlie and Dan for making sure that Duffy didn't come to too much harm on his stag night; and to Duffy's mum for everything she's done, especially for sorting out the catering – you have her to thank for the wonderful Moroccan-style chicken starters. And finally, I've got a surprise for my husband. For the past few months he's been under the impression that we're having a band playing at this evening's reception, but we're not – we're having the Derek G Mobile Disco Experience instead. And yes, Duffy, I made sure before I hired him that he's got

'Come On Eileen', 'Three Times A Lady' and even 'The Birdie Song'. That's all I've got to say really, but before I sit down, I'd like to take this opportunity to thank my husband, who is the most special person in the world . . . he's kind, gentle and . . . and . . . a . . .

The Groom

That's exactly why women aren't supposed to give speeches at weddings – they just burst into tears. Mel, her mum, my mum, Vernie, have been shedding tears all morning. It's only because I shed all mine last night watching *ET* that I'm the only one in the house with dry eyes. There's nothing in the world that I want more than to be with Mel for the rest of my life. Now it's not my intention to shuffle off this mortal coil until I'm oh, what shall I say, eighty, ninety? I want to see for myself whether one day we will all be drinking blue drinks, wearing shiny silver spacesuits and taking winter breaks on Mars. I wouldn't mind living for ever, which of course will mean being married for ever. Which is as great as it sounds. This is what I've spent the whole of my life not searching for, mainly because I didn't know I needed it. A few hours ago Mel promised to love and cherish me for the rest of her life. She didn't say obey, which is okay, because I don't want to control her, I just want her to want to be with me and me with her. I know I sound like some sort of New Man, fully in touch with his emotions, able to cry at romantic comedies starring Meg Ryan and capable of having women as friends without harbouring secret desires to see them naked. It's not true – well, apart from the naked women friends thing – I'm still me. I still don't like it when she talks when the TV's on. I'll admit I don't understand her all of the time. But I know I wouldn't want it any other way, because I've seen the other ways. And so, I'd like for you to join me in a toast – to Mel, my wife, the best a man can get.

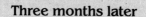

Three months later

She's gorgeous

'Isn't she beautiful?' said Mel holding her up for all to see.

'Gorgeous,' said Vernie, taking our baby in her arms. 'Absolutely gorgeous. Look at her eyes – the way they sparkle.'

'Duffy,' said Julie, 'don't you want to hold her?'

'Er,' I uttered noncommittally, 'I'm not sure about this. I've never held a . . . you know . . . anyway, she looks a bit fragile to me. What if I drop her? Maybe later, eh? When Mel's mum and dad arrive. Give them the chance to see their granddaughter in one piece before I start juggling with her.'

'No,' replied Mel firmly. 'You're going to hold her now. You've been making up excuses for the last two hours. It's time for the two of you to bond.'

'My hands are really sweaty. She needs to be held by someone with a better grip than mine.'

'Are you seriously intending not to hold her until she's more robust?' asked Mel. She turned to hand me my daughter. 'Here you go, Daddy.'

'It's not difficult,' reassured Julie as I took her from Mel's hands. 'Just be gentle with her.'

My baby was oblivious to the fact that someone new was holding her. Her eyes were firmly closed and her mouth was pouted just like her mum's when she's having a sulk.

'Have you thought of a name for her yet?' enquired Mum. 'I can't believe you've left it this long.'

'We wanted to wait until she was here before we named her. It didn't seem right calling her something without seeing her.' Mel looked up at me and smiled. 'We're open to suggestions. What does everyone think?'

'I don't know,' said Mum, 'I've never been all that good at thinking on my feet.'

'She looks like a Philippa,' said Julie. 'Or maybe a Jane. Or maybe even a Philippa-Jane.'

'Elvis!' said Dan and Charlie in unison.

'I reckon Jackie,' said Vernie, carefully balancing Phoebe in one arm in order to thump Charlie playfully with the other. 'There hasn't been a world famous Jackie since Jackie Onassis. The world needs another one as soon as possible.'

'What do you think?' said Mel, directing her question towards me. 'You're her dad, you should have a whole list of names by now.'

I looked fondly at the new addition to the Duffy family, who was still resting peacefully in my arms. *She's beautiful, I thought. No doubt about it. This has got to be the best-looking baby there has ever been. She needs a name that sums up her personality. Something that says, hello, I'm smart and funny and irresistible – just like my dad.*

'I know exactly what her name is,' I said, looking into her tiny face. 'Mel chose it a long time ago, and as ever, she was spot on. I think we should call her Ella.'

'I can't believe you remembered!' said Mel fondly. 'You're right, she does look like an Ella. So Ella Elvis Duffy it is.'

'Elvis?'

'Of course,' said Mel with a flourish. 'She's a Duffy, isn't she? So she's bound to be a star.'

Don't miss Mike Gayle's Number One bestselling
first novel MY LEGENDARY GIRLFRIEND.

'A funny, frank account of a hopeless romantic'
THE TIMES

'The male Bridget Jones'   EXPRESS

'Full of belly laughs and painfully acute observations'
INDEPENDENT ON SUNDAY

Meet Will Kelly. English teacher. Film fan.
Pot noodle expert. Ex Boyfriend.

Still in love with The One, Will is desperate to discover
if there can be An-Other One. In his decrepit flat where
he can't even manage to cook spaghetti hoops without
setting off the communal smoke alarm, his lifeline is the
telephone. Will realises that with a single call, friends can
either lift him from the depths of depression or completely
shatter his hopes.

There's Alice (who remembers his birthday), Simon (who
doesn't), Martina (the one-night stand), Kate (the previous
tenant of his rented hovel). And of course his Ex, Aggi –
the inimitable Aggi. His Legendary Girlfriend.

Or is she?

Two men, three women and a donkey called Sandy . . .
basically it's your classic love hexagon.

Hodder & Stoughton Paperbacks